CRASH DIVE!

Admiral Jack Boxer joined Carson in front of the console that displayed the area directly above the *Manta*. He knew the Arctic ice cap was a constantly shifting mass, breaking apart, grinding together again, leaving open leads of water and raised pressure ridges that mottled the surface.

Carson pointed to a lightly shaded area on the screen. "The ice here looks no more than a foot thick."

Boxer called to the Dive Center. "Whitey, bring her up slowly. I just want to break the surface."

The *Manta* shivered and rose several feet. A scraping, crunching sound was heard throughout the ship and then they broke surface.

Suddenly the intercom squawked. "Conn, this is sonar. Two targets approaching, Skipper! Speed four zero knots and closing!"

Boxer hit the klaxon siren. "Dive . . . dive," he began . . .

ACTION ADVENTURE

SILENT WARRIORS (1675, $3.95)
by Richard P. Henrick
The Red Star, Russia's newest, most technologically advanced submarine, outclasses anything in the U.S. fleet. But when the captain opens his sealed orders 24 hours early, he's staggered to read that he's to spearhead a massive nuclear first strike against the Americans!

THE PHOENIX ODYSSEY (1789, $3.95)
by Richard P. Henrick
All communications to the USS *Phoenix* suddenly and mysteriously vanish. Even the urgent message from the president cancelling the War Alert is not received. In six short hours the *Phoenix* will unleash its nuclear arsenal against the Russian mainland.

COUNTERFORCE (2013, $3.95)
Richard P. Henrick
In the silent deep, the chase is on to save a world from destruction. A single Russian Sub moves on a silent and sinister course for American shores. The men aboard the U.S.S. *Triton* must search for and destroy the Soviet killer Sub as an unsuspecting world races for the apocalypse.

EAGLE DOWN (1644, $3.75)
by William Mason
To western eyes, the Russian Bear appears to be in hibernation — but half a world away, a plot is unfolding that will unleash its awesome, deadly power. When the Russian Bear rises up, God help the Eagle.

DAGGER (1399, $3.50)
by William Mason
The President needs his help, but the CIA wants him dead. And for Dagger — war hero, survival expert, ladies man and mercenary extraordinaire — it will be a game played for keeps.

Available wherever paperbacks are sold, or order direct from the Publisher. Send cover price plus 50¢ per copy for mailing and handling to Zebra Books, Dept. 2535, 475 Park Avenue South, New York, N.Y. 10016. Residents of New York, New Jersey and Pennsylvania must include sales tax. DO NOT SEND CASH.

#18: ICE ISLAND

IRVING A. GREENFIELD

ZEBRA BOOKS
KENSINGTON PUBLISHING CORP.

This book is sincerely dedicated to Mr. Michael Bergman, whose advice helped to bring it to completion.

Irving A. Greenfield
Staten Island, New York

CHAPTER ONE

Admiral Jack Boxer maneuvered his crippled *Los Angeles* class submarine, the *Halsey,* through the narrow Strait of Hormuz in the Persian Gulf, leaving the blazing hulk of the Iranian sub *Hezbullah* floundering in her wake. From his vantage point on the sail's bridge, Boxer looked back at the orange glow of the burning wreck against the gray evening sky until it was finally swallowed up and extinguished by the sea. "Good riddance," Boxer commented to Mark Clemens, his executive officer.

"Roger that," Clemens replied with a half-smile. "It was them or us."

"Could have been avoided. They were out of their league in that old diesel. Well, that's the way it goes." Boxer shook his head. "They go out all crazed, ready to martyr themselves in their holy war against the Great Satan."

"Meaning us." Clemens remarked, looking northwest toward Qeshm Island. There was no longer any sign of the Iranian submarine that had stalked them for two days and almost succeeded in capturing Major Roland Jones and the survivors of his small band of Rangers. He turned his attention back to the bridge's command module before him, conscious of their position on the tiny screen as they entered the Gulf of Oman.

"Meaning us." Now that the immediate danger of the Iranian sub and its sister ship, the Soviet *Alpha* that now lay smoldering on a beach in the United Arab Emirates was past, Boxer's attention drifted back to thoughts of Francine Wheeler, his fianceé. She had been gang raped and left in a state of catatonic shock by two men who worked for Julio

Sanchez, his sometimes ally, sometimes enemy. Now Sanchez was his enemy. An adversary to be hunted down and killed.

". . . Skipper?"

"Huh?"

Clemens cleared his throat. "I asked if you'd like to go below and catch forty. You've hardly slept in the last three days."

Boxer studied his EXO's boyish face in the fading light. Clem was old for his age, Boxer mused. That's good. He was a good exec. "Why don't you take a break. I'll take us out into the Arabian Sea. Then I'll catch a few hours sleep before we rendezvous with Admiral Rodgers."

"Aye, aye, Skipper. I could do with some shuteye, myself. I'll be back to relieve you in three hours."

"Roger that, Clem." Boxer watched Clemens's tall, lanky body slip through the hatchway into the command room belowdeck. With the diving gear damaged and forcing them to sail on the surface, and the ventilation system shut down, the hatch was being left open to circulate some fresh air below. Even at 1900 hours, the ambient temperature was still ninety degrees.

Boxer used night-vision glasses to scan the horizon ahead, as the waning sun slipped away behind him to the west. There wasn't another ship visible for at least ten miles. Good thing, he thought. With the *Halsey* crippled and unable to dive, they'd make an easy target for a cunning predator.

Boxer became aware of some noise below, and turned to see the shaven head of Rolly Jones protrude up through the hatch. "Evening, Skipper." Jones worked his muscular hulk up onto the bridge, a steaming cup of coffee in each hand. "Thought you might like some refreshment."

"Nice of you, Rolly. Thanks." Boxer sipped the steamy black brew. "That hit the spot. How're your men doing?"

"The survivors? There're just seven of us left, out of

twelve. Out of the seven, Evans and Tinker are busted up some. They'll probably ship out once we get aboard the *Rickover*. Kaplan can't hear anything. His ears have been ringing since we blew up the *Hezbullah*. He'll be going home, too. That leaves me and Sergeant Rivera, Mean Gene and Shorty."

"You've got a fine group of men, Major. You're all heroes in my book. Sorry you had to lose so many."

Rolly took a sip from his coffee. "We, uh . . . the four of us, that I just mentioned . . . We, uh, got to talkin' it over, and uh . . . we . . ."

Boxer said, "Why not just come out with what you want to say?"

Rolly Jones shrugged. "We just want you to know that we'd like the opportunity to serve with you again, Skipper."

Boxer smiled. "You just might get your chance sooner than you think, Rolly"

"Huh?"

"What I'm going to tell you now goes no further than the two of us for now. That clear?"

"Loud and clear, Skipper."

"Up to about a year and a half ago, I commanded a state-of-the-art hunter-killer sub called the *Barracuda*. We transported a strike force, similar to your Rangers, to trouble spots around the world, on missions much like this one."

"Well, if you don't mind my asking," Rolly scratched his bullet head, "why'd you switch to a conventional tub like the *Halsey?*"

Boxer's face took on a grim expression. Visions of his former exec, Cowley, along with some of his other former men lay sprawled on the deck of the *Barracuda,* lying dead in their own blood. They, and the *Barracuda* were victims of some unknown assailant, a mystery never solved to Boxer's satisfaction. "She sank. Lost a lot of good men. The best."

"Oh. Sorry. I was just . . ."

"It's time for us to develop a new class of submarines, one that will put us years ahead of anything the Ruskies have to offer. And we're going to need a new strike force. The meanest, toughest bunch of sons of bitches we can muster." A smile crept across Boxer's face. "And it occurs to me that you and your men seem to fit that bill."

Roland Jones beamed.

"And I'd be proud to have you boys on any crew that I get to command."

Rolly Jones, a rock-hard mountain of ebony, afraid of no man, was clearly flustered. "I . . . I don't know what to say, Skipper."

"Don't say anything, Major. Your deeds speak for themselves."

Rolly stood tall and erect. "Thank you, sir . . . er, Skipper. My men would like that very much."

Boxer nodded. "Why don't you get some rest. We'll rendezvous with the *Rickover* at oh-two-hundred and transfer aboard. This ship won't make it home on her own steam."

"Right. See you later."

As Rolly Jones departed, he was replaced by the chief of the watch and two enlisted men, all outfitted with night glasses. Chief Perez said, "Good evening, Admiral."

"Chief. It's a clear night. Shouldn't have any problem spotting trouble tonight."

"Right."

Boxer swept the horizon with his glasses, being especially wary of anything unusual on their port side, overlooking the Iranian Coast. The hairs on the back of his neck began to prickle, leaving him with an uneasy feeling. And then it happened.

A fierce explosion lifted the *Halsey*'s bows fifteen feet

into the air. Flames shot out of the forward torpedo compartment. The *Halsey* slammed down hard onto the surface, and began to settle at the bows.

Boxer was knocked off his feet. He crashed into the chief and an enlisted man. "Mine," he yelled. "We hit a mine."

The chief did not respond.

"Turn him over," Boxer said to the rank.

The young sailor felt for a carotid pulse. There was none. When he removed his hand, it was covered with sticky blood. He nudged the chief's body into its back. The skull was caved in and the neck hung at an odd angle. "He's dead, sir."

Boxer grabbed up the MC mike. "All hands, we've struck a mine. DCO report on damages."

There was no reply, only an intermittent squawking.

Boxer threw down the mike with disgust, and scurried down below. In a moment he was surveying the scene in the command room. Clemens was trying to pull himself to his feet. Men and equipment were strewn everywhere. He picked up the intercom mike and shouted, "DCO, this is Admiral Boxer. Report damages at once."

"Conn, DCO. The forward torpedo room took a direct hit below the waterline. Damages are extensive."

"Casualties?"

"Ten, twelve men down, Skipper. Probably dead."

"Seal off the forward compartment. And try to save any survivors if you can."

"Aye, aye, Skipper. We're working on that right now. And, Skipper . . ."

"Yes?"

"The smoke is getting thick up here. With the air scrubber down, the men won't last here much longer."

"Roger that. Try to get the men aft. And open the forward hatch."

Rolly Jones stumbled into the command room. A trickle

11

of blood oozed from his brow. "You all right, Skipper?"

Boxer nodded. "You?"

"Okay. My Rangers are all okay. How can we help?"

"Get the men off, Rolly. The wounded, first. I'll radio Admiral Rodgers to pick up the survivors, and take the *Halsey* in myself with a skeleton crew."

"Right, Skipper. I'll have my men set up and man the life rafts. Can we get your crew up on deck?"

Boxer keyed the MC. "DCO, report."

"Conn, DCO. We have twelve DOAs, all from the forward torpedo compartment. That's sealed tight, now. Smoke's getting worse up here now."

"Send all essential hands back to the control room. Get the rest up on deck."

"Are we abandoning ship, Skipper?"

"Just the wounded, and non-essential crewmen. Move the men out fast, DCO. Major Jones is standing by on deck to assist you."

"Aye, aye, Skipper."

Boxer stood aside as Rolly Jones led Sergeant Rivera, Mean Gene and Shorty through the bridge hatch. The Rangers carried scuba gear and coils of braided lines out to the deck. Crew members handed up the containers holding the emergency life rafts. Boxer was pleased to see his men working like a well-oiled machine, even under such adversity. He keyed his radioman. "Patch me through to Admiral Rodgers. Code ten."

"Aye, aye, Skipper."

What seemed like ages slipped by. Boxer called all his officers and chiefs into the control room, advising them as to who were needed and who were to abandon ship. Reluctantly, those chosen to leave gathered up their belongings and climbed up on deck.

"Skipper, I have Admiral Rodgers on line for you."

Boxer put on a headset and spoke into the microphone.

"Boxer here, sir."

"What's the situation aboard the *Halsey,* Jack?"

"We struck a mine, Admiral. It tore out the torpedo room. We're taking on water and settling at the bows. There's still fire and smoke in the forward compartment."

"You'd better abandon ship, Jack. I'll send some help right away."

"Aye, aye, Admiral. All hands not essential to saving the *Halsey* are being placed aboard life rafts. I'll try to bring her in with just a skeleton crew."

"Are you sure you can get here safely?"

Boxer lied. "Aye, aye, sir. We can make it."

"Okay, Jack. Help is on the way."

"Thank you, Admiral."

Boxer picked up the intercom mike. "Mahoney, make course one two five degrees."

"Aye, aye, Skipper. One two five degrees."

"EO, what's the max we can get out of her?"

"Eight, ten knots, maybe, Skipper."

"Okay, give it the max."

"Yes, Skipper."

The *Halsey* no sooner got underway when the second explosion stopped the sub in its tracks.

"DCO, conn. What the hell's going on?"

"Not sure, Skipper. Something blew in the torpedo room. We're taking on water again."

Boxer's expression was grim. He turned to Clemens, his exec. "Looks like that's it for the *Halsey,* Clem. I'll stay on board as long as possible till help gets here. I won't abandon her here except as a last resort."

"Count me in, too, Skipper."

"Thanks, Clem. Help seal off all bulkheads forward of the control room."

"Right, Skipper."

Suddenly, Rolly Jones jumped down into the control

room from the bridge. "Skipper, we're under attack. Three enemy speedboats closing fast on the life rafts."

"Get to the heavy machine-gun on deck. See if your men can hold them off long enough for me to get off some torpedoes."

"Aye, aye." Rolly was back up and out on the bridge in a moment.

Boxer could hear the staccato machine-gun fire through the open hatch. He keyed the stern torpedo room. "TO . . . Load and arm tubes eight and ten."

"Aye, aye, Skipper."

"FCO . . . Prepare to fire eight and ten. Slave them in on your sonar."

"Right, Skipper. We're at T minus ten."

Boxer watched the digital timer on the firing console tick off the seconds until the release of the fish: nine . . . eight . . . seven . . . six . . .

"They're on top of us, Skipper. I can't get off a clear shot. We'll hit the men."

"Abort . . . abort."

FCO slapped his palm against the Fire-Control Abort switch. The digital display stood at three.

"TO," Boxer called into the MC. "Disarm eight and ten."

"Aye, aye, Skipper."

"Clem, you've got the conn. I'm going to see what I can do." Boxer dashed into the Ranger's quarters and returned in a few seconds clutching an M-16. "Try to get some more armed men on deck."

With that, Boxer climbed the steel ladder inside the sail, and made his way to the bridge with his weapon. He looked over the edge. Three enemy speedboats were converging on the *Halsey*. Their eight-man crews were firing small arms at his men bobbing helplessly on life rafts. Heavy machine-gun fire was directed at his sub.

Shorty manned the sub's machine-gun. He returned the

fire of the speedboat closing amidships. Rolly lay prone on the deck, firing his M-16 at the boat fast approaching the blown-out bow. Boxer wheeled and sprayed the third enemy vessel as it swung around to the stern.

A battle cry rose to a feverish pitch. The lead Iranian boat launched itself into a life raft filled with submariners. Men screamed. The raft exploded. Bits of bodies and black neoprene flew in all directions, then settled onto the surface. The Iranians went wild.

So did Boxer. "Get them," he shouted.

Shorty spun his weapon at the fast-closing craft and let loose a prolonged burst of fire. Rolly and Boxer fired at the same boat from their vantage points. The Iranian vessel flipped over, dumping its crew. Boxer's men dove in after them. There would be no prisoners taken. They set on with their grisly task with a vengeance . . . an eye for an eye . . . a limb for a limb . . .

The remaining two speedboats altered course and fired on Shorty at the heavy machine-gun. Boxer watched as Shorty's legs jerked, then turned red with blood. Shorty continued to fire.

One speedboat cut ahead of the other, took a broadside sweep at the *Halsey*, firing all they had at the big man at the machine-gun on deck. Shorty's body bucked and jerked, torn apart by the enemy bullets. Still he hung on . . . still firing, now on instinct alone.

Boxer fired down from the bridge. Rolly chased after the speedboat, running along the *Halsey*'s deck. He aimed at the pilot manning the twin outboards. "Die, Motherfucker. Die." He loosed a burst of his M-16.

The pilot spun and slumped. The speedboat immediately slowed and turned one-eighty degrees into its own wake.

Rolly emptied a clip at the stunned Iranian crew. "That's for Shorty, fuckers." He slammed home a fresh ammo clip and finished the job.

"Behind you," Boxer shouted.

Rolly hit the deck just a hair below the enemy's fire. The remaining speedboat was closing in fast. Boxer climbed down to the deck, shooting short bursts at the Iranian crew. Rolly stayed on the deck, as the Iranians continued their fusillade just over his prone body.

Boxer directed his return fire from behind the sail. He noticed several objects heading their way, hovering just above the horizon. The unmistakable sound of copter blades was barely audible above the din of the firefight. It was choppers, all right. Ours or theirs?

Boxer fired a burst at the fast approaching speedboat. The Iranians kept coming. It seemed to Boxer that they were headed directly at him, straight for the sail.

Rolly fired from his forward position on deck. Still the Iranian vessel came.

A near miss sent Boxer running to safety behind the ship's sail. He could see and hear the enemy fire ricocheting off the steel plate. The copters loomed closer overhead, the din of their blades almost blocking out all thought. Ours . . . They're ours. Thank God, they're our choppers. He chanced a glance at Rolly, ready to flip him a thumbs up sign.

Rolly suddenly stood up and fired in a rage, throwing caution aside, almost running toward Boxer's position as he fired at the Iranians racing to their destiny.

Boxer heard the horrible crunch of the speedboat colliding with the sub. He didn't have time to react. The ensuing explosion split the *Halsey* in half amidships, threw Boxer forty feet through the air. The ringing in his head lasted until he hit the water. He felt a tremendous pressure on his chest, as the sea enveloped him. The ringing was replaced by a dizziness . . . his head seemed to be spinning . . . thoughts of dying clouded his mind . . . he couldn't concentrate on anything . . . Rolly . . . Clem . . . Francine . . .

Stark . . . Chuck and John . . . then nothing. Not ready to die, yet, he thought as he settled deeper and deeper below the surface. Not ready to die . . .

CHAPTER TWO

Not ready to die, yet. Not ready to die . . . Boxer sat bolt upright, felt a tugging at his nose, his throat, his right forearm. What the . . . where . . . ? He tried to speak. His voice would not come.

The white room. The woman dressed in white is screaming. What's wrong?

"Doctor, Doctor Abramson, come quick. He's awake." She's talking about me.

The woman in white came running back into the white room followed by a man in a green scrub suit. A doctor. She pointed at Boxer.

Dr. Abramson hastened to Boxer's side, felt for a carotid pulse, checking the beat against his watch. "Seventy-four. Not bad at all."

The woman in white noted the measurement on a clipboard at the foot of the bed. His bed. Boxer stared at them, back and forth, from one to the other.

"You're okay, now, Admiral Boxer. I'm Dr. Abramson." He pointed to the woman in white. "Nurse Bender. She's been keeping an eye on you. Frankly, you startled her. She didn't expect . . ."

Boxer tried to speak again. Again the words wouldn't come.

"Of course we never gave up hope that—Oh, press your finger here when you want to say something." Abramson indicated a spot on his own throat. "I'm afraid we had to perform a tracheotomy. Life or death, you know. We'll close it up, now that you're back with us."

Boxer covered the opening in his trachea as he was

shown. "Whe . . . where am I? My men? Rolly?" The odd sound of his voice surprised him.

"Easy, now, Admiral. Take it easy. Nurse, give me a hand here, will you?"

"Yes, doctor." Nurse Bender went to Boxer's side, plumped several pillows behind his head and back, and adjusted the tubing that was causing him some discomfort.

Boxer forced a smile at her.

She smiled back, adjusted the IV drip, went back to the foot of the bed and made some notes on the clipboard. "I'll get you all spiffed up. You've got some important company here to see you."

Boxer asked the question with his eyes. Who?

"Surprise. He'll be here in a few minutes. Comfy?"

Boxer didn't answer. His eyes went to the doorway, where his important visitor had just entered.

Admiral Stark stood there in his full dress whites, leaning slightly on a cane. "Welcome back to the living, son." He made his way to Boxer's bedside.

Nurse Bender hustled over to him and offered a chair.

Stark settled into the seat, pulling the chair closer to the bed. He put his hand on Boxer's arm. "Thought you wouldn't make it for awhile, there," he offered. "Glad you did, though. I'd really hate to lose you. As bad as having to bury a son."

Boxer covered the trachea opening. "Where am I, Admiral Stark? What's happened to me?"

"You're in Bethesda, Jack. Government hospital, reserved for VIPs like yourself."

Boxer smiled.

Stark continued, "Well, Jack, you were very lucky. One of our rescue copters dropped a crew in after you just after you were blown off the *Halsey*. Got to you almost immediately. That's what saved your life. Another minute, two at the most, and I'm afraid you'd have been a goner."

"Have I been here long?"

"About a week here in the hospital. Before that, you spent some time aboard the *Rickover* with Admiral Rodgers before they flew you home."

Boxer grabbed Stark's sleeve with his free hand. "My men?"

Stark cleared his throat. "Some didn't make it, Jack. Captain Clemens is due to be released from Walter Reed. He suffered a concussion. Your navigator, Mahoney, is okay. So are most of the men who were aft of the control room. Your forward torpedo crew took the most damage. Almost none of them made it."

"Whitey, the cob?"

"Amos White, Chief of the Boat," Stark said, shaking his head. "He's too mean and tough to go down like that. In fact, he was one of the heroes. Helped get the survivors off the sinking sub and onto life rafts. Major Jones and his boys did well for themselves, too. Too bad that one of them got shot up so badly."

A flash of memory brought back the vision of Shorty at the heavy machine-gun, firing at the enemy, his own body being torn apart in return. No retreat. No surrender.

"Brave men, all," Admiral Stark continued. "The *Halsey* is on the bottom of the Gulf. Not enough left to salvage, so we destroyed her."

Boxer shook his head. He managed, "I'd like to see us get back on track. It's time we had a new super-sub to replace the *Barracuda*. That *Alpha* was almost too much for us."

Stark leaned closer. "This is very confidential, of course, but I understand that we're to do just that. As soon as a certain Admiral Jack Boxer is well enough to get back to work on helping develop the prototype."

"No shit. Well get me out of here so we can get started."

"I wish it were that easy, son. Dr. Abramson figures it will take at least another three, maybe four weeks till you're anywhere near fit again. You just concentrate on getting your strength back. I'll be by to visit you now and then."

Boxer fought back a tear forming in his eye. "Thank you, Admiral. I appreciate everything you've done."

"Nothing," the old admiral said as he hefted himself from the chair. "Nothing at all. Take care of yourself."

Nurse Bender entered just as Stark left the room. Boxer said to her, "Quite a guy, the admiral."

"More than you could imagine," she replied. "He's been here almost constantly since you were admitted last week. Hardly even goes home to sleep." Before Boxer could say anything, she added, "Oh, there are some others here to see you. Only for a minute, now. Dr. Abramson wants to close up the trachea now that you're feeling better."

As Nurse Bender stepped out, she was replaced by Major Roland Jones, whose muscular hulk filled the doorway. Rolly was at least six-four, a black Buddha with a shaved head and biceps the size of most men's thighs. He entered the room wearing a broad smile above his neatly pressed cammos. He was followed by Corporal "Mean Gene" Greene, and Sgt. Carlos Rivera, the only survivors of Rolly's Rangers in the Persian Gulf.

"Evening, Skipper," Jones said.

"Hello, Rolly." Boxer held up his hand to the others. "Gene, Carlos. Nice of you to visit."

"We been checkin' in on you every day," Mean Gene offered. "We didn't think you were going to make it."

Rolly shot a cross look at Gene.

Boxer smiled, and closed the opening in his throat. "Thanks for the vote of confidence, boys."

Rolly smiled, and allowed his men to relax a bit.

"The boys and me would like it if you'd join us in a little celebration when you get up and about. Captain Clemens thought it might be a good idea to talk things over, sort of get it all out of our systems."

"That would suit me just fine, Rolly. Thanks for thinking of me, guys."

"Nothing to it," Rivera replied.

"In fact, we brought you a little get well present, didn't we men?" Rolly motioned to the door with his head.

Mean Gene stuck his head out the doorway, said a few words and was followed back into the room by two very beautiful young women wearing Navy topcoats. Rolly said, "Admiral Jack Boxer, I'd like you to meet Sherree and Loralee." As he spoke, his men helped remove the women's coats, revealing very provocative, mini-sailor outfits.

Then he headed for the door, motioning with his head for his men to follow him. As he left, he said, "Ladies, cheer up Admiral Boxer."

Boxer looked puzzled at the two women, then at Rolly Jones.

"Compliments of Carlos, Gene and myself, Skipper. And of course, Strip-o-gram. See ya."

Boxer's mouth fell, then broke into a smile as Sherree and Loralee plied their trade to the beat of the portable cassette player they'd brought along. As piece after skimpy piece of clothing was taken off and tossed onto his hospital bed, Boxer's smile broadened. He lay there in the bed, unable to move, his eyes taking in the undulations of the two charmers as they bumped to the beat. He started to look heavenward for relief as the strippers got almost naked and started doing naughty things to themselves, and to each other. He broke out in an uncontrollable guffaw as Nurse Bender walked back into his room, saw what was happening, shrieked and dropped her bedpan before she went running down the hall after Dr. Abramson.

"Nice of Admiral Stark to let us use his shore house," Rolly Jones remarked as he slipped into the front passenger seat of the black BMW.

"He looks after me as if I were his son. Didn't have any of his own, so in a way, I guess I am. My folks are gone, and he has no relatives left, so we're sort of family to each

22

other." He unlatched the back doors from the console. "Hop in, guys."

Mark Clemens climbed in behind Rolly. Mean Gene walked around and sat in the seat behind Boxer. He ran his hand over the leather upholstery. "Hey, neat car. Yours?"

Boxer swallowed hard. The words were hard to say. "Belongs to a friend."

Mean Gene sensed he'd trod on hallowed ground, and kept quiet. Boxer broke the silence. "Well, our last weekend of R & R, before we have to become full-time sailors again."

"Me and Gene been working out with the SEALS at their special training station outside of Norfolk. I'm supposed to be given a new command soon, a tie-in with you, Skipper. That's all I been told so far. That, and to be ready for anything."

Boxer pulled away from the curb and made his way into the bustle of D.C. traffic. "You couldn't pick a finer bunch to train with than the SEALS."

"Right. Rivera's there right now, screening some recruits. I'll go down there after our weekend and make my final selections."

Gene nodded his head. "Yeah, then we gonna work their asses off till we're left with the toughest."

Boxer smiled. "It's a mean world out there."

"Don't I know it," Mean Gene replied.

Mark Clemens sat quietly watching the scenery and the famous landmarks along their route. They passed the Jefferson Memorial, crossed the bridge into Virginia, and headed south. With his carrot-top crewcut and freckled baby face, he looked like a child amongst the others. In fact, he was older than both Rolly and Mean Gene. And he'd be in line to command his own sub, which he'd turned down in order to be Boxer's EXO on their new assignment.

What he knew was that they'd be in on the development of a new class of sub. Similar to the *Barracuda*, he guessed,

23

but better. He'd know more after Boxer was briefed by the CNO on Monday.

". . . And a trout stream like you wouldn't believe," Boxer was saying. "There's plenty of fishing tackle to go around, and a very well stocked bar. Name your favorite beer, and I'll bet the admiral has it. We'll just have to stop for food along the way. There's a general store a few miles north of the property that we use."

The mood of the four men was good. Boxer was up to strength again, though he still got occasional dizzy spells. And loud noises were definitely out. That brought back the pain, and the memories. Other than that, he felt good again.

Clemens had gotten over his concussion, his other wounds healed over, though the scars left in the mind by almost going down with the sub would remain with him for awhile.

Rolly and Mean Gene were as strong as ever, in spite of the loss of their comrades. In fact, it had a toughening effect on their character, honing their will to survive.

"Anybody else gettin' hungry? There's a sign up ahead," Gene said.

"Sure, why not?" Boxer replied. He followed the signs for food and fuel along the feeder road off the interstate. After a few minutes they came to a dark rough-hewn building with a sign above which read SQUIRE'S INN, and the silhouette of a knight in armor. Boxer pulled onto the gravel parking area. "Well, what do you think, men?"

"Can't always tell a book by its cover," Gene said, obviously hungry enough to eat anywhere.

"What the hell," Rolly shrugged.

The four of them got out and headed for the heavy wooden entrance door. A small sign on the door stated, NO SHOES, NO SHIRTS, NO SERVICE. That brought a smile from all of them. They went inside, quickly adjusted to the dim lighting, and took a table in the corner. A pretty waitress dressed as a serving wench came to take their order.

"What's on tap?" Rolly asked.

"Bud, Bud Light, Miller and Coors," she recited. She had long blond hair done up in a braid that trailed behind her all the way down to there. She smiled at him.

"Coors it is, then," Rolly smiled back.

"I'll have the same," Gene said.

She looked at Clemens. "Scotch, rocks."

"And you, sir?"

Age breeds reverence, Boxer mused. She didn't call anyone else sir. "Stoli, straight up, please. And a lunch menu."

"Sure thing. I'll be right back with your drinks."

She returned quickly, placed their drinks in front of them, and a basket of fresh popcorn to munch on while their burgers were prepared. They were finishing their meal and on their second round of drinks when the gang came in.

"The Barbarians" was the name of the motorcycle gang, according to the fancy signwork on the backs of their black leather jackets. Nine . . . ten . . . eleven . . . twelve of them, Boxer counted as they pushed through the door and bullied their way to the bar. The smarter patrons backed away, found seats elsewhere. The unlucky few were shoved out of the way.

The leader, a large scruffy two hundred fifty pounder with black wooly hair on his head and exposed arms and ponderous belly slammed a fist on the bar and shouted, "Buds for the boys."

Some of the others laughed, as if that were the funniest thing they'd ever heard.

The bartender started pulling beers as fast as he could. Not fast enough for the leader. "Faster. C'mon, move your fuckin' ass. We're thirsty."

The barkeep would place a mug of beer on the bar, and Big Wooly slid it down to his men. "Faster," he ordered.

25

"They'll be done drinkin' down theirs before I get mine. And if that happens, your ass is grass."

"I'm working as fast as I can, Johnny."

The big man slammed his palm on the bar. "It's Johnny Ace. And don't forget it."

"Sorry." He kept up the supply of beers as fast as he could.

Johnny Ace slid the mugs faster and harder, trying to smash into the previous mug before his men lifted them off the bar. Finally, he succeeded, dousing several nearby patrons with beer and derisive laughter.

"My, how clumsy of me," he guffawed, to the accompaniment of his merry men.

The frightened bartender said, "Drinks are on the house, boys. No charge for the beers. Don't worry about the mess. I'll clean it."

His job of intimidating the bartender out of free drinks over, Johnny Ace turned his attention to the patrons. "Hey, anybody here own that fag BMW outside?"

Boxer and the others looked at each other, but remained silent. So far it was only talk.

"Nobody? Good. Then nobody will give a shit about the footprints we put on it." That set his gang to laughing again.

Not having provoked a fight yet, Johnny Ace peered at Boxer's group and continued, "Hey, we don't like no niggers in here."

Veins popped out on Rolly's shaved head. Boxer placed a hand on his forearm. Rolly said. "It's okay. I'm in control."

Boxer said. "Let's get going. No sense in letting these assholes spoil our weekend." He motioned for the waitress for their check.

"I got to take a leak," Clemens said. "Be right back." He got up, tossed a ten on the table, and made his way around the bar to the men's room.

The waitress with the long blond hair gave them the

check, then took it back to the bar to make change. Johnny Ace began to harass her. He took hold of the end of her braid and pulled just a little, to let her know who's boss.

She grabbed her braid from the middle and tried to pull it away from him, but in vain. "Let me go."

Johnny Ace laughed. "Know what they used to call a serving *wrench* like this back in old England?"

Some of his gang shrugged.

"A piece of ass," he bellowed.

Boxer was having difficulty controlling his temper.

Gene nudged him with an elbow. "Hey, Skipper. Clem's been gone too long just to take a piss."

"Maybe he had to do more than that."

"Maybe . . . maybe not. I'll be right back." Gene got up and made for the restrooms.

Johnny Ace pulled the girl closer to him, got a beefy arm around her, hugged her against his belly. He reached around and roughly grabbed her behind. "A piece of ass. That's what I want."

The blond waitress pushed him off, unsuccessfully. He reached for the front of her square-cut bodice and tugged at it. "Watcha got there, baby. Haw haw haw."

Some of the cronies laughed along with him. Someone pinched the woman's ass. They were having a grand time with her.

Boxer stood up. He pushed his chair away and headed for the bar. Rolly Jones was a step behind him.

Mean Gene pushed open the door to the men's room and went inside. He heard the sounds of a beating before he turned the corner. Two punks from the gang held Clemens up against the onslaught of a third. A lanky greasy haired punk in a sleeveless leather jacket was pounding Clemens's stomach. The two goons yanked him up by his head, and he was beaten in the face. Clem was a mess. An eye was swollen, his lip was split. Blood trickled down his chin.

The punks were taunting him. "What's the matter,

Howdy Doody? Mommy let you out by yourself?"

"He's not by himself."

Mean Gene's voice caught the one doing the beating by surprise. The punk turned to face the voice.

Gene spun quickly. His foot swung high in an arch and caught the jaw of the greaser. The jawbone cracked. The greaser went down holding his face, crying in pain.

The other two split up, circled to either side of Gene. Clemens sank to the floor.

Gene let them get closer. Suddenly, he charged the one closest to the wall of mirrors above the sinks. His foot shot out sideways. The punk's knee snapped, and he went down.

Gene snapped a downward blow of his fist against the nose of the third goon. He thrust his taut fingertips into the punk's throat.

The biker clutched at his neck. Blood spurted from his broken nose. He watched the small, wiry guy with the short hair glare at him through crazed eyes. He tried to protect himself against what was to come.

"Motherfucker." Gene smashed at the nose again. And again.

The punk stumbled backward into a toilet stall.

Gene kicked him in the groin, spun him around when he doubled up clutching his balls, and stuffed his head into the toilet. Gene held the head under long enough to make the biker think twice about getting up.

The second punk was back on his feet, limping slightly where he'd been kicked. He brandished a six-inch blade, and crouched low, ready to lunge at Gene.

Mean Gene just smiled. "Thanks, asshole. Just the excuse I need to kill you."

The punk couldn't believe it. He was holding the knife and the guy threatens to kill him? His attention was distracted just enough.

Gene lashed out a long kick to the solar plexus. The biker dropped the knife, clutched his stomach. Mistake

28

number two. Gene straightened him up with a fist, turned him facing the wall and grabbed a handful of hair. "Vanity will be your undoing, asshole," Gene said, and slammed the punk's face into the mirror. Broken glass and blood fell into the sink below.

Gene went to Clemens and helped him to his feet. "You okay, Clem?"

"Felt better," he managed. "Thanks."

With Clemens hanging on for support, Gene made for the door. He stepped into the room just in time to hear . . .

"I said, 'Leave the lady alone.' "

Johnny Ace turned to his gang behind him. "You hear that, boys? Leave the lady alone." He turned back to face Boxer.

Wham. Boxer's fist found its mark. Wham. Left handed version of the same. Johnny Ace stared blankly. Wham. A right cross knocked him senseless. A leg sweep sent him sprawling down.

Rolly was on the next closest biker before he could react. He grabbed a handful of throat and squeezed. Tears came to the biker's eyes; tears that pleaded to be let go because the mouth couldn't speak. Rolly slammed the guy's face into the bar.

A punk hoisted a bar stool and swung it at Rolly. He stopped it and brought it down hard on the punk's head.

The remaining half dozen bikers tried to retreat toward the exit. Mean Gene cut off their escape.

Someone pulled a knife. Clemens watched from the bar. He picked up a full bottle of beer and hurled it at the guy's head. Strike one.

"Nice one, Clem," Boxer said. He, Rolly and Mean Gene closed in on the remaining five bikers. The battle was short and sweet. Five up and five down.

Boxer surveyed the room. Not a biker was left standing. Someone started to applaud, then another, until all the patrons not involved in the fighting were giving them a standing ovation. The waitress walked up to him. "I don't know how to thank you."

"You don't have to. They got what they deserved."

The bartender came over to them. Boxer said, "Sorry about the mess. I'll pay for the damages."

The bartender smiled. "Don't worry about it. I'm insured. I just wanted to tell you that your food and drinks are on me. Maybe the *Barbarians* will find someplace else to terrorize from now on."

Boxer put a hand on the barkeep's shoulder. "Maybe they shouldn't be terrorizing anyone again. Thanks for the chow."

The four of them walked back into the parking lot. Someone, indeed, had walked on the BMW with muddy boots. Mean Gene became infuriated. He walked up to a row of motorcycles parked nearby and kicked at one. The row of six toppled like dominos.

Rolly said, "That goes for me too," and kicked over the remaining half-dozen bikes. He and Gene stood there looking at each other, panting from the exertion. Rolly said, "Mean Gene, you thinking what I'm thinking?"

"Does, 'burn your bridges behind you,' mean anything to you?"

Gene ripped the bottom third off his undershirt, removed the gas cap on the nearest bike and stuffed in the cloth. Rolly did the same to another motorcycle, near the bottom of the pileup. Then he struck a flame on his Marine Corps Zippo lighter. "Semper Fi," he said, lighting the first wick.

"You can say that again. It's music to my ears."

Rolly did, and lit the second wick. "That ought to do it."

Boxer watched the flames for a moment. "We'd better be going."

"Right." The four of them piled into the BMW, and pulled out of the parking lot to the crunching sound of the gravel underneath. The first gas tank exploded as they pulled out onto the feeder road. The second bike blew as they passed by the front of the Squire's Inn. They watched the pile of burning motorcycles behind them as they sped back onto the interstate. Finally, once again they could relax. Boxer asked, "Everyone okay? Clem?"

Clemens smiled through split lips, touched his swollen eye, and said, "I'll be all right, I guess. But this is sure a strange way to spend a weekend of R & R."

CHAPTER THREE

"Morning, Admiral Boxer." The young Marine sergeant snapped to attention and saluted crisply. "Sgt. John Englert, sir. I'll escort you to Admiral Mason's office."

Boxer returned the salute and followed the sergeant onto an elevator, and felt himself descend the two levels to the sub-basement. He followed the Marine down the familiar gray corridor, finding himself wishing that he was being escorted by Lt. Kathleen Carson, whom he'd met on previous visits to the CNO. He smiled, standing there while Sergeant Englert fed his coded passcard into a slot on the doorjamb of Mason's suite of offices. "Admiral Jack Boxer here to see Admiral Mason," he spoke into an intercom.

The heavy steel door clicked open and the two men went inside, to a vast room filled with computer equipment purring away, clerical workers busy at their desks, and more workers monitoring banks of consoles filled with electronic maps and charts. They were greeted by a lieutenant commander, Mason's personal aide, at the door to the inner office. "Admiral Boxer's here, sir."

"Send him in," Mason barked in his customary gravelly voice.

Boxer straightened his tie, set his cap on just so, and went inside, closing the door behind him. He stood at attention and saluted perfunctorily. He didn't care much for Mason, as a person or as the CNO.

Mason replied by touching his finger tips to his forehead. He was hatless, his steel gray hair cut short in military fashion. Mason had a round face with fleshy jowls, and a short, stout body. "Sit down, Boxer."

Boxer took a chair across the huge teak desk from Mason, tucking his cap under his arm.

Mason uncovered a humidor on his desk, helped himself to a fat cigar, and offered one to Boxer. "Thanks, but I'll stick to my pipe if that's okay with you."

"Suit yourself." Mason deftly cut the tip with a pocket knife and lit up, drawing deeply until an even white ash formed on the cigar. He blew a smoke ring at the ceiling, and waited for Boxer to finish lighting up. "A nice bit of work you did off Iran."

The compliment surprised Boxer. "Thank you, Admiral. Mission accomplished, but at too great a price. We lost too many men."

"Not to mention a damned good three-hundred million dollar submarine, to boot. Try to be more careful with the hardware, next time. We're going to be playing for bigger stakes."

"Meaning . . . ?"

"Meaning the president wants us to develop the ultimate underwater fighting machine. A state of the art submarine capable of outperforming anything the enemy can throw at us. A hunter-killer that can take on and destroy any Russian sub, out-run and out-fight any ship sent to neutralize it, that can remain at sea for a half a year at a time if necessary, and—"Mason paused for emphasis, "strike fear into the souls of the Ruskies and Chinese with first-strike ICBM capability."

"Whew. No small order, there."

"President Spooner would like to be able to deploy a small, elite strike force from the sub. You already know Major Jones. He'll command the strike force."

"Good choice, Admiral. Rolly Jones fears nothing in this world. Nothing. He's a born leader, not afraid to make the tough calls, either."

"You're to begin work on the project, code name *Manta*, at once. You'll have one of our best engineers assigned to you. The three of us will be the only ones with the big picture. Everyone else will have access to the project according to their specialty on a need to know basis, only."

"Suits me fine. Except that I have some unfinished business to attend to."

Mason realized that Boxer wanted to go after Julio Sanchez, for the trouble he had caused Francine Wheeler and Admiral Stark. He wasn't about to let that interfere with the president's wishes, especially when his own ass was on the line. "Save your personal vendettas until we're into the production stage. Then you can do whatever the hell you want to. If you want to go get yourself killed, I'm sure I can find someone else to command the new sub."

Boxer gave it some thought, decided to put his personal feelings on hold for the time being. "Okay," he said. "Fine."

"You'll have the best brains in the industry available to you for consultation. What I want from you is a wish list of the features that you want on the *Manta*. We'll proceed from there."

Boxer's face broke out in a broad grin. "Thank you, Admiral."

"Don't thank me, Boxer. The president wants you on this project. So be it. Now I want you to meet your engineer." Mason buzzed Lt. Commander Wilcox seated outside. "Get me Carson."

Carson? Could it possibly be the same Lt. Kathy Carson that Boxer had been thinking about a few moments ago? He smiled at the thought.

The smile broadened when Carson the engineer turned out to be none other than the young lieutenant j.g. whom Boxer had admired the last time he'd visited the CNO. Carson saluted and smiled back. "How do you do, Admiral

34

Boxer. I'm happy to be working with you on this project."

Boxer returned the salute. Before he could reply, Mason growled, "I'll have no griping about working with a woman on this, Boxer. Carson's the best we have available."

Boxer looked very serious. "No problem at all, Admiral. I'm sure Lieutenant Carson will do just fine."

Mason blew smoke toward the ceiling, ending with a perfectly formed smoke ring. "Why don't the two of you take the rest of the day to get acquainted. Carson, show Admiral Boxer around your office and the CAD programs you can run off the mainframe. Project *Manta* starts officially at oh-eight hundred tomorrow."

"Aye, aye, sir." Carson saluted.

Boxer looked at Mason, his eyes asking if there was anything else.

"That's all, now," Mason grumbled. "Dismissed."

Boxer saluted as before, and held the door open for Lieutenant Carson as they left Mason's office. "Pleasant fellow," he whispered to her when they were out of earshot.

She blushed in reply. "Project headquarters is down the hall. We have our own staff, access to any computers we need, the motor pool at our disposal, the works."

"Big time."

Carson smiled.

When they entered their new quarters, Carson said. "Well, Admiral, how do you like it?" with a sweep of her arm.

"First of all," Boxer replied, "You're going to wear yourself out calling me Admiral Boxer all the time. My men call me Skipper, and that'll be just fine for you, too."

Carson blushed again. "Well, if you insist. And, please, Lieutenant Carson is a bit stuffy, also, if we're going to be working together like this. Feel free to address me by my given name."

"All right, Kathleen, isn't it?"

"My close friends call me Kit."

Boxer smiled at her. "Kit Carson. Okay, then. Kit it is. This is quite a place."

"Yes. I think it will work out just fine."

Boxer checked his watch. It was almost 1300. "Anybody here as hungry as I am?"

"Count me in, Skipper. Shall we go up to the commissary?"

Boxer said, "Rank has its privileges, Kit. I know a great little restaurant in Georgetown. Shall we?"

"Aye, aye, sir . . . I mean Skipper. My pleasure."

"My pleasure, darling," Richard Baxter said, clicking his champagne glass against Lori-Ann's. "I propose a toast to the three month anniversary of our marriage. Thanks to you, it's actually working out all right. Happy, darling?"

Lori-Ann Collins was indeed happy. As she smiled, her eyes took in the splendor of the dining room in one of D.C.'s most magnificent restaurants. A few short months ago, Jacques would have been off-limits to her. But now, as the wife of a distinguished career diplomat from a wealthy family, the world was hers. A far cry from the austerity of the Russian orphanage of her youth. Her sexuality had taken her far. "Yes, Richard. Very happy. Thank you."

"You're very beautiful, you know. Perhaps, had I known you sooner, well, who knows?" He smiled at her, his eyes taking in all that she had to offer. She wore an elegant off-the-shoulder cream colored silk gown, cut very low in front to reveal the tops of her lush, pear-shaped breasts, the trace of her nipples toying with the edge of her bodice. Her long raven hair flowed flawlessly onto her bare shoulders. Her high cheekbones and almost green eyes and sensuous lips gave her face a cover-girl quality. To Baxter, she was just perfect.

And she was the perfect cover to hide the fact that he'd been a homosexual since the age of fifteen. When his position as Undersecretary of State for Eastern Europe had been endangered by hints of his sexual preferences, she had come through for him, in fact, suggested this marriage. Now, they were both off the hook, he at State, she, at the CIA, for having a gay boyfriend. The marriage had shaken off their critics. The approaching figure of Andre, the maître d' broke his concentration. "Ah," he said to Lori-Ann, "Let's see what Andre suggests for dinner tonight, shall we?"

Andre nodded at Lori-Ann, and turned to Richard Baxter. His usually jovial face now quite somber, Andre bent forward and whispered in Baxter's ear. Then he handed him a folded note.

Baxter read it quickly, then looked up at Lori-Ann, the color suddenly drained from his face. "It's my parents. There's been an accident."

Lori-Ann's fingers went up to her lips. "Oh, my God. Is it serious, Richard?"

Baxter stared at her for a moment.

"Richard? Are you all right?"

"Oh, sorry. Yes, it seems as though they were badly hurt. They're at the hospital in Georgetown."

Andre cleared his throat. "I've taken the liberty of having your driver bring the limo out front, Monsieur Baxter. Perhaps you'd better go look after them. I'll take care of things here."

Baxter stood up rather shakily. "I'm grateful, Andre." He held out his hand to Lori-Ann as the maître d' pulled back her chair for her.

The ride to the hospital took less than fifteen minutes. Baxter flashed his credentials at the swarm of police officers milling around the emergency entrance. A burly uniformed policeman took his arm and said, "Right this way,

Mr. Baxter. The sergeant would like to see you."

They came to a heavy-set man in a tan raincoat who was speaking to several other plainclothes types, busily jotting down his words in little notebooks. The heavy-set man stopped in mid-sentence when the patrolman approached escorting the well-dressed young couple.

"I have Mr. Richard Baxter and his wife here, Sergeant."

"Detective Sergeant Francis X. Murphy," he said, extending a hand to Baxter. He tipped his hat to Lori-Ann. "Ma'am."

"How . . . how are my parents, Sergeant? Are they all right?"

Murphy put a consoling hand on Baxter's shoulder. "I'm afraid I have bad news for you, sir." Murphy took a deep breath, and let it out. This part was never easy. "I'm afraid they're both dead. Never knew what hit them."

Baxter stared at him, too stunned to speak.

"An eighteen-wheeler rammed their limo broadside out on the beltway. The truck burst into flames, killing the driver and your parents. Their chauffeur is in critical conditions upstairs."

"But . . . how . . . how could this happen? Johnson, their driver, was a professional. He never took risks."

Murphy shook his head. "Don't know. Forensics is working on it now. Seems as if the truck driver lost control. But with him dead, too, perhaps we'll never know."

Baxter stood there with tears running down his face. Lori-Ann removed a handkerchief from her bag and daubed at his tears. She put her arms around him, squeezing him to her body, tried to comfort him as best she could. In a way, she really felt sorry for him. Now, they were both orphans, though suddenly enormously wealthy orphans at that. And maybe the fat detective would never know what caused the fatal accident, but she felt sure that she did. The professionalism of the double murder, and subsequent neutralization of the truck driver-killer were the hallmarks of her KGB control, Richard Frumpkin. She shuddered slightly, and held on tighter to her husband.

CHAPTER FOUR

Igor Borodine awoke at 0600, donned his best uniform, spit-shined his shoes for the third time in two days, checked his appearance in a mirror, and tiptoed past the sleeping figure of his wife, Tanya, hoping not to waken her. He paused by the cradle holding his infant son, Viktor, pulled the tiny blanket up onto the child, and smiled. He never imagined himself being a father at the age of thirty-eight, having gone through a twelve year childless marriage to his first wife, Galina. Well, he thought as he straightened his tie again, mustn't keep Admiral of the Soviet Fleet, Gorshkov, waiting.

"Igor, is that you?"

"Who else?" Borodine walked quietly to his wife's bedside. "You have another man who comes to visit you in your bedroom, my dear?"

Tanya smiled as Borodine touched her cheek with the back of his hand. "Silly. You know you are the only man in my life. Not counting Viktor Igorovich, trying to sleep over there while his father does his best to rouse him. Come kiss me good-bye."

Borodine sat at the edge of the bed, careful not to ruin the crease in his trousers. He bent forward and kissed his wife quickly on the cheek.

"A kiss, Igor. That is not a kiss."

He found her lips and planted a long, languishing kiss, teasing her with his tongue.

"Why Igor, I didn't know you cared," she giggled. "Now hurry. You don't want to be late for your meeting with Comrade Admiral Gorshkov."

Borodine decided to walk the nine blocks from his apartment in Moscow to the offices of the High Naval Command. The late summer sun warmed him as he strode briskly through the bleak sameness of the concrete jungle that made up the neighborhood. That the old admiral had called him to a special meeting was a good sign, a sign that he was returning to the good graces of the Politboro. He was sure that heads had rolled when he proved what could have been a fatal flaw in the proposed new *Brezhnev* class sub prototype. That was too bad, he thought, but countless lives of good submariners could have been lost, to say nothing of billions of ruples, due to malfunctioning nuclear power plants aboard the subs.

He arrived at Gorshkov's office ten minutes early. He was made to wait only fifteen minutes before being admitted by the admiral's secretary, an overweight captain with a sour, jowly face and a five o'clock shadow even at 0800 hours. Gorshkov rose as he entered, and Borodine snapped a formal salute. Gorshkov extended his hand, which Borodine shook. The Admiral of the Fleet was a stocky man in his late sixties with a ruddy complexion, a full head of gray hair and steel gray eyes.

"Good morning, Admiral Gorshkov."

Gorshkov sat down. "And good morning to you, Igor Alexandrovich. It is good to see you looking so fit again."

"I'm feeling just fine, sir."

"And your family?"

"Well, Admiral. The baby's doing just fine."

"And your beautiful wife?"

Borodine smiled. Was the old admiral warming him up for the kill? Surely he was not summoned to headquarters to report on the well-being of his family. Still, he could not rush Gorshkov. "Tanya is as well and beautiful as ever, Comrade Admiral. And very grateful for the maternity leave so she can look after young Viktor herself."

"An admiral's wife has certain privileges, Igor. It is a small price for the Motherland to pay to the wife of a man who saved our submarine fleet from possible oblivion because of his expertise and the candor to express it."

Borodine shrugged, "It was nothing that anyone else couldn't do."

"Unfortunately, most bureaucrats wouldn't risk standing up to their superiors on an important matter like this one. It would be someone else's ass on the line, not theirs. In fact, it might put them in a position to take over for their bosses, should they fall from power. But not you, Comrade Borodine."

Borodine sat there, waiting patiently.

Gorshkov asked, "Breakfast?"

"Some coffee would be nice, thank you."

"Not tea? No matter. We have some fine Costa Rican coffee, which we get through our comrades in Nicaragua. I think you'll like it." He buzzed his intercom, and barked, "Coffee for Admiral Borodine and myself."

"Yes, Comrade Admiral," was the reply on the desk speaker.

Gorshkov reached into his desk and produced two fat cigars, placing them in front of Borodine. "Help yourself to a smoke. They're Cuban."

Borodine hated to smoke cigars so early in the morning, but he didn't want to displease Gorshkov, who seemed to be in an especially good mood. The older man took a cigar cutter from his pants pocket and clipped the ends off both their cigars. Soon each man had lit up and was blowing smoke toward the ceiling fan, when the secretary entered with a silver tray bearing a silver pot and two glass cups set into silver holders, as well as real cream and sugar.

Borodine sipped his black coffee while he waited for Gorshkov to mix his with two spoons of sugar and an unhealthy amount of cream. The old man tasted his concoction, and leaned back with a smile of approval. He said, "The reason I've called you here today is to promote you to director of the new design team on the *Brezhnev* prototype."

Borodine didn't reply. It didn't make much difference to him one way or the other.

"And to direct you to test the new sub upon its completion. Congratulations, Igor. You'll be going back to sea, again."

Borodine's face broke into a wide smile. "Thank you, Comrade. That's wonderful. I don't know how to . . ."

"No need to thank me. I chose the best man for the . . ."

Suddenly, an intensely loud klaxon siren reverberated through the entire underground office complex. Gorshkov looked up at the wailing speaker on his wall. "Your friend, Comrade Kakusky has arranged for one of his air-raid tests. The KGB tries to keep us in a continuous war-alert stage. Well, let's get started. Help me empty the safe."

Borodine helped Gorshkov fill three large briefcases with the contents of a small safe on the rear wall. "Oh, yes. The fabled underground network."

"Come. Through this door." The two of them stood before an elevator door. They entered the car and were soon descending a shaft a hundred meters below the sub-basement offices. "The others with Code Armageddon clearance will soon join us," he added.

Gorshkov led the way to an underground subway system. They climbed into an electric car and followed the gray concrete concourse about a half mile, where they stopped at the opening of a vast bunker carved out of the subterranean trap-rock. Even with a functioning air conditioning system, Borodine couldn't escape the pervasive smell of mildew, or the chill caused by the high humidity. The overall feeling was reminiscent of his early submarine training years in the old *Whiskey* class SSK's.

Sentries, armed with AK-47 assault rifles checked their credentials, challenging Borodine's right to enter. "He is my assistant," Gorshkov insisted. "Stand aside, and let us pass."

The sentries hesitated a moment, then gave way to Gorshkov's scowl. The two admirals made their way down a gray painted concrete block hallway and entered a room set in on the right wall. Several dozen men and an elderly woman were seated or milling about a long lacquered table. Borodine recognized several of the Chiefs of Staff and some of their assistants. Valentine Kakusky, the Deputy Director of the KGB's Second Directorate was present, as was his boss, Marshal Svedrovsky, the Director. Kakusky came forward with a clipboard.

Gorshkov nodded, and said, "Comrade Kakusky."

Borodine chose not to acknowledge the man at all. Kakusky had been responsible for his desk job in the first place. He'd forced Borodine out of active sea duty because of a flap over the baptism of his child, Viktor, in a Roman Catholic church in Poland. Borodine would never forgive the man for that.

"Comrade Admiral Gorshkov. You have made excellent speed in getting here. Congratulations." He turned to Borodine. "If necessary we could fight a protracted nuclear war from these quarters. The imperialists have nothing that even comes close."

Borodine made no comment, though he was duly impressed.

"So," Kakusky continued, "I understand that you have been put in charge of our new state-of-the art submarine class."

Borodine nodded, but still said nothing.

"Since I am in charge of overall security for the project, perhaps we can meet in the near future to enhance our mutual understanding?"

Borodine was about to object when Gorshkov replied for him. "Of course, that would be in the best interest of the project." He turned to Borodine. "I'm sure we can spare some time for you and Comrade Kakusky to meet."

The stern look on the old admiral's face left no doubt in Borodine's mind that he must comply. "Certainly, Comrade. I will make time available next week for Comrade Kakusky."

Kakusky smiled, and nodded his satisfaction. "Very well, then. I shall pay you a visit on Monday. Good day, then, Comrades."

As the KGB man walked away, Gorshkov stepped closer to Borodine and whispered, "The cooperation was mandatory. Just be sure to watch your ass."

"Believe me, Comrade Admiral," Borodine countered, "I intend to do just that."

Lt. Kit Carson sat before an ultra-high resolution CRT display screen, her fingers resting lightly on the keyboard on her desk. Boxer sat beside her. He opened a small, leather-bound notebook. "My wish list," he explained.

"Very well, Skipper. Your wish is my command."

Boxer smiled. He was beginning to like Carson a great deal. "Okay, I'd like to use the *Shark* as a starting point. We'll modify her, based on my experiences since then."

Carson keyed in some figures, and in a few moments, a three-dimensional line drawing of the *Shark* came onto the screen in front, side, and top views, as well as profile. By pressing certain key combinations, she was able to rotate the profiled image through any angle.

"First of all, I'd like more speed. We want to outrun anything the Ruskies have. At least fifty-five to sixty knots flank speed submerged."

Carson entered some data into her computer. "That may

not be possible, Skipper."

"Try. At this point, I just want to come up with the best sub that we can. Later, we'll work around any existing limitations. Next, I want a safe diving depth of at least three thousand feet."

Kit Carson looked at him, smiled, then turned to her computer and entered the criteria.

Boxer smiled back. "The CNO is adamant on ICBM capability. So, we need at least a half-dozen tubes for ballistic missiles."

"That contradicts your earlier request, Skipper." Carson was shaking her head. "You're asking for the speed and maneuverability of a SSN, and the performance of a boomer."

"And while you're at it," Boxer continued, "I want facilities to transport a strike force of at least a hundred men."

"What you're asking for is . . ." Lieutenant Carson played with the keyboard, and came up with a huge, bulbous cigar-shaped submarine on her display screen. ". . . That monster. It's closer to a Soviet *Typhoon* class than the *Shark*. At least five-fifty to six-hundred feet long. You're looking at an unacceptable length to breadth ratio of twelve or more to one."

She continued to query the computer with her keyboard commands. "She would weight in at twenty-five thousand tons dived, would require a tremendous power plant, and the men to keep it humming. I'm afraid that instead of getting the best of the boomers and hunter-killers, we've come up with a turkey." Carson was obviously getting flustered. "Respectfully, Admiral, I just don't buy this design."

Boxer broke out in a big smile. The lady knows her stuff, and isn't afraid to show it. "Agreed, Lieutenant. An eight to one ratio is the maximum acceptable. We need to scale her down, completely computerize her. That will eliminate fifty men, whose living space will be used instead by my

46

strike force."

"Oh."

"Power the *Manta* with liquid metal cooled reactors. That will save additional space."

She started to type in data into the computer. "We've never really proven them to be safe."

"The Ruskie *Alfas* have been using them for a decade. We'll prove them safe. Kit, I want a crew no larger than forty men, officers and petty officers only. Anything that can be performed using shoreside personnel will be handled at the base."

Carson agreed. "That will certainly free up personnel. I'm beginning to like this new sub, Skipper."

"Our main objective is to be able to deploy a strike force to any trouble spot in the world. We'll need to be able to fight our way in and out, and at the CNO's insistence, deal a death blow to the enemy with our ICBM's."

"Aye, aye, Skipper. That's a tall order, but I'm up to it. I assume we'll keep the retracting sail from the *Shark* class."

"You assume correctly, Kit." Boxer was clearly pleased with his new assistant.

"The *Shark* was the prototype we studied in my submarine engineering classes at the Academy," she said. "Even though the design was almost eight years old by then."

Boxer blushed. Carson must have just entered high-school about the time he was putting the *Shark* through her sea trials. "Why don't we give the design boys your data, Kit. Give them something to work on. I have some more ideas I'd like to see implemented, but that can wait till we have a better idea of the hull design."

"Sure. Well, I guess that's about it for today."

Boxer packed his notes into a leather briefcase and slipped into his white uniform jacket. "Can I drop you off somewhere? I've got a car with me."

"Just home, I guess. I'm turning into a regular couch

potato."

Boxer opened the door for her. "What? All these men around and no date? No special guy?"

She shook her head. "Being an officer, I can't date the enlisted men. And the officers . . ." Carson shrugged in exasperation. "They're afraid the CNO will take their heads off if they get involved with one of his staff." As they walked down the corridor toward the elevator, "Or maybe it's just me. Maybe I just turn guys off. I wish I knew."

"I can assure you," Boxer said with a grin, "that is not the case. You're beautiful, bright, self-assured. No, I think you'll make the right man, when he comes along, very happy." He stepped aside to her let enter the elevator car.

On the way up she said, "Sure. Here I am twenty-five years old and no prospects. My mother says I'll never get married. She says guys feel threatened by me. Heck, I'm just a girl trying to do the best I can to make it on my own."

They both saluted the Marine guards as they left the Pentagon building. Inside the black BMW Boxer said, "No sense in both of us eating alone. Will you join me for dinner tonight? I know some good restaurants in D.C."

Carson beamed. "I'd love to. But let me cook for you. We can pick up some steaks and salad fixin's at the Big D."

"You sure it's no trouble?" Boxer couldn't remember his last home-cooked meal.

"No trouble at all. I don't live far from here, and the supermarket's a few blocks from my apartment."

While Kit picked out a pair of thick T-bones and assembled the makings of the salad, Boxer found a well-stocked wine department and picked out a vintage Bordeaux and a Beaujolais to go with dinner. He joined Carson and paid for the provisions.

They were at Kit's apartment in less than ten minutes. It was a three room affair, with a large eat-in kitchen, a bedroom behind a closed door, and the living room which was done in grays with pink and burgundy tones as the main color accent. Boxer was impressed with its clean lines and comfortable, tasteful touches.

It definitely bore a woman's touch, with its pink throw cushions on the white, overstuffed sofa and chairs, fresh flowers in a vase on a glass coffee table, and framed watercolors of floral still-lifes. On a short wall abutting the kitchen, Boxer noticed several framed photographs of people, presumably family. One of the subjects was a distinguished-looking man in a lieutenant commander's uniform. Hmm, Navy family, Boxer mused.

"Why don't you make yourself comfortable, Skipper. There's a bar in the living room, if you'd like a drink."

"Thanks," Boxer said, folding his jacket neatly over the arm of a chair. "What'll you have?"

"Rum and Coke, please. You'll find some Meyers dark rum."

"Fine. Any vodka?"

"I think so."

Boxer was pleased to find a bottle of Finlandia. Not Russian vodka, but the Fins were right up there. He returned to the kitchen with their drinks. He added ice from the freezer, and topped Kit's glass off with Coke from the fridge. She had removed her jacket and tie, and was standing there making the salad in her stocking feet. Boxer waited till she was done and handed her the drink.

They clinked glasses. "Let's see." Boxer thought a moment. "Here's to our new association. May we design the best submarine ever built."

"I'll drink to that." Kit sipped her drink. "Mmmm, perfect. I'd better put up the steaks. Dinner in ten minutes."

Boxer went back into the living room. He found the overstuffed chair as comfortable as it looked. In a moment, she joined him. She noticed him staring at her family photos. "That's Mom and Dad when they were just married.

49

That's Dad in uniform."

"Is he still in the service, or did he retire?"

Tears welled up in Kit's eyes. "He was killed in the Persian Gulf on escort duty. His ship was damaged by an Iranian gunboat on a suicide raid. They went right for the bridge. Dad never knew what hit him."

"I'm sorry."

"Me too. I really miss him. I was just a kid when he got killed, but I promised myself that I would try to carry on in his footsteps. Become the best naval officer I could."

"I'm sure he'd be proud of you."

Kit wiped her eyes. "Smells like the steaks are done." She went into the kitchen. "Rare okay?" she called back.

"Perfect. I'll open the wine."

They each ate a large portion of salad. Boxer watched in amusement as Carson made light work of the thick steak. Together, they polished off the Bordeaux and half of the Beaujolais. Kit made coffee and they brought it into the living room. Boxer settled into the sofa, and she sat down next to him. They were both feeling the effects of the alcohol.

Carson pointed to the group of photos. "See that good-looking blond guy? Looks like an actor or a model? That's Richard. We were engaged."

"You don't have to talk about it if you don't want to."

Kit sipped her coffee. "It's okay. In the past now. I met Richard at a party. One of my friends introduced us, and we really hit it off. He's so worldly. And so handsome. And there I was, fresh out of Annapolis." She tucked her feet up under her, and turned to face Boxer.

She continued, "We dated a lot. Hot and heavy, you know. Got engaged. Mother just loved that. We set the date, invited all the relatives . . ." Carson's voice trailed off. "And then I caught him cheating on me. I stopped off at his place unexpectedly one day. And there was the man of my dreams, my future husband, in bed with another man."

Boxer nearly choked on his coffee.

She laughed, and put down her cup. "Took me almost a year to get over Richard. Funny thing is, I read in the society column recently that Richard got married. Beautiful woman, too. I understand she works for the CIA. I guess I'll never figure out what went wrong. Maybe I drove him into the arms of another man."

As the tears began to well up in Kit's eyes, Boxer hugged her to him and held her. "Don't go kicking yourself in the pants over him, Kit. Sometimes these guys need a beautiful woman to cover their homosexuality, especially if they work in sensitive jobs."

"Do you think so?" She wiped her eyes, but continued holding Boxer. "You could be right. Richard works for the State Department, you know. Anyway, thanks for the shoulder to cry on." Kit hugged Boxer, then said, "Well, I'm glad I got that off my chest. Maybe sometime you'll tell me your life story, too."

"Maybe."

They looked at each other a moment. Kit moved into Boxer's arms, they embraced, and kissed each other passionately, she holding on tightly to him, he caressing her back and shoulders.

Finally, she looked into his eyes and said, "I've never gone to bed with an admiral before. Do you think we . . . ?

Boxer picked her up and carried her into the bedroom. He placed her down gently on a queen-size platform bed.

Kit turned on a small night-light. "You can put your clothes on that chair," she pointed. "I'll turn down the covers."

Boxer slowly undressed, while he watched her take off her clothes and toss them in a heap on the floor. When she was down to her white, lacy bikini panties, she hooked her thumbs under them and slid them provocatively down her legs.

Boxer noticed that she had a fine, athletic body, muscular and well proportioned, but with curves in all the right places. It looked like she worked hard to keep fit. Kit had a narrow waist and nice long legs. She had full, firm-looking breasts with large nipples, which had become hard and erect.

And speaking of erect, Boxer felt himself becoming excited by what he saw. They came together on the bed, embracing tightly, exploring each other's bodies with their hands, and then their tongues. Boxer licked her nipples, running his tongue around them, taking them into his mouth and sucking eagerly.

She must have been very sensitive there. She lay back, her hands fondling and stroking his manhood.

Boxer continued licking his way down her taut belly. His hands gently parted her thighs, and he worked his tongue over her clit, toying and playing with it as she writhed beneath him. "Oh . . . oh . . . it's sooooo good, darling."

She slid under him and took his turgid penis into her mouth, stroking and fondling his scrotum as she sucked. As demure as she had been previously, Boxer found her to be a wild woman in bed.

The more Boxer drove her into ecstasy working his experienced tongue into her love nest, the more she responded in kind. They were driving each other into a frenzy. "Oh . . . darling . . . I want you in me. I want you on top of me — please."

Boxer took a missionary position above her. She held his turgid shaft and guided him into her, wrapping her muscular legs around his waist. "I want you to come in me."

Boxer lunged into her warm moistness, developing a rhythm with her movements, at first, long, deep, leisurely strokes that picked up in intensity as she used her legs to quicken his pace, faster, harder, deeper into her. She cried out, "Now . . . oh darling, now. Come in me now. Ooooooohhh. So good, my darling. That was so good."

Boxer brushed a wisp of hair from her face and kissed her. "That was good for me, too. Thank you."

"That was wonderful. I don't remember the last time I've felt this good." She held Boxer tightly. "Well, ready to do it again, Skipper?"

Again? Boxer's heart was still pumping from the exertion. Oh, well, he told himself. What the hell. "Sure. Just give me a moment to catch my breath. Oh, and Skipper's a bit too formal under the circumstances, don't you think?"

She giggled.

"Call me Jack."

"C'mon, Jack," she teased, drawing him close to her. "What are we waiting for?"

CHAPTER FIVE

Igor Borodine entered the outer office of his suite at exactly 0750, ten minutes earlier than required, in order to organize his work before the day officially began. He was met inside by an embarrassed Lieutenant Velikaya, his personal secretary. Velikaya was standing there, red-faced and shrugging his shoulders. Borodine realized the young officer had no authority to keep out Valentine Kakusky. The Deputy Director of the KGB's Second Directorate would have had him arrested and probably shot for his impertinence.

Kakusky smiled and said, "Good morning, Comrade Admiral. I commend you for arriving at work ten minutes early. I am here for our little chat."

"Comrade." Borodine nodded a greeting and proceeded to his office. He turned his head toward the secretary. "Tea for the deputy director and myself. And some of those biscuits that I've been saving for an important occasion."

"At once, Comrade Admiral."

Kakusky made no move toward Borodine's office. Instead, he said, "It's such a lovely morning, Comrade. Why don't we take a nice walk, instead." He patted his belly. "It will do my body more good than having breakfast."

Borodine sensed Kakusky's desire for privacy, so he rebuttoned his jacket and retraced his steps. "Lieutenant, when Comrade Captain Viktor Illyavich arrives, inform him that I am out with Comrade Kakusky. I shouldn't be more than a few hours."

"Yes, Comrade Admiral."

Kakusky smiled, stroked his goatee beard, and held the door open for Borodine. He noticed how deftly Borodine had left a warning message for his executive officer, Viktor, should he not return in a reasonable time. But then, Borodine had always been clever. Not as clever as he, though. Not a chance of that.

As they reached the street level exit, Kakusky put his arm around Borodine's shoulders and they walked toward Gorky Park. "Now we can speak freely, Comrade. It is said that the walls have ears."

"You would know that, Comrade. It is not something that I am concerned with."

Together they crossed the street and entered the park. They strolled along a path that led to the river. "That is a problem, Comrade. Security is everyone's business. I shall have my people working along with yours on all stages of the new prototype project. We don't want the imperialist Yankees or their stooge allies getting information on our new submarine."

Even though they were out in the open air, Borodine was careful what he said, for Kakusky could easily be wearing a recorder, or have his men nearby monitoring their talk with high-powered listening devices. "That is something we do not want, Comrade. We want the first encounter that our enemies have with the *Sea Demon* to be their last. However, these submarine designers are very talented, artistic people. I wouldn't want their creativity stifled by your agents breathing down their necks."

"Like it or not, my men will be in on all aspects of the design and construction of your submarine. No one is to be absolutely trusted under these circumstances."

Borodine stopped near a large rock to retie his shoelace. A quick glance behind him verified what he had already felt through the prickling of the short hairs on the back of his neck. They were being followed by at least one man, who stopped abruptly and tossed a crumb to a group of swans near the water. A second man sat on a park bench, seeming to be reading a newspaper. Maybe so, maybe not. Borodine took a chance on boldness. "Comrade, don't turn around abruptly, but I think we are being followed. Are you armed?"

Kakusky broke into a broad grin and slapped Borodine on the back. "My dear Comrade Borodine. I have no need to carry a weapon when I have my two bodyguards following me. Not as discreetly as they presume, though. I fear they will have to be replaced. Amateurish of them being found out by someone with as little concern for security as you have admitted having."

Borodine said nothing. He had scored a minor coup by discovering Kakusky's agents, and had slapped the deputy director in the face with it.

"There is something else to discuss, Comrade Borodine. We have to discuss the placement of a scuttling device to blow up the sub should it ever be in danger of being captured by the enemy. There is to be no surrender. Ever. Under any circumstances. If ever put in a position to surrender or be destroyed, the captain of the *Sea Demon* must choose the latter, and preferably by his own hand."

Borodine was livid. "You can't just snuff out the lives of two hundred good men just to save the ship from being captured."

"I can and I shall, Comrade. And for this reason, I shall insist that you are never to be the captain of that submarine. I know that you don't have the balls to do the job if it needs doing."

Borodine stopped and turned to face Kakusky. "I have been selected to take the *Sea Demon* on her sea trials, Comrade. By the admiral of the fleet, himself. And I was assured that this had the blessings of the Politburo. You don't have the power to oppose their selection,

Comrade."

Kakusky toyed with his beard. Though he was almost a head taller than Borodine, his almost womanish body made him no physical match for an opponent such as the admiral. He had to rely on guile, and the fear that his position in the KGB usually instilled in others. "I don't think that I will have to resort to that."

Borodine stood there facing him, hands on hips.

"If you recall, Comrade," Kakusky continued, "I have some very interesting videotape of you and the young American slut, Trish Kinkaid, who happened to be the granddaughter of the CIA director at the time. How unloyal of you, Comrade."

"That's in the past. It was just a sexual thing when I was stationed in the U.S.A. The admiral of the fleet is aware of what went on. It was just something that happened, as far as she's concerned."

"And what about your wife's concern, eh? I've taken the trouble to have the voices dubbed in Russian, and made to seem much more recent. How do you think Tanya, correct me if I'm wrong, Comrade, but it is Tanya, isn't it? Yes? How would Tanya view an affair with this young, beautiful woman and her faithful husband? You get my point, Comrade?"

Borodine grabbed Kakusky's lapels and nearly lifted him off his feet. "You bastard. You stay away from my wife. You go near her and I'll—" Borodine didn't finish his sentence. He was still wary of a hidden recorder. And Kakusky's two agents had come running down the path and were almost upon them. Borodine released his iron grip and shoved Kakusky away from him.

The two agents arrived seconds later, taking positions between their boss and Borodine. Their hands clutched 9 mm automatics in shoulder holsters. Kakusky needed only to say the word. But he didn't want to kill Borodine in cold blood in public. He would pick a better time and place. After he had publicly disgraced the man and destroyed his family. "Consider what I have just said, Comrade," Kakusky said. He smoothed out the wrinkles on his jacket lapels. I will contact you again in a few days. Good day." Kakusky turned and led his two men along a short path to the street, where he had a waiting car.

Borodine cursed to himself, and contemplated his next moves during the walk back to his office. This time, he told himself, that bastard has gone too far.

At 4:35 PM, Lori-Ann Collins arranged the files on her desk into three neat stacks, and locked each stack into a separate drawer in her desk. She tidied up her workstation, and slipped her white linen suit jacket over the low-cut navy silk blouse. Her white linen skirt was slit high up above her left knee, and revealed a flash of thigh with every movement she made. She smoothed the close-fitting skirt over her curves, extremely pleased with herself.

"Night, Miz Collins."

"Oh, goodnight, Maria. I'll lock up." She waved after the last of the typists in the pool left the large office.

Maria waved back. "I think the director's still inside."

The buzzer on Lori-Ann's desk sounded, confirming that fact. She watched the typist close the door behind her, then locked the door. "Miss Collins, will you step into my office before you leave?"

Well, here goes, she thought. Time to face the music. She knocked on Tysin's door.

"Open."

She opened her blouse further, to show off more cleavage, and walked in, careful to expose as much thigh as possible. May as well get the old buzzard horny. "Yes, Henry?"

"Sit down, my dear. Time we had a little chat about your future here."

58

She pulled up a comfortable chair to the side of his desk, and stretched out her arms, her breasts straining against the confinement of the sheer blouse. She separated her legs enough for him to look up her skirt if he tried hard enough. May as well pour on the charm. "I really like my job here, Henry."

Tysin took the cue, and leaned forward to peer at her bare thighs. She was wearing silk stockings held up with a lacy garter belt. "You have a fine way of showing it. I thought we had an understanding, dammit, a relationship. And you go run off and marry some millionaire. I gave you an apartment, clothes, money . . . anything you wanted, and this is how you repay me?"

She spread her thighs even further, the skirt hiking up her long, sensuous legs. She smiled, watching his eyes follow the progress of the white linen material exposing more and more of what she had to offer him. "Henry, there was nothing I could do. Richard and I were engaged. It was a perfect cover for us. Who would suspect a married man like yourself having an affair with a woman engaged to be married. Frankly, I thought Richard was just using me as window dressing, to further his career. He surprised the hell out of me." She opened another button of her blouse, revealing most of her breasts barely tucked into a white half-bra.

"Well, you both sure surprised the hell out of me, too."

"Henry, darling, he just proposed to me over lunch one Saturday. Didn't even give me time to make an excuse. He just drove us to a J.P. and we were married. Just like that. Of course, we had to have a church wedding after, to please his dear mother."

"Too bad about them getting killed like that. Nasty business. Scares the hell out of me when I see those eighteen wheelers barreling down the highway like they own it. They're just accidents waiting to happen."

"Well, Henry, I just couldn't walk out any time I wanted to, and tell Richard I had a date with my boss, you know. I just had to bide my time. It was so frustrating for me."

Tysin smiled. "Do you . . . do you think that maybe we could, er . . ."

"Why Henry, I just wet my pants thinking about us together. Richard's nice and all, but he's not half the man you are in the love-making department."

Tysin wheeled his chair next to her and kissed her passionately on the lips, all the while sliding his hand up her skirt and playing with the milky white flesh above her stockings.

She responded by slipping her tongue into his mouth, and letting her hand rest in his lap. She found the bulge and fondled it, caressed and stroked it beneath the cloth of his trousers.

He loved every second of it. As his fingers found their way to her crotch he let out a sigh. She wore no panties beneath her garter belt. He slid two fingers against her clit. She was sopping wet. He pushed in further until she squealed with delight.

Lori-Ann unzipped Tysin's fly and found his throbbing member. Her fingertips traced the distended veins on his shaft up to the head of his penis. He felt ready to explode.

Tysin was beyond himself with delight. A few minutes ago, he was about to fire Lori-Ann for jilting him, and now she was helping him to soar to new sexual heights. He fumbled with his free hand to open her blouse completely.

"Let me, Henry. Let me help you." She stood up and removed her jacket, folding it neatly on her chair. Then she slowly opened each button on her blouse, letting him see more and more of her firm, white flesh. She reached behind and undid the fastener and zipper of her skirt and let it fall to the floor. She watched Tysin's eyes taking her all in. She deftly stepped out of the skirt, turned her back to him and bent at the waist to pick it up. She heard his gasp as she exposed her bare bottom to him as she did. When she turned back around, Tysin was fumbling with the buttons holding his pants on. "Let me, Henry, darling. Let me take care of you."

As he stood there, she undid his buttons and belt, and tugged Tysin's pants down to his ankles. Next, she pulled down his striped nylon mini-briefs. Strange for a man who dressed so conservatively as the director, she thought. Well, everyone has his own little secrets. She cradled his manhood in her hands and leaned forward, taking the tip into her mouth. She made a slurping sound as she sucked, licked all around with the tip of her tongue, then took him all in.

Tysin stood there almost mesmerized, her willing slave. Finally, he got up the nerve to say, "Do you think you could, uh, turn around again . . . like you did before? I'd like to . . ."

"Oh, yes, Henry. Yes. I want you in me."

Tysin swept some things away from the top of his desk. Lori-Ann let go of his manhood after giving it a little squeeze, and turned her back on him. She bent over, crossed her arms on his desk to cradle her head. "Now, Henry. Do it now."

Tysin approached her from behind, finding her opening with his fingers. She reached beneath her to guide him in. "Oh, Henry," she cooed. "You're so big."

Tysin was almost delirious with pleasure, and almost ready to pop. A few lunges into her from behind and he felt himself coming. He started to moan.

She pushed back against him with each stroke, and contracted her vaginal muscles rhythmically. He was spent in less than a minute.

He fell against her body, exhausted from his brief

performance. "Sorry . . . I'm sorry, Lori-Ann. Didn't mean to . . ."

"Oh, Henry. I enjoyed you so much. I just hope it was as good for you as it was for me. Now let me help you clean up."

It took about fifteen minutes for them to remove the traces of their lovemaking, and get themselves dressed. When Lori-Ann was satisfied that her appearance was just right, she flicked a non-existent speck from her skirt and said, "I know for a fact that Richard works late almost every Tuesday night. Perhaps we could go back to seeing each other again at the apartment?"

Henry Tysin straightened his tie. "Yes. That would be very nice. Tuesdays." He let the thought sink in. "Yes. Wonderful."

"Well, then, I'd better be going. I don't want Richard to miss me." She got up to leave. She looked back with a provocative smile. "Oh, by the way, Henry, what did you want to see me about?"

CHAPTER SIX

Boxer slipped his passcard into the security slot on the door jamb outside of the *Manta* design room. The code was changed frequently as a precaution. He heard the tumblers fall into place, the lock clicked open and he let himself in. He was surprised to see Lt. Kit Carson already working at her station. Boxer always tried to make a point of being the first on the job, to get a head start on the day, and get a better sense of how the others approached their work.

"Jack . . . I mean Admiral. You startled me. I didn't expect you for another half hour."

"Good morning, Kit. It's oh-seven-thirty. Did you sleep here last night?"

"I just wanted to put the finishing touches on the basic hull so you wouldn't have to waste any time on preliminaries, today."

Boxer walked up behind Carson and planted a gentle kiss on her neck. "Thanks."

Carson blushed a bit. "Uh, Admiral?"

He tucked his hand under her chin and lifted her face till their eyes met. "Yes?"

"About the other night—I guess I was out of line."

"Don't be sorry. The other night was wonderful. It's been months since I've been with a woman. You made me feel like a man, again."

"I, uh, heard through the grapevine about your . . . uh . . . about Francine. I'm really sorry. I feel like a real heel making a play for another woman's fiance."

"Don't Kit." Boxer closed his eyes for a moment. Visions

of Francine played in his head; the visions of the Francine Wheeler he loved and was about to marry, and of the Francine who was left catatonic on the floor of Julio Sanchez's luxury yacht. He sat down next to Carson. "The other night," he continued, "when you told me about your fiance being a homosexual, then marrying another woman. Well, you said, 'Maybe someday you'll tell me your life story.' Well, today I just might. At least the latest chapter or two."

Kit held his hands. "Jack, don't do this to yourself. I'm really sorry I started this whole thing. There's no need for you to hurt yourself any more."

"It's okay, Kit. I want to be fair to you. Let me start off by saying that I loved Francine Wheeler in a way far different, on a much higher level, than any one else before her. Including my ex-wife, Gwen." Boxer paused a moment to collect his thoughts.

"She was bright, articulate, self-assured, beautiful . . . very beautiful. She understood that the nature of my work would mean long separations, and that there were some aspects of my job that I could never talk about to her. You can understand that."

Carson nodded. "Of course. We've both had to deal with secrets that we could never reveal to anyone outside the job. Richard had a hard time with that, though he was often tight-lipped about his work at State."

"And then someone wanted to hurt me a great deal. They could have killed me. That wouldn't have been too difficult. They could have me tortured. Wouldn't be much fun to watch. But no, they tried to destroy the three people who meant the most to me in this world. They nearly beat old Admiral Stark to death. Kidnapped Francine, then used her for a punching bag, repeatedly gang raped her, abused and tormented her, and left her a sobbing shell of her former self, afraid of any man."

He paused to regain his composure. "Wouldn't let me go

near her. I had to put her in a sanatorium in Northern Italy where she gets constant care and therapy. She even retracted in fear of the male doctors in the beginning. Even now, months later, it's difficult for her." He continued, "She hardly speaks, eats only with assistance. She's coming along very slowly."

"That poor woman. How could I do what I did to her?" Carson pleaded.

"That's just the point, Kit. I want very much for Francine to come back again to the way she was. I maintain her brownstone in Georgetown, and her car. The BMW is hers. I make the payments, pay for the upkeep. I even set up a trust fund to care for her at the Piedmont for as long as is necessary . . . or as long as she lives. And if she gets well, and wants to come back to me, I'll probably marry her as we planned."

Carson let out a sigh of despair.

"But Kit, I've got to take charge of my life again. We've got a sub to build, and I want it to be the best we can make it. I have a life to live, too. I have to work, eat, drink, sleep and . . . yes, Kit. I need to be a man again."

"But I feel that I used you, Jack."

Boxer shook his head. "No. You didn't use me, Kit. And I didn't use you. We did what we did. It just happened. It was wonderful. I'd do it again, gladly, and without a trace of guilt. Kit, you're a wonderful woman. You're vivacious, perky, smart . . . very smart I believe. You certainly know your job, from the looks of that model on the CRT. Let's just be ourselves, let things happen if they will, and enjoy them when they do."

Carson looked at him. "Thanks, I guess, would be more appropriate. I hear footsteps down the hall. The staff is about due to start work. I'm sorry that I dug into your past and caused you such pain. I just didn't want to show any disrespect for her."

"Roger that, Lieutenant. I read you loud and clear. Now

I suggest we get some coffee and get down to work on the *Manta*. Let me tell you about the electronics."

Borodine climbed up the two flights of steps from the tile-covered subway station and stepped out into the night. He paused there on the sidewalk long enough for his eyes to adjust to the darkness. There were few streetlights in this part of Moscow. He was in a section where the dregs of society lived and worked at the most menial of jobs, for they lacked the skills, or the intelligence to acquire the skills to better themselves. In this part of the city, nobody cared if you lived or died.

Borodine walked two more blocks until he came to the street whose name matched the one on the piece of paper in his pocket. He headed west. He had come alone, as requested. Took public transportation instead of the official car to which he was entitled by his rank and station. Wearing civilian clothes was his own idea, lest someone recognize him in this distasteful neighborhood and get any wrong ideas about him. He was being very careful, very discreet, yet he hated all this spooky business. That was for the KGB. That was for the man whom he was about to meet, Valentine Kakusky.

The bastard had him by the short hairs. Couldn't get him out of the service fairly. He was still the best submariner the Motherland had. Even Admiral of the Fleet Gorshkov would attest to that. No. Kakusky had to resort to blackmail and threats against his wife. Well, we shall see, Borodine fumed. We shall just see.

He glanced at the scrap of paper once more, pocketed it and walked to a narrow alleyway, hesitated and then entered it. Almost at the very end a small electric bulb glowed white over a doorway with three steps leading to it. The alleyway stank of garbage and urine. The ancient brick walls bore the filth and grime of a century of abuse and neglect. He hoped that Kakusky had a good reason for meeting him in this foul and Godless place.

He mounted the three steps, and opening the door he found himself inside a very long, narrow hallway. And at the end of the hallway, not only was he affronted with the garish glare of high-intensity strobe lights, but what was unmistakably the intense blare of American rock and roll music. What better way to keep the drones in their place; suffocate their senses with this cacophony of sounds and mind-destroying lights. He'd seen such effects on the burned-out faces of American teenagers on his official visits to New York and Washington.

He entered a room where he was assaulted by the sights and sounds of young people gyrating to the music. He stood there watching the mindless minions play out their sex fantasies in their wildly colored, tight-fitting clothes that did little to hide their bare midriffs or shoulders, or the fact that many of the women wore no bras to constrain their movements.

He stood motionless and searched the tables along the wall, where he expected to see the man he had come to meet. All of the tables were occupied. He thought of leaving. Maybe this was not such a good idea at all. He felt a presence behind him and was about to turn around when . . .

"Don't turn around," the deep voice said. Borodine felt something hard jab him in the back just under the shoulder blade on the right side. "You see that woman coming toward you? The red blouse, and short skirt?"

Borodine turned his head back. He smiled, and asked, "You mean the pretty thing with the large . . . ?"

Before the man with the deep voice caught on, Borodine had spun around with his left elbow slamming into the man's face. "Ohhh. My nose . . ."

Borodine continued his spin. "Deep Voice" was holding his broken nose with both hands. A small automatic handgun crashed to the floor. Wham. Borodine smashed his right fist into the man's jaw. The guy's head jerked back. Borodine cocked his arm and threw a punch with all his weight behind it. "Deep Voice" 's larynx shattered, and he was "Deep Voice" no more, a broken man with a broken face. Borodine stooped to pick up the gun, and slipped it into his jacket pocket. He watched as two men came by and carried the hapless man out of the room.

"You're a brave man," the pretty girl in the red blouse with the large, pear-shaped breasts was saying to him. Her nipples were large, pink buds, straining against the diaphanous material that tried to constrain them. Then her hands were pressing the muscles of his chest and arms. "And so strong. Come, dance with me."

Borodine realized that she was the key to unlock the door to the whereabouts of the mysterious Kakusky. He reluctantly took the woman in his arms and let her lead him onto the dance floor.

She threw her arms up over her head and nearly shook her breasts out of the low-cut blouse in time to the beat of the music. "Dance," she commanded.

Borodine stood there looking at her, surprised by her aggressiveness, almost mesmerized by the bouncing breasts, but not sufficiently cowed to bow to her orders. "If you can find some suitable music, a little slower, and more civilized than this garbage, then yes, I will consent to dance with you."

Apparently, the girl had her orders to dance with him. She shouted something to a tall, thin youth, finger-snapping in time to the music coming from a stereo by his side. A new tape was installed, slightly more to Borodine's liking. He held the girl to him.

"My name is Maria. You are making my job tonight very difficult. Someone is here to see you. When we finish the dance, you will notice a table against the wall occupied by the man you have come to see." She smiled up at him, and rubbed her breasts against his chest. "Meanwhile, why not enjoy the dance?"

Borodine felt uneasy dancing with this young woman, whom he was certain was one of Kakusky's agents. As soon as he was in a position to spot Kakusky at the table, he excused himself and walked off the dance floor.

Maria stood there pouting, with her hands on her hips, playing the jilted lover role to the hilt. In truth, she was really pissed. There wasn't another man in the room who wouldn't give anything to have been in Borodine's place, and the steel hard man treated her like an unwanted parasite to be cast aside just like that. That shit.

Borodine pulled up a chair and sat opposite Kakusky at the round bistro table. "I've always wondered what kind of man would find the beautiful Maria so offensive. A pity, Comrade. She makes a wonderful bedfellow, I can assure you." The deputy director smiled and stroked his beard.

"I don't like all this sneaking around business. Let's get down to what we're here for."

"We will. First, though, a drink." Kakusky had a bottle of 100 proof Stolichnya vodka on the table before him, and two glass tumblers.

Borodine shrugged.

Kakusky unsealed the bottle and poured three fingers of the vodka into each glass. He slid one across to Borodine, and raised the other. "To your health, Comrade."

Borodine stared into his eyes, neither making a move for the drink, nor returning the toast.

"Ahem. Well, then, I shall drink alone. No sense letting this good vodka go to waste." Kakusky drained off half the drink.

Borodine indicated the surroundings with his head. "I didn't realize you had such exotic tastes, *Comrade*. These friends of yours?"

Kakusky finished his drink, put the glass down and reached for Borodine's. "You mind? Shame to just leave it here."

Borodine shook his head.

"Some of them work for me. Maria, of course. A few of the others. And of course, we own the place. It's one of the best we have. And Maria's one of our top agents. She usually gets what she goes after."

Borodine watched Kakusky drink off half the vodka from the second glass. "A little blatant for me. So, let's get down to business, shall we?" He didn't know how this meeting would go, but Borodine knew for sure that he wasn't going to disgrace himself out of the service to please this bastard Kakusky. Blackmail or not.

Kakusky downed the remainder of his drink. "Not here. Too loud." He stifled a burp. "Can hardly hear oneself belch, heh, heh." He was obviously amused with himself. "This was just to meet you, make sure you followed my instructions by coming alone. My people have ascertained that you are indeed alone. A wise move on your part, Comrade. Anyone fool enough to spy on us would soon find himself in a labor camp in Siberia, if he were lucky. Or dead if he weren't. Shall we go now?"

Borodine rose with the KGB deputy director. "Where to?"

"An apartment not far from here. More private."

Borodine made no move to leave.

"I would appreciate it if you'd join Maria, now, and escort her outside. She'll walk you to her nearby apartment. I'll follow you shortly, at a discreet distance, of course."

Borodine walked to the young woman and simply said to her, "It's time to leave."

She linked her arm through his and together they walked down the long hallway to the door, and outside. "I'm glad you changed your mind about me," she teased. "I kind of like you." She squeezed his biceps. "The way you took care of poor Pietre."

70

"He was an amateur."

"Just the same, you made fast work of him. Comrade Kakusky will not be pleased with him. A shame. We were to be married."

"And that's the way you react to him being beaten and made a fool of? Just, 'A shame'?"

She held on tightly to his arm. "Oh, Pietre's a nice boy. Big and strong. Not like you, though."

"Comes from experience," he muttered.

"I find that one man is seldom enough for me, Comrade. I have an insatiable appetite when it comes to men. Perhaps you'd like to put that to the test, sometime, eh?"

"Perhaps under different circumstances." Borodine was just playing for time. No sense upsetting her until he'd dealt with her boss. "This visit is strictly business."

"Well," she said, coyly. "Perhaps when you're finished with your business?"

Borodine simply smiled at her. He wondered if she was to be part of the package. His consolation prize for resigning from the Navy. Over his dead body, he said to himself.

She led him down another alley, and stopped abruptly at a metal door set into the wall. "We are here." She unlocked the door and opened it for him. Borodine stepped aside and allowed her to pass in front of him and lead him up the stairs. Always the tart, she brushed her breasts against him as she squeezed past him, and swished her behind provocatively as she climbed the flight of stairs to her apartment door.

It was a nice, cozy, three room flat, well kept and neatly furnished, considering the sleazy neighborhood they were in. The KGB provides for their own, he figured. She led him to the parlor, and tried to help him off with his jacket. "I'm just fine, thank you."

She shrugged. "As you wish. Care for a drink?"

"Not until I'm finished with my business with your boss."

71

She took him by the hand. "Come, I'll show you my bedroom."

Borodine followed her into the next room, first checking around with his eyes for hidden dangers.

"Well, how do you like it?"

He didn't. It had the tacky appearance of a harem chamber, with flimsy woman's underthings strewn here and there, and several 11x14 photo enlargements of Maria, posed in various stages of undress. She turned to face him, smiling. "Recognize me?" She reached down and loosened the fastening on her blouse, and shook her breasts free.

Borodine watched as her large, pink nipples distended and got hard. "Yes," he said, uneasily. "They are certainly a good likeness of you."

"Pietre's a photographer by trade. He took those of me. Pity he's so jealous. He just hates when I show them off. Sent one poor bastard to the hospital. Of course, he's afraid of the deputy director."

Borodine heard the apartment door open and shut. He motioned to the kitchen with his head. "In here," Maria called.

Kakusky joined them in the bedroom. "I trust you were made comfortable, Comrade?"

Borodine nodded.

Kakusky motioned to the semi-nude photos on the wall. "You like?"

"She's very lovely."

Maria smiled.

"Maria, take off your clothes, and get on the bed."

"Wait a minute. No need for that, Comrade," Borodine blurted out.

Maria froze.

The KGB man's face suddenly became a perverse, tortured mask. "I said, 'Take off your clothes and get on the bed.' I won't say it again."

Flustered, Maria started to undress. She undid the red

silk scarf at her neck and handed it to Borodine. Then she removed her blouse, and tossed it on the floor.

"Beautiful. They really are beautiful," he said. "Now the rest."

Maria reached behind and undid the fastening and zipper of the mini-skirt. It fell to the floor. She was wearing scanty bikini panties, red, to match her blouse. And like her blouse, she slipped them off and tossed them in a heap on the floor.

"Good. Very good. Now get on the bed. On your back, slut. C'mon, spread your legs. We want to give the admiral the best show we can."

"Now, see here, Kakusky . . ." Borodine turned around to find himself staring down the barrel of a short-barrel 38 caliber revolver, powerful enough to stop any man, and small enough to conceal in a pocket. "If this is your idea of how to get me to resign, it won't work. I've already told my wife about the videotape that you have of me and Trish Kinkaid. Your cheap tricks won't work this time. If this is an attempt to embarrass me, it won't work."

"I have already anticipated you not cooperating with me, Comrade. So I'm not here to embarrass you. I'm going to kill you. Now hand me Pietre's Walther PPK."

"You're mad, Kakusky. All this power has addled your mind. You won't get away with this."

"I think otherwise, dear Comrade Igor. It seems that you were here having your way with the lovely Maria. No . . . fucking her would be more appropriate, don't you think. Now hand it over, butt first." He pointed the revolver at Borodine's face.

"Don't do this. I beg you." Borodine swallowed hard. Kakusky had the drop on him. To try something now was certain death. He handed over Pietre's automatic pistol.

"Yes, beg for your life, Comrade. You see, her crazy, jealous husband, whom you beat up in front of a room full of people tonight, came home, found you both naked in bed . . . fucking . . ." Kakusky checked to make sure there was a full clip, and slid back the chamber of the automatic. Then he slipped his own handgun back into his jacket pocket. "He shot both of you right there on the bed. Luckily, I was coming here to check on my best agent when I heard the shots. I found poor Pietre lying on the floor in his own blood, his head blown off with his own gun. Pietre was very fond of this Walther."

Borodine was sizing up his chances of overcoming Kakusky. The deputy director had a chambered round in the gun, but not aimed at him yet. Maybe—

"Would you be so kind as to open that closet, Comrade?" Kakusky pointed to the bedroom closet with the pistol. "Move, please. That was just a rhetorical question."

Borodine moved to the closet and opened the door. The bound and gagged body of Pietre slumped out onto the floor.

"Ah, there's the culprit now."

"You're mad, Kakusky. Insane."

"Flattery will get you nowhere, Comrade. Kindly remove your clothes. It's such a bother to undress a dead man."

Borodine didn't move. Maria lay there, terrified, trying to cover her nakedness with her hands between her legs.

"I said, spread 'em, slut." With that, the Walther PPK barked, and Borodine watched incredulously as the bullet bored a hole in Maria's forehead. Her head jerked back down against the pillow. The gun barked again, gouging a bloody hole through her left breast. The once beautiful body jerked one last time, and settled against the covers.

"May as well get the jealous lover out of the way." Kakusky moved to the terror-stricken young man tied up helplessly at his feet. He placed the tip of the gun barrel into Pietre's ear and fired. The head jerked to the side. Bits of bone and gray matter spewed from the gaping hole where the bullet exited the other side. Kakusky smiled tightly, and showed no other emotion. "And now for—"

But Borodine was already moving. A backhand caught Kakusky's face, sending him reeling. Borodine smashed a fist into the man's gut, then another. The Walther dropped to the floor. Both men lunged for it. Borodine got the gun. Kakusky got a knee in his groin for his trouble. He was doubled up, writhing in pain.

Borodine tore off the man's jacket and shirt and threw them on the floor at the side of the bed. Kakusky had lost his spirit, and didn't offer much resistance. "Does it hurt, Comrade? Let me help you." With that, Borodine opened Kakusky's trousers and yanked them down to his knees. One push, and Kakusky was lying on the bed next to the dead girl. Borodine wrapped Maria's red scarf around the gun butt and aimed at the KGB man. "There's only one way to deal with a madman like you. And that's to pay you back in kind."

Borodine fired a round into Kakusky. He watched as a disbelieving expression strained Kakusky's face as he felt the fire, the pain, the sticky blood where once was his manhood. The grimace became a death mask when Borodine fired the coup de grace into him.

Borodine heaved a great sigh. What a tragic loss of lives. And for what? He removed the bonds that bound Pietre, wiped his own fingerprints off the gun and wrapped Pietre's hand around it. He took one last look at the carnage behind him and quickly slipped outside.

CHAPTER SEVEN

"Ready for lunch yet, Skipper?" It was 1400, and Boxer and Lieutenant Carson had been at it since 0730. The workers assigned to the *Manta* project were just now returning from lunch. Boxer had been living on black coffee, Carson on tea.

"I'd just as soon work through. You go ahead if you like, though. You need to keep up your energy level."

Kit Carson said, "Why don't we send for some sandwiches. I'd like to get on with the electronics equipment, too. The sooner, the better."

"Great." Boxer gave their lunch order to an aide. Then he turned his attention back to the design console. Carson had punched up the revised CAD image of the new sub. An elongated teardrop shape had replaced the unwieldy cigar form of the former model. She worked the keyboard to turn the profile image through a three-hundred and sixty degree azimuth. The *Manta*'s hull shape looked very sleek, very fast, very maneuverable. "Watch this." Carson fiddled with a dial at the end of the keyboard.

"Well, I'll be damned," Boxer exclaimed. The monitor produced an animation of the sail retracting, then extending to its full height. "That's terrific."

Kit Carson smiled. "Thanks. That's what I was working on so early this morning."

"Kit, are you familiar with the *Turtle,* the sub that I took on a raid against Libya several years ago?"

"Sure. Retractable treads to climb up onto the beach. My understanding is that it was more of a dog than a turtle."

"Performance-wise, yes. It proved to be a clunker. I lost

most of my men on that mission." Boxer closed his eyes for a moment. Any thought about that fiasco instantly brought back the images of his men impaled on stakes along the Libyan beach. He fought to regain his composure.

"You all right, Skipper? The color drained from your face. You're white as a ghost."

"It's ghosts that do this to me, Kit. Sorry. There was one good thing to come of the *Turtle* design, at least in my opinion. That was the protective skin that we put on her. A double skin, actually. The inner skin is a viscous liquid while the ship is on the surface normal conditions. But when dived, the liquid gels, then gradually solidifies until at four hundred feet it is completely solid. It also solidifies instantly upon impact. It won't hold back a nuclear armed torpedo, but at that point, the sub would be a goner, anyway."

"Is that part of your wish list, Skipper?"

Boxer nodded. "If it can be done, I would like to add the *Turtle* skin."

Carson fiddled with the computer. "It will add some weight, but at the same time, some extra strength. We might be able to modify the space between the titanium alloy outer pressure hull and the high-tensile glass inner hull. I should be able to reduce the hull size by the thickness of the *Turtle* skin. That will keep her in the same configuration as before. You'll still have your eight-to-one ratio: four hundred feet from bow to stern, and fifty feet at the widest point, at this line here, through the bridge."

"I'm impressed. And I don't impress easily."

Carson beamed. "Thanks. Oh, here comes lunch. I may turn into a bear before your eyes."

Boxer smiled back. "I'm hungry, myself." He took a bag from the enlisted man. "I got ham and cheese, roast beef and turkey sandwiches. I hope that's okay."

"Fine. I'll have the ham and cheese and the turkey."

Boxer grinned. "You really are hungry. I'd better not

work you so long next time. We'll run out of food. How do you keep your great figure and still eat like a football player? I'd go to fat in no time."

"Diet soda," she smiled. "Pass the potato salad, will you?"

Boxer ate his rare roast beef on roll with ketchup while he watched Carson polish off her lunch. Finally, she said, "Okay, back to work, or we'll never get out of here tonight. Would you pass me another pickle, please?"

Boxer helped her clean up the workstation, and they got back to the sub design. "How about the missile tubes?" he asked her.

"Right here," she pointed to the bulge in the teardrop shape. "Three starboard, three to port. Any more than that and we'll have to compromise maneuverability, or cut down on the size of your strike force."

"Not acceptable. We'll go with the six tubes. Any more than that would be superfluous, anyway. I could start World War III with those six ICBM's. Next: Install the UWIS, and the COMCOMP, of course."

"Of course, Skipper. They're standard features as far as I'm concerned. And everything that can possibly be automated will be. You'll have AUTONAV, AUTODIV, AUTO-HELM, as well as automatic Fire Control. The torpedoes can be loaded by two men with the use of the AUTOLOAD. All systems can be operated by an officer or a chief, instead of a team. I would suggest a crew of forty, using two shifts. That way, you can also cut down on bunk space in favor of more working room."

Boxer nodded his approval. "What about the power supply?"

"The engine room is more labor intensive, though most of the work is maintenance. You can punch in your desired speed from the COMCOMP. Of course, all systems can be backed up manually. It would be advantageous if some of the officers could cross-train with the EO. That would free up some crew, also."

"Kit, what about damage control?"

"Your DCO will need some staff, too. Perhaps the ship's quartermaster can help. He won't be tied up with meal prep. That's mostly automated, too. Everything's pre-portioned, freeze-dried, nutritionally sound, calorically correct with regard to each sailor's needs based on weight, proportion of muscle to fat, and activity level. The food's everything but delicious." She laughed and munched on her pickle.

Boxer said, "That may be okay for a short haul, but the men will really miss having fresh food occasionally. It's important for morale. Could you imagine yourself eating pre-packaged freeze-dried food for very long? No pickles. No potato salad. C'mon, Kit."

She blushed. "Well, maybe we can make some provision for the pickles. Besides, you'll still need a baker for mid-rats, and desserts. And I put in some nice touches, like the high-pressure steam shower. It converts a small amount of water into a luxurious three minute shower. It sprays in from the cylindrical inner lining of the shower stall as well as overhead with enough pressure to rinse off and feel really clean."

"A Hollywood shower with a cupful of water. Not bad. How about some Gucci upholstery in the wardroom? The men would enjoy that."

Carson giggled. "Maybe for the captain's quarters. Oh, by the way, both the sonar and radar are integrated with the UWIS through the COMCOMP. You'll be able to differentiate aircraft and missiles on a screen on the COMCOMP. In fact, I think you'll be almost invincible."

Boxer became a little somber. "Nothing's invincible, Kit. Anything can happen. And I've seen many things go wrong with these subs."

Carson was somewhat taken aback. "Like what? What could possibly defeat the *Manta?* I think I've thought of everything."

"First of all," Boxer said, "the *Manta* will be her own worst enemy. Anything this complex will have problems, not necessarily of your design. Fittings can deteriorate. Bearings break loose. Electrical systems break down. The propeller shaft is probably the weakest link. I think we should install an auxiliary propulsion system to take care of emergencies."

She thought about that for awhile. "All right, I guess. I just don't like to think of the *Manta* as vulnerable."

"Better to expect the worst," Boxer replied. "And hope for the best. How soon till this gets to the production stages?"

Carson did a quick calculation in her head. "About a month, I guess. If I really push them," she indicated the two dozen designers, engineers, naval architects and draftsmen assembled in the office complex.

Boxer nodded. "Push them, then. I want to be on hand to supervise the production. Meanwhile, I've got a long awaited leave due me. I have some unfinished business to clean up."

"Aye, aye, Skipper. I've really enjoyed working with you. I also appreciated the companionship."

"So did I, Kit. And you're eminently qualified for the job. You keep up the good work, and I wouldn't be surprised if you became our first female admiral." Boxer got up to leave.

Carson jumped out of her seat and crisply saluted.

Boxer returned the salute. "Good-bye, Kit. See you in about a month."

"Good-bye, Skipper. I'll be ready for you when you return."

Boxer turned that around in his head a moment, smiled, and turned away. Carson called him back. "Oh, Skipper," she was holding the remains of his roast beef sandwich in her hand, poised to bite into it. "Are you finished with this? It would be a shame to let it go to waste."

Lori-Ann Collins strolled along the tree-lined residential street in one of D.C.'s nicer neighborhoods, stopping occasionally to window-shop at some very fashionable boutiques that were interspersed with other shops and well-kept brownstones and brick apartment buildings. She paused at a cozy bookstore, several doors in from the corner. The overhead sign read Odyssey Bookstore. In gold leaf on the glass door read, WE SHIP ANYWHERE IN THE WORLD. She walked in, to the tinkling chime of a strip of bells hanging from the door.

A professorial type behind the counter, dressed in tweeds and a yellow sleeveless sweater, pushed the wire frame glasses up his nose, and smiled at the beautiful, fashionably dressed woman. "And how may I help you today?" he asked, good-naturedly.

"I'm looking for a special book, for a dear friend, but it's long out of print. It's called *The Ancient of Days*. I understand that you might have a copy."

The fifty-ish man ran his fingers through his thinning, gray hair, his brow furrowed in thought. "No, I don't believe we do. Perhaps the owner, Mr. Frumpkin, will try to special order it for you. I'll go ask him."

Daniel Frumpkin smiled at the request. It was one of the first novels he'd read in this country when the KGB had sent him here to spy. He often used it as a signal between himself and the agents he controlled from his bookstore. "It might take some doing, Stuart. And I'd better take a deposit. Would you please ask him to come back here to the office while I check on its availability?"

"Er, it's a she, Mr. Frumpkin. Very nicely endowed, if I say so myself." He made a double handful motion in front of his chest, and smiled wryly.

Frumpkin was amused by his usually prissy assistant's

display of levity. "That's fine, Stuart. Please show the lady in while I look up the title."

Frumpkin smiled when Lori-Ann entered his office. The smile faded when she closed the door behind her. "You could dress more discreetly, you know. It won't do for old Stuart to spend the afternoon and the night dreaming about the hot-looking dame who came in here for a special order. Next time you come in here, dress like a student, or a schoolteacher, dammit."

Lori-Ann's good mood was gone in an instant with Frumpkin's verbal slap in the face. "Sorry, Daniel. I was trying to blend in with the neighborhood."

"You look like you were trying to blend in with the hookers downtown. It's fortunate for you that we're in a public place. Stuart's going to spend the rest of the day giving me the business about the foxy chick who came into my office looking for a book. Haven't you learned anything these last ten years in this country?"

"I said I'm sorry."

"Don't be insolent. I understand that the U.S. Navy is designing a new super submarine to rival anything that we have. In three weeks, when your specially ordered book arrives, I want the plans for that sub inside it when we ship it to your dear friend in the U.S.S.R. Understand?"

Lori-Ann was embarrassed. "But how? I don't have any contacts in the Navy?"

Frumpkin stood up behind his cluttered desk. "I'm losing my patience with you. Use your influence with Tysin. Or with your husband. He must have contacts at Defense. I want to put a man in when they go into production, so we've got to get to an official, or a contractor. Use whatever it takes: bribes, sex, threats, blackmail. I want those plans."

Lori-Ann cringed at the thought of having to use her body every time Frumpkin wanted someone hooked. Tysin was an old fart who couldn't find his dick with both hands if she didn't hand it to him first. It was a good thing she had a fertile imagination to turn her on during his ministerings.

Sex with Frumpkin was another thing. He was a mean, sadistic bastard, delighting in inflicting pain and humiliation on her. She was much happier under her old control. At seventy, Leo was thankful for anything he got. Not Frumpkin.

"I'll do my best, sir. But I doubt that my husband Richard will collaborate with us. He may be a wimpy, gay ass-kisser, but he's not a traitor. I don't think he'll turn."

"We shall see," Frumpkin fumed. "We shall just see about that." He paused a moment, then had an idea. "I want to meet him. Bring him to the apartment."

"Tysin's apartment? What if it's bugged? Are you crazy?"

Frumpkin became livid with rage. His face turned scarlet and he shouted at her, "Don't you ever call me that."

Lori-Ann cringed at the outburst. She noticed his cheek begin to twitch.

"Of course it's bugged. By me, idiot. Just get him in there, sit him down on the sofa and turn on the television. Do you think you can handle that?"

"Yes, but . . . but . . . then he'll know that I'm a . . . that we're both working for the Motherland. After that, there'll be no turning back."

Frumpkin moved closer to Lori-Ann, glaring at her, his face turning deeper red. "Perhaps you didn't hear what I ordered you to do. I want those plans here in three weeks. I want a man at the shipyard during the production so we can do whatever we can to sabotage the sub. Do you understand?"

Lori-Ann just stood there, unable to move, unable to reply.

"Put it this way. Just one submarine of this type is enough to reduce Moscow, Leningrad, Kiev, or any number of our major cities to rubble. It can destroy an aircraft carrier, can destroy our own ballistic submarines. In short, it is capable of starting a third world war all by itself. And winning it, if they are lucky. Do you think I care one whit about how your faggot husband feels about you, or me, or for that matter, whether he lives or dies? Frankly, my dear, I don't give a damn."

"If you put it that way, I—"

"That's the way I put it, and that's the way you should look at it, too. Like a good agent. You're getting too used to the decadent lifestyle the rich Americans lead. Don't worry about your husband. He will cooperate with us. If not, we will employ someone else to assist us. And you will become a very wealthy widow. The ultimate capitalist revenge."

CHAPTER EIGHT

Boxer arrived at the CNO's headquarters at precisely 0800. He was led immediately to Mason's office by Captain Preston, the CNO's aide. Admiral Charles "Chi-Chi" Mason rose from behind a huge walnut desk as Boxer entered.

"Morning, Admiral." Boxer saluted and stood at attention.

Admiral Mason returned the salute. He was a short, stout man with a full head of salt and pepper hair which he wore short in military fashion. "What's on your mind, Jack?" He indicated for Boxer to have a seat.

"I'm putting in for a month's leave, Admiral. I've got more than enough time coming to cover it."

"This is a bad time for it, what with the *Manta* project full under way, don't you think?" Mason helped himself to a cigar from a humidor shaped like an old oaken cask from ships of times past. "Smoke?" He offered Boxer the humidor.

"I'll stick with my pipe, if you don't mind, sir." Boxer fished in his jacket pocket for the well broken-in meerschaum that his son John had given him as a Christmas present some years ago. "The design stage of the *Manta* is finished. Now it's up to the production staff. Incidentally, Lieutenant Carson's top notch. She's done an excellent job with the design. I'd like to nominate her for a promotion to full lieutenant."

"Agreed. Carson derserves the promotion. As for your leave, I'm afraid I have to put it in abeyance. I'd like to see the *Manta* built and tested before you take a vacation, Boxer."

"Not a vacation, Admiral. If you recall, earlier this year I was hunting down Julio Sanchez for what he'd done to Admiral Stark and my fianceé, Francine Wheeler. You asked me to put it off because of the trouble in the Persian Gulf. I did. Now, it's time to lay this problem of mine to rest once and for all. It should be accomplished in time for the later stages of the *Manta*'s production."

Mason was getting pissed. "I only assigned you to the Gulf on orders from the president, himself. For all I cared, you could have gone and gotten yourself killed chasing down that damn spook, Sanchez." His tone softened a bit. "Besides, Stark is feeling much better, now. And I understand that your girlfriend is recuperating in a hospital in Italy. Why don't you just let the thing lie? Get on with your life."

Boxer realized that there was no sense prolonging this discussion with Mason. The man was an unfeeling boor. "Admiral, let me put it to you this way. Julio Sanchez will be a thorn in my side forever, an albatross around my neck, an itch that constantly needs scratching. I'll have no peace until I bring him to justice. And I mean that in the biblical sense: an eye for an eye. So I intend to do just that, sir. If you grant my furlough, I will take care of Sanchez, and get back to work on the *Manta*." Boxer paused, and blew a smoke ring toward the ceiling. He noticed Mason was munching on the end of his cigar, his jaw working furiously.

"If not . . . and I don't mean this as a threat, Admiral, believe me," Boxer continued. "I will resign from the Navy, thereby making what I do no one else's business but my own." He took another pull from the pipe and let the smoke waft upward. "You can explain to President Spooner why the *Manta* is being assigned another skipper in mid-production."

Mason slammed his fists on his desk. He jammed his barely smoked cigar into an ashtray. "Dammit, Boxer. You always were a hard-assed bastard. You're insolent, arrogant and downright vindictive." He quickly lit up another cigar. When he had a good ash working, he continued, pointing the cigar at Boxer. The gray ash fell off onto the desk. "Look, son. Don't fuck with me. I'm giving you one month off. You go do what you feel you have to do. Just be back here when we start to build the *Manta,* just in case the president happens to inquire as to your whereabouts. Understand? Because I will tell him that you have chosen to give a personal vendetta more significance than his pet project, and if that pisses him off, well, then you had better retire before he gets a chance to bust you down to ensign. And if he asks me to do the honors, well, I'd relish the idea. Now you'd better get the hell out of here before I lose my sense of humor."

Boxer tapped out his pipe in the ash tray on the desk, and tucked it back into his pocket. Then he pulled himself up out of the chair and snapped a salute. "Thank you, sir. Is there anything else?" he asked stolidly.

"No," Mason shouted. "Yes, dammit, there is something else. I'm sending Major Jones and his crew up to Fort Greely. I want them to cross-train with the Snow Troopers."

"Fort Greely, Alaska?" Boxer asked. "That's a far cry from Camp Lejeune, North Carolina. They'll have quite an adjustment to the cold."

"They'll be just fine. Those men are tough. And they don't question orders. They will march straight into hell from the North Pole if I order them to. Besides, they missed out on sea duty in the Antarctic with you last year. The training will do them good."

"Guess you're right, Admiral. Never know where our orders will take us. Will I have time to pay them a visit before they ship out?"

"You've got less than a week. Oh, and another thing. You got me so pissed off I almost forgot. Tysin wants to see you.'"

Boxer shrugged. "About what?"

"He didn't say. Doesn't have to. He's the head of the CIA. He wants to see you, you go see him. That's an order. Now get out of here."

By virtue of his status as Undersecretary of State for Eastern Europe, Richard Baxter and his wife, Lori-Ann were seated in the row of prestigious box seats at the Kennedy Center's gala performance by the Russian virtuosos, Perlmutter and Roschkov. The ancient Perlmutter, a frail, wisp of a man was the undisputed master of classical piano, while the younger of the pair, Roschkov, a red-haired and bearded cherub, had debuted as a violin prodigy at age six, and was now at age twenty-nine closing in on his mentor, Yaakov Mandelbaum. No wonder the Soviets won't let their Jews emigrate, Baxter mused. The loss of talent such as this would be astronomical.

The recital ended with a flourish by Roschkov, and the black tie audience went wild. The duo received a standing ovation. Baxter turned to Lori-Ann and said, "Marvelous, aren't they? A shame they're not Americans. They'd be worth millions."

Lori-Ann was stunning in a backless white silk gown that plunged in front down to here, and must have seemed to the congressmen and other dignitaries and their women that it was being held to her lush body by magic. She whispered in her husband's ear, "Money's not everything, you know, dear. Some people master their skills for the joy of being the best there is. And these two certainly are."

After three curtain calls, the audience filed out of the huge, modern theater. When the Baxters had climbed into their rented limo, Lori-Ann put her arms around her husband and kissed him passionately on the lips. He responded with only mild enthusiasm. "Honestly, Lori-Ann," he mumbled.

She cuddled close to him and said, "I have a surprise for

you, Richard. Have the driver turn up Nineteenth. I'm going to take you to a friend's apartment. There's something there I want you to see."

"I don't think so, Lor . . . The Symingtons are having a little party, and Bruce will be so disappointed if we don't show."

"The hell with Brucie, dear. I'm more important than he is, anyway. I'm your wife, aren't I?"

"Ours is a marriage of convenience, Lori-Ann. We both know that. And Bruce is so sensitive. He'll be terribly hurt if we don't go to his party."

Lori-Ann slid her hand into Baxter's lap, letting it come to rest on his testicles. She tightened her grip on his balls, applying just enough pressure to make him wince. "Put it this way, Richard. Certain parts of you are very sensitive, too. And you'll be terribly hurt if we don't go to my friend's apartment." She gave a little tug to add credence to her request.

"Ooh. All right. If it means that much to you. Will we still have time to make a late showing at the Symingtons?"

"That all depends on you, darling."

Baxter pressed the intercom switch. "Driver, turn up Nineteenth. There's been a change in plans."

The driver, who'd watched the scene take place, chuckled to himself. If it was him back there with Miss Yum-yum, her tits almost falling out of that dress, shit, he'd go anywhere she wanted to get some of that. Shit, he wondered, what's the matter with some of these big-shot stiffs anyway? They must have their dicks up their asses not to want to spend all their time in the sack with a babe like that one. He adjusted his rear-view mirror back to the traffic behind him, and drove them to the address the stiff had given him. You'd think they could afford a better neighborhood, though, he thought, as he pulled up at the curb. "Here you are, folks. Watch your step."

The driver climbed out to open Lori-Ann's door. Baxter

followed her out and paid off the driver, adding a ten dollar tip. He asked, "Do you want me to wait around?"

"That won't be necessary," Lori-Ann told him. "We'll call if we need another ride, thank you."

The two of them took the elevator to the third floor and Lori-Ann opened the apartment that Tysin had left in her name. It was her first trip back since her wedding.

"Nice little place," Baxter said, looking over the apartment. "Tastefully done, if you're on a small budget. Whose is it?"

Lori-Ann smiled at him. "Belongs to an old friend, dear. Needed a place to get away from it all once in a while. Lets me use it whenever I want." She approached him and put her arms around his neck again. "Tonight's the first time since we got married." She loosened his black bow-tie, and slipped his tux jacket off one shoulder. "Make yourself comfortable, darling."

Baxter removed the jacket and folded it neatly over the arm of an upholstered chair. "What's the purpose of coming here tonight? I don't get it?"

She undid the top two buttons of his pleated shirt, and tugged him after her toward the sofa. She sat next to him and slid her hand over his crotch again, this time unzipping his trousers. He was taken aback. "What?"

Lori-Ann reached into his fly, groping a bit before finding what she wanted. "Ah," she said, stroking him, still in his pants. "Don't you just feel like sucking some guy's cock, sometimes? I do." She looked up at him dreamy-eyed.

"C'mon, Lor, quit fooling around. What's up?"

"What's up?" She smiled and came up with his throbbing penis in her hand. "See for yourself, dear." With that, she undid the tie behind her neck and the dress lost its magic; the top fell off with a little shrug of her chest. She leaned over and took the tip of his penis in her mouth and licked it with her tongue.

He tried to pull away.

"What's the matter. Don't you like me any more, Richard?" She went down for more.

"C'mon, Lor, cut it out. Sure I like you. It's just that I don't like that."

"Here," she said, handing him his turgid penis. "Hold this for me a moment, will you? I want to show you something."

Baxter sat there on the couch, dumbfounded, his penis in his hand, watching her get up from the sofa still naked to the waist and pop a video cassette into the VCR above the television. "This one always makes me horny," she told him.

Lori-Ann sat back down beside him, and reached for his penis. He pulled it out of her reach. She chuckled, "We going to have a tug-of-war, darling?"

He slid farther away from her on the sofa, now feeling that he wasn't going to be pleased by what was going to happen, wondering what had gone wrong with his two month old marriage of convenience.

Lori-Ann pressed the remote controls. The set turned on, followed by a blur of black and white specks. "No FBI warning on this porno flick, Richard. And wait till you see who stars in it."

Baxter looked at her strangely. "I don't know any porno stars, Lor. What the hell are you talking about?"

"Shh," she pointed her fingertip to her lips. "The fun's about to start."

Richard sat there, a little frightened, but curious enough not to leave. Then the action began. It looked like the setting of a birthday party for a very handsome young man in his late twenties. Birthday cake on the table, balloons, but on closer inspection, the balloons appeared to be inflated condoms. The birthday boy took off all his clothes while watching himself in a full length wall mirror, and started playing with himself. The doorbell rang, and two more male model types entered, kissed the host, and undressed each other. And so on, until there were about eight or nine of them.

Then they took turns stuffing each other's orifices with anything they could think of, including their penises. The movie went on and on. Richard cringed, pulled himself into a fetal position at the edge of the sofa, as far away from Lori-Ann as he could.

She sat there watching the movie until it was finished. Her hand had gone up under her dress at the start, and never left till the end. Finally, she snapped off the set and turned to Baxter. "Well, happy birthday, darling. And I thought you told me you didn't like it when I did that to you. What's the difference who sucks on . . ."

"Cut it out, you bitch. Why are you hurting me this way. You knew what I was when you married me. It was your idea. To save face for both of us, you said."

"But Richard, didn't you like it? It sure looked like you were enjoying yourself, the way I saw it."

"Enough. Stop it. You didn't want to marry me. You just want to use me. I don't know your motives, but I'm going to have this marriage annulled. And I'll use my influence to get you thrown out of the . . ."

"You'll do nothing of the kind."

Frumpkin's baritone voice startled Baxter. His penis went limp in his hand. He cringed and tried to cover up, protect himself from . . . whom?

Frumpkin stepped from the now open doorway to the bedroom behind the TV. He'd been watching and taping the two of them with his hidden cam-corder. "I'd like to discourage you from doing any such thing to Lori-Ann. In fact, I think cooperation is in order. That is, if you still like your job at State."

"Who are you, you bastard." Baxter tucked himself back into his pants and zipped up his fly. "I'll have you arrested for this. You can't do this to me."

Frumpkin laughed. "Can and will, dear boy. And if you resist us, the Secretary of State will have a copy of this tape in his office by morning. Lori-Ann, cut that out and get dressed. You look like a slut."

"Hey, we don't have to take this." Baxter was only half convinced of that.

"And a copy to the NSA, Defense, the president. I'll bet you didn't know that President Spooner just loves a good porno film now and then. He and some of his friends, some Cabinet members, a senator or two. I wonder how long it will take them to figure out who the birthday boy is. A minute or two, wouldn't you think?"

Baxter saw his career, his life going down the tubes in front of him. He contemplated suicide for a moment. Just a moment. He was too much the coward to do it. He let out a sigh of exasperation. "What do you want?"

Frumpkin beamed ear to ear. "Now that's better. Much better. You've come to the conclusion that I'm powerful enough to do what I say I can. That's good, because it's true. I can deliver. And I want you to deliver for me. And then we'll call it even. I'll let you off the hook."

Baxter doubted he'd be let off that easy. Usually, when these slime set their hooks into you, they're too greedy to let go. But he'd have time to figure his way out of that. For now, he'd have to go along. "Deliver what?"

"A submarine. That shouldn't be too difficult. Most of the subs in that class are built by the Symington Electric Boat Works in New London, Connecticut. And, correct me if I'm wrong, dear boy, but I believe I saw young Brucie Symington enjoying himself at your birthday party."

Baxter knew he'd been had. "What do you want me to do."

"I'll let you know. I will want certain documents concerning its design within a few weeks. You can have your friend Brucie work on that. Just tell him to get the papers, not why. I'll have Lori-Ann let you know exactly what I want."

Baxter turned all his fury on Lori-Ann, sitting there on the sofa, tying the front of her gown back in place. "You cunt. You're a fucking spy for these people. You set me up and drew me into their lair."

Frumpkin shook his head. "Calm down, Richard. She's in the same boat as you are. She didn't want her boss, the director of the CIA, to know that she was a nymphomaniac. Things like that scare people like him. Makes them think that the nymphos can't be trusted, because they can be turned so easily, isn't that so my dear?" No sense making her out to be his agent, Frumpkin figured. Better to make it seem to Baxter that they were co-conspirators. They might get along with each other better, for as long as he found Baxter useful.

Lori-Ann had tears in her eyes. "I'm really sorry, Richard. He did the same thing to me."

Baxter put a consoling hand on hers. "It's okay. I can see that now. The bastard." He turned back to Frumpkin. "What now?"

"I'll be in touch. Work out a plan to get Symington into and out of the project room with the plans I ask for. Now, both of you, get the hell out of here. You make me sick."

CHAPTER NINE

Major Roland Jones worked his men hard. He had his four squads of ten men doing push-ups on the wet Carolina clay that had been drenched the night before by a sudden thunderstorm. As the men pushed off the ground, red mud dripped off their faces, chests, trousers. Rolly was closest to Mean Gene Greene, leader of squad three. He heard the tough little corporal shout the cadence, "One-forty, one-forty-one, one-forty-two . . ."

Sgt. Carlos Rivera led squad one. He and Gene were the only survivors of the fighting in the Gulf. Now they had forty of the best men they could muster from the Marines, SEALs, Army Rangers and Special Forces. The group had been narrowed down to platoon strength from over five-hundred candidates. The toughness of their missions dictated that they be headed by a major, and Rolly Jones filled the bill as no other man could.

Along the way they'd picked up Sgt. Tony Snappiello, whom the men called Snappy. He was barking orders to squad two. Snappy had been a street-smart kid from Brooklyn before Uncle Sam got him. He was as tough as they came. And rounding out the squad leaders was Corporal John Silverman, tall and wiry at over six-five. The men couldn't resist dubbing him Long John Silver. But not always to his face.

Rolly looked off beyond his men to see a figure in a Navy dress white uniform with the stripes and bric-abrac of an admiral. It took him a moment to recognize Boxer. He snapped to attention and shouted above the din, "Atten-hut."

The four squad leaders spotted Boxer and came to attention. "Admiral present," one of them shouted.

At once, forty men jumped to their feet and stood at attention. Red mud ran down their faces and bodies, yet not one man showed the slightest sign of discomfort.

Jones saluted as Boxer came upon them. Boxer returned the salute as he marched closer. The remainder of the men saluted when he faced them. Boxer said, "At ease, Major."

"Yes, sir." Rolly relaxed just a little, about as close to at ease as he got. No one else moved.

"That goes for your men, too, Major."

"I'm trying to maintain tight discipline, sir."

"That was an order, Major."

Jones did a crisp left-face and shouted at his men, "At ease, men."

They relaxed about as much as their major had.

Boxer smiled slightly. "I haven't met most of your men, Major."

"Yes, sir. Admiral Boxer, this rag-tag, sorry-looking bunch of sadsacks is one day going to be worth of the name Rolly's Rangers. At this point, it's in name only. But we're working on it."

Boxer knew better. These men were as tough as you could get. He'd done his homework, and asked around before coming out to the borrowed training grounds at the Marine Corps base. None of the other Marines would fraternize with them, would, in fact, move out of their way when approached by them, even in a two on one confrontation. The way Rolly pushed his men, dying would be an easy way out for them.

"I hope you work fast, Major. Scuttlebutt has it that you're moving out soon. And call me Skipper."

"Yes, sir. Skipper. Sorry, Skipper. When the training's so tough, the discipline gets very tight. It's hard for me to switch it on and off. It's different when we're aboard your sub. These men are pretty wound up. And yes, I got my orders to go to Fort Greely, Alaska next Monday. Sweat our balls off one day, freeze 'em off the next."

"Greely's our Northern Warfare Training Center. The CNO wants your men ready for anything. Ever been to the Arctic?"

"No, Skipper, I haven't."

"Well, the Ruskies live with the cold as a way of life. They have no problem with it. We have a small, elite company of men called the Snow Troopers who guard our Northwest frontier against the Russians. Their training is similar to yours, except for the underwater work. They're all airborne troops. Your men will cross-train with them."

"No problem, Admiral. My men ain't afraid of anything on this earth. Or in the sea, or in the sky. Some of these guys have airborne training. The rest will learn."

"Good. They'll also learn to sleep in snow caves, to march at night under the stars, live off the land. Then they'll train with Eskimo scouts on St. Lawrence Island, just over thirty miles from Soviet soil, and later parachute onto the polar ice."

Rolly Jones smiled. "We can handle it, Skipper. No sweat."

"You can't sweat up there, Rolly. It will freeze your skin. When it gets down to thirty below, the men not only do frequent head counts, they also count each other's fingers and toes."

"We'll make you proud of us, Skipper. I know we can

do it."

Boxer clapped Rolly on his muscular shoulder. "We've got to do it, Rolly. The Ruskies think they own the Arctic. We've got to have a presence up there to counter them. They've got more men up there. We've got to be better. Anyway, I just wanted to stop by to say good-bye and wish you and your men good luck."

"Thank you, Skipper." Jones straightened up and saluted. Boxer saluted back, then offered a handshake. Rolly engulfed Boxer's hand with his massive paw with a smile. "We . . . the men will do anything for you."

"Thanks, Rolly. I appreciate that. Now, as you were."

"Yes, sir." As Boxer walked off, Rolly shouted to his men. "Okay, you mothers, back into the dirt. The party's over. Squad leaders, start them at one-fifty."

Boxer had to hand it to Tysin. When the director wanted to see you, he made sure it was a command performance. The Sikorski helicopter lifted off from Camp Lejeune, North Carolina with Boxer and two CIA agents aboard, Will Montgomery and Everett Pierce, along with the pilot. Boxer knew Monty and Pierce for several years; they were part of the design team for his first super-submarine, the *Shark*. Pierce was the man who implemented the UWIS and most of the other fancy electronic equipment. Monty was in charge of overall security for the *Shark* project.

"Glad to have the old team back together, boys."

"Likewise, Jack," Pierce answered. "Fine piece of work you did on the *Manta*'s hull design. In a face-off, it'll run rings around any of the Ruskie boomers, fare at least as well or better against any of their *Alfas* and their super-sub program is years behind ours now, thanks to your Antarctic mission."

"I agree, Monty, that the *Manta* is a fine looking sub, a one-of-a-kind that might begin an entire new class. But it's not my doing. The *Manta* is the work of a very fine young naval architect, Lieutenant Carson."

Monty said, "Well, he did an excellent job, Jack. No doubt about it."

Boxer smiled, "Carson's a twenty-five year old woman, who also happens to be a fine naval officer. I'm sure she'll be pleased to hear herself praised by you gentlemen."

"World's sure changing for the better," Pierce quipped. "Not only are they making the Navy personnel smarter, but they're putting them in nicer packages."

They all got a chuckle out of that, including the pilot, seated next to Monty. Pierce continued, "Monty and I will be taking over the project at this point, Jack. Symington's got the bid, so we go straight to New London after our chit-chat with the director. If this Lieutenant Carson is as good as she seems, we'll see to it she goes along with us. We want to integrate the electronics into the hull design from the start, so we know it's right."

"We're really committed on this, Jack," Monty added. "The president wants the new sub yesterday, so we're running late already. We know Symington can do the job for us. They built the *Barracuda*, and designed the hull for the *Turtle*. And, they're being given monetary incentive to finish early, so they won't be inclined to drag things out."

"You running security, Monty?"

"Yes, I am, Jack. In fact, that's the gist of our meeting with Tysin. There's word of a security breach already. I can't say any more about it now. Don't want to steal the boss's thunder, you know."

They spent the next few hours in the air trading anecdotes and reminiscing until they touched down on a landing pad inside the Langley complex. A marine escort ushered Boxer, Monty and Pierce past the sentries, directly to the director's underground offices. The pilot stayed with his helicopter. It was Lori-Ann Collins who announced their presence to Tysin. "Why, Admiral Boxer, so nice to see you again," she flirted.

Some things never change, Boxer mused. The sun rises, the sun sets, and Lori-Ann, Tysin's secretary, is still busting out of the most provocative outfit she can find. "The pleasure is mine, Miss Collins."

"Please call me Lori-Ann, Admiral. It seems like we're already old friends."

The intercom buzzer on her desk phone sounded. Lori-Ann put the headset to her ear. "Yes, sir. I sure will, Mr. Tysin." She turned to the three men. "The director will see you in the blue room, gentlemen. If you'll please follow me?"

She turned her back and guided them down a hallway within the director's suite of offices. Monty and Pierce glanced at Boxer with sheepish grins, reading his reaction to the over-ripe body in the skin-tight yellow jersey dress. The three of them followed her, never taking their eyes off her, watching her behind undulate with each step.

She stopped at an unadorned door, apparently a good distance from any other rooms. "Well, here we are, gentlemen. Have a pleasant meeting." She stepped aside to let them pass, but not enough to keep her from brushing those full, pear-shaped breasts against Boxer, enough to let her be sure that he'd gotten the message.

The three men entered the room and took seats at one end

of a highly polished teak table. There were yellow legal pads, pencils, water pitchers and glasses in front of each of them. At the other end of the table was a high-backed, leather upholstered swivel chair. Must be the throne, Boxer figured. He's got his lady-in-waiting. Lord knows he's got enough jesters serving him. I guess that makes us the knights of the round table, he chuckled to himself. A moment later, a door opened behind the throne, and Henry Tysin entered the room. Immediately, Pierce and Monty stood up at their places. All rise, here comes the judge, Boxer thought. He remained seated.

"Be seated, gentlemen," Tysin said, by way of greeting. "Boxer, I guess you know why I sent for you?"

"Good afternoon to you, too, Tysin. Yes, Monty and Pierce filled me in on the chopper."

Tysin stared directly at him. "You can speak freely, here, Jack. The blue room is soundproof, and Monty and Pierce's credentials are exemplary."

"Just as long as the conversation remains among the four of us, Tysin. And no one else." Boxer emphasized the word no.

Tysin scowled at him. "Meaning?"

"Just that."

"I can assure you that nothing we say will leave this room. Behind me is a shredder, and next to that is an incinerator for the shreddings."

"Nothing recorded?"

"Nothing. Now, the problem. I have it from one of our people very highly placed in the Kremlin that plans are underway by the Soviets to steal the plans for the *Manta*, then sabotage it if possible. That will give the Ruskies the benefit of our superiority in submarine design. And if they succeed, it gives us a rusting hull on the ocean floor."

101

"Sir, may I . . . ?" Monty had his hand raised.

Tysin nodded.

"Jack, we don't have anywhere near the kind of secrecy that was possible when we built the *Shark*. That was the first of its type, and we caught Ivan with his pants down."

Boxer smiled at the memories of those times, of taking the *Shark* on her sea trials with nothing in any ocean that could touch her. It didn't take long before the Russians had their *Sea Death*, and Igor Borodine to command her.

"Now, what with the press hounding us, and the 'No Nukes' and other environmental groups protesting anything nuclear, it's tough to keep anything under wraps."

"We have to try, Monty. The standard Soviet *Alfa* is one of the best subs in the world today. One of them almost got me in the Persian Gulf. If they develop another super sub, and they've got to be close, things will be mighty nasty down there."

Tysin interjected. "They are on the verge of a breakthrough, Boxer. Our source has it that they aborted their plans at the last moment during the Persian Gulf fiasco that you referred to. And we would have had nothing to counter with except an old *Los Angeles* class."

"The question is," Pierce said, "How do we stop them?"

"Uncover their spy before they get what they want, sir. But how?"

"Give them the plans," Boxer said.

"What?" Tysin growled. "Are you out of your fucking mind?"

"It seems to me, sir, that if you're going to go fishing, you're going to need some bait."

"Sound like the fish catching the fisherman," countered Tysin. "I don't get your point."

"I think I'm beginning to get it, sir," Monty responded. "Give them the plans . . . but not the real plans, I'll bet."

Boxer smiled. "Right, Monty. The *Shark* has been declassified for some time, now, Tysin. In fact, the young designer who worked with me on the *Manta*'s hull shape told me they use the *Shark* as a teaching tool, now, at the Academy. We feed the *Shark*'s plans to the Ruskies, but make them think it's the new prototype."

"Yes. Yes, indeed," Tysin said, beaming from ear to ear. "The Ruskie high brass will certainly realize they've been duped, and heads will roll for it. I doubt that any of their field agents would be able to tell the *Shark*'s plans from the *Manta*'s. Damn, that's really good, Boxer. Hate to admit it, but it's a good idea."

"If you liked that, sir, you'll love the next part."

Three pair of eyes homed in on Boxer. Six ears fine-tuned to his every word.

"We leak different plans in different areas. Each phase of the operation leaks a slightly different version of the *Shark*'s specs. Carson's group at headquarters gets one variation, Tysin, your office staff gets another. Monty and Pierce, you'll make it easy for someone to pick up still another modification up in New London. That ought to make it easier to find our spy."

"Or spies," Monty added.

"Or spies," Tysin mimicked. "Well, gentlemen. This meeting has been very productive. Monty, Pierce, you'd better get on up to Symington's. We don't want to waste any more time. Boxer, please stay behind."

Boxer shook hands with his former colleagues, and watched them leave the room. When the door had been closed behind them, Tysin motioned for Boxer to sit down. "What's up, Tysin?"

"It has been brought to my attention that you have a little vendetta planned."

"I won't deny that. I'm going to bring Julio Sanchez to justice for what he did to Admiral Stark and my fianceé. I have some time off due me. That makes the entire affair my problem, not anyone else's. If you catch my drift."

"It is my understanding that you are planning to consort with Bruno Morell, a known traitor, Commie spy, and enemy of the state. That makes it my business."

Boxer replied, "Bruno claims he was set up by Sanchez to be the fall guy in the Libya debacle. There is some evidence that he may be telling the truth. And Sanchez's henchman confessed to the kidnapping under Sanchez's orders."

"Sanchez sometimes works for us. I prefer to believe his version of the story."

Boxer couldn't believe what he was hearing. "You mean you've been in touch with Julio since the kidnapping?"

"I told you, he sometimes works for us. Some of my best leads come from him."

"Sure," Boxer retorted. "He'd be in a good position to know what the Ruskies are up to. He'd deal with anyone for a profit. No, Tysin. Sanchez is my man. I'm going after him, and neither you nor anyone else is going to stop me."

"Don't count on that, Boxer. We have a warrant out on Morrell. We're offering a bounty of half a mil for Bruno, dead or alive. Think about that, while you're running around with him."

"Half a million dollars? Whose idea was that?"

"Why, mine, of course." With that, Tysin got up from

his comfortable chair and left the way he came in, leaving Boxer sitting there alone.

"Of course," Boxer said to the empty room. "Who else?"

CHAPTER TEN

Boxer took TWA flight 401 to Rome, arriving in late evening. He slept on the train during the journey north, and was at the door of the Piedmont Sanatorium near the Swiss border by 0600, Italy time. He dismissed his taxi driver and announced himself to the receptionist.

"Yes, of course, Admiral Boxer. It is always a pleasure to have you visit with Signora Wheeler. It is certain to brighten her spirits." She noticed the huge bouquet of local flowers he carried. "As I'm certain the beautiful flowers will. Oh, and I have a note for you, left here just two days ago." The middle-aged woman handed over a sealed envelope.

Boxer looked at the hand-addressed envelope of fine quality eggshell colored paper. "Couldn't someone here have notified me of this? You have a list of numbers where I can be reached."

"That would have been my choice, Admiral. But the man who delivered this insisted that it wouldn't be necessary. He said that you would be visiting here within a few days, and that would be timely enough for this message."

Boxer pocketed the note. "Grazi, Signora. Now, if you'll please take me to Miss Wheeler?"

"Si. With pleasure. Dr. Garipalli is with her now."

Boxer crinkled his brow. "Garipalli? The woman doctor?"

The matronly receptionist looked rather sadly down at her feet. "Si. She still does not trust any of the men. But . . ." Her face lit up as she said, "I'm sure that will all change now that you are here. Come, I will bring you to her."

They found Francine Wheeler and Dr. Garipalli on lounge chairs on the terrace, chatting and looking out at a beautiful valley below in this mountainous area. Boxer found the view to be breathtaking. He also found Francine to have regained much of her former beauty, even dressed in a plain pale green hospital gown, and devoid of any makeup. Her long red hair was pulled back and allowed to fall to her shoulders. His escort cleared her throat, and Garipalli turned to face them.

"Ah, look Francine, it is Admiral Boxer come to visit you." Dr. Garipalli was a dark-haired woman in her late thirties, about ten years older than Francine. She was a handsome woman, Boxer thought, although her years in this very difficult profession had added many lines of worry and sadness to her face.

Francine looked at Boxer impassively, at first, then with a glimmer of recognition she allowed herself a slight smile.

"Admiral Jack Boxer," Garipalli coached her. "Your fiance."

No response.

"He saved you, and brought you to us. Jack Boxer," the doctor tried again.

"Hello, Francine. How are you doing, darling?"

"Jack. Yes . . . Hello Jack. I'm okay."

Garipalli noticed the bouquet Boxer had been carrying at his side, and added, "Francine, look at those beautiful flowers. I doubt that he brought them here for me."

Boxer smiled and handed them over. Dr. Garipalli and Francine fawned over them, folding the tissue wrapping paper back and admiring them, enjoying their beauty and fragrance. "You are very fortunate, Francine, to have a man who loves you so much, and brings you beautiful things."

Francine smiled at Boxer again. So far, so good, he figured, at least this was a little encouraging. Last visit, she huddled up in a fetal position and wouldn't let him near her.

"Well?" the doctor asked. "Aren't you going to say thanks for the flowers?"

"Grazi," she said, softly. "Thank you for the flowers. They're very beautiful."

Boxer moved closer and held out his hand to her. "I'm glad you like them.

She recoiled from him.

"Go ahead, Francine," Garipalli prodded. "Jack is your friend. It's okay to hold his hand."

Suddenly, Francine's face lost its color and she shrieked, "Nooo. No . . . nooo . . ." She bolted from her chair and ran off screaming toward her room. Dr. Garipalli looked at him and shrugged an apology before running off after her.

Boxer did not follow. He knew that it was too soon. The wounds to her psyche had not sufficiently healed. It was best to go.

"Leaving already, Signor?"

"Yes," he told the receptionist. "I must have upset her. Will you please order a taxi for me?"

"Yes, of course. At once, Admiral Boxer."

Within minutes, Boxer was seated in the back of a yellow taxi.

Tipped off by the receptionist, the taxi driver spoke in English. "Where to, Signor?"

"To the train station," Boxer answered. Just then, he realized he still hadn't opened the note. "Wait just a minute, please."

Boxer produced a small pocket knife and slit open the

108

envelope. It contained a two sentence message on matching eggshell paper. Boxer's eyes quickly scanned the note. It read, GO TO THE PLACE WHERE I FIRST GAINED YOUR TRUST. I WILL TAKE YOU HUNTING. It wasn't signed, but Boxer had no doubts that it was written by Bruno Morell. Place where I first gained your trust. Boxer tossed the enigma around in his head for a moment, then smiled at the obvious answer. "To the station," he ordered the driver. "I've got to catch the train for Rome."

The driver at the sanatorium had been very cautious, what with the tricky mountainous roads. The driver of the yellow taxi in Rome drove like a man possessed, speeding, cutting off other vehicles, darting in and out of traffic, all the while cursing and gesturing obscenely at the traffic. Boxer was thankful to arrive at the American Embassy alive. He paid off the driver. As soon as he was safely on the sidewalk, the driver directed the obscenities at Boxer, possibly because he didn't feel that the tip was adequate. Boxer's Italian wasn't very good, but it seemed that the taxi driver was questioning the origins of his family.

Boxer decided to walk the half-mile to the apartment where he'd been snared by Morell last year, and then offered Bruno's gun as a show of good faith. That was the place where he decided to trust Bruno Morell. He climbed the long flight of stairs and very carefully entered the flat.

It was sparsely furnished: a wooden table and two wooden chairs in the kitchen, a worn sofa and upholstered chair in the tiny living room, and upon Boxer's inspection, a single cot in the bedroom. The floors were worn linoleum, the unprotected lightbulbs glared harshly. Well, Boxer thought, nothing to do now but wait. If Morell knew he was going to The Piedmont sanatorium, then it was a cinch he'd know when Boxer arrived at his apartment in Rome.

The wait took about an hour. Boxer heard a telltale creak from one of the old wooden steps and pressed his body flush with the wall to the side of the door. The door opened, and a man entered with gun drawn. Boxer grabbed the gunhand, bent it backward until the blued automatic crashed to the floor and twisted the man's arm twice. Nicky Capoletti flipped head-over-heels onto the linoleum floor. Before Boxer could recover, Aldo Fagiole, Morell's other bodyguard had a gun pointed directly at his head. Bruno followed him in, laughing as he entered at Nicky Capoletti's expense.

"So I see at least I taught you something, my friend. It's a good thing for Nicky that you weren't armed."

Boxer was relieved. "Hi Bruno. Sorry, Nick. For a moment there I thought my number was up." Boxer's hands were over his head. "Mind if I put my arms down, now?"

Bruno chuckled. "Ease up, Aldo. Admiral Boxer's on our side now, remember?"

Fagiole returned his nickel chrome 9mm automatic to his shoulder holster. "You could'a fooled me there for a while, boss. Hiya, Boxer. Sorry about the hardware."

Boxer nodded, while Nicky got back to his feet, and brushed off his brown silk suit. "What's on your mind, Bruno? Your message seemed urgent."

The joviality left Bruno's voice. "I have located Julio Sanchez. I am going to hunt him down and kill him. I thought you might like to go along."

"You thought right," Boxer said. "Where is the bastard?"

"The little weasel is running a white slavery ring. He

kidnapped—there is really no other way to describe it," Bruno went on. "He duped or physically abducted about a dozen beautiful young women in Cannes last month during the film festival. The place swarms with would-be starlets, groupies, and the like. He had his pick."

Boxer was shaking his head. Sanchez had Francine abducted and brought aboard his yacht. Then she was brutally beaten and gang raped into submission. He realized that she might never recover from the ordeal. And now, Sanchez was continuing this evil practice.

"I understand that his yacht, with the women aboard, is already through the Suez Canal and steaming toward the slave auctions in Al Qunfudah, in Saudi Arabia."

"Slave auctions? C'mon, Bruno, they've been outlawed for over fifty years."

"Some ideas die hard, my friend. Don't be naive. A beautiful young American or Western European woman in good health, and with a great body can bring in twenty, twenty-five grand, easy. And a natural blonde, or a redhead, forget it. Maybe twice that. And the buyers will know if the hair color is natural before they buy, believe me. I've been there. And once inside of Saudi Arabia there's as much chance of those girls ever getting out of some sheik's harem as there is of hell freezing over."

Anger caused Boxer's face to redden. He was livid with rage. "Can we stop him, Bruno?"

"We're gonna try, Jack. We're gonna fly into Jiddah, and pick up some weapons. Then it's on by Land Rover to the slave auctions." He paused a beat, to let the seriousness of his next statement sink in. "We'll have to fight our way out."

Boxer took in a deep breath and let it out. "Okay," he asked. "When do we start?"

Bruno Morell clapped him on the shoulder. "We're on

111

our way, my friend. We're on our way."

The aging Saudi 727 landed in Jiddah's international airport early in the morning. It was already almost ninety degrees when Boxer, Morell, and Morell's two bodyguards climbed down onto the tarmac. They were dressed in loose-fitting khaki colored safari clothing. Morell quickly donned a traditional Arab headdress which covered the sides of his face, and his dark complexion and prominent nose made him appear to be a native Saudi.

Boxer adjusted his pith helmet. He, Nicky and Aldo would have to pass as Europeans, although he thought the dark-featured Aldo Fagiole could pass for an Arab in a pinch. They checked into a hotel where Bruno Morell began calling his contacts to arrange for the things they would need to escape, once they abducted Sanchez.

They had decided to travel at night, both to hide their intentions and to escape from the incredible daytime heat. An hour after dusk, the four of them headed south along the coastal route in two rented Land Rovers. At 0300, the lead vehicle sputtered to a halt. Bruno Morell jumped from the passenger seat and kicked at a front tire. "Fuck," he sputtered. "C'mon, Nicky, get the stuff." Bruno removed the two gallon jerry can filled with water and placed it in the rear of the second halted Rover.

"What's up, Bruno?" Boxer asked.

"Fuckin' rental cars. I think the fuel pump sprung a leak. Fuckin' gas spilled out for the last half a mile." Nicky dumped their personal effects into the second vehicle, and climbed into the back seat.

"Thought I smelled gas," Boxer added.

"That's why I insisted we take two of these Rovers instead of one. What if we'd all been riding in that piece of shit," he snarled, pointing a finger at the disabled vehicle in front of them. He climbed into the rear passenger seat behind Boxer and muttered, "C'mon, Aldo, you waitin' for an invitation? Let's get the fuck out of here. We got business up ahead."

They reached Al Qunfudhah by 0800, local time. Boxer could feel the sweat trickle down his underarms already. He hated to think about the heat of the afternoon.

Bruno went right to work making his contacts. "We'll be moving out this afternoon," he said. "Let's get something to eat."

Bruno had Nicky gas up the Land Rover in case they would need it for their return to Jiddah. It would be one of several escape routes. The four men walked along a broad thoroughfare until Bruno turned into a narrow street lined with many shops and stalls. They stopped at a small restaurant where they were seated at an outdoor table. *"Safsouf,"* Bruno ordered from the fat shop owner who doubled as waiter.

The fat man returned in a few minutes with a platter piled high with a garlicky grain dish that reminded Boxer of the kasha that his old friend and nemesis Borodine loved so much. It smelled wonderful.

"What's this stuff, boss?" Aldo was inhaling the odors with his nose a few inches above the mound of food. "Smells like garlic and mint."

"Get your nose out of there, Aldo. That's called tabulleh. It's like a cereal. They mix it with lots of garlic and tomatoes, lemon juice, and mint. Here, watch me." Bruno broke off a thick lettuce leaf from the pile that bordered the grainy food. "You scoop it up like this, and eat it." Bruno shoved it into his mouth and closed his eyes while savoring the wonderful taste. "Delicious," he proclaimed.

The others followed suit, everybody digging in and

shoveling the delicious meal into their mouths. Suddenly, Bruno froze and stared at Nicky Capoletti. "Hey, Nicky, eat with your right hand. They think it's very impolite to eat with their left hands."

"Sure, Bruno. What's the difference? Right, left. Who cares?"

Morell looked around him, making sure that none of the natives were watching them. "They do," he said in a stage whisper, motioning around him with his head movement. "Out here in the desert, there ain't enough water to go around. So they eat with their right hand and wipe their ass with their left."

That brought chuckles from the two bodyguards. Boxer almost choked on his mouthful of food. Bruno continued. "They do almost everything with their right hand, shake hands, eat food, everything. The left hand has got only one function. So Nicky, don't mistake your mouth for your ass, okay?"

Nicky was embarrassed, but joined the others in laughter. After all, Bruno was the boss. After the meal, they munched on dates and drank tiny cups of rich, syrupy Arabian coffee. After paying off the restaurant owner, and thanking him for the delicious food, Bruno got up and said, "It's time to go now."

They drove to the outskirts of the city and parked the Land Rover in the shade. It was now noon. The small thermometer mounted in the vehicle read 112 degrees. They waited in the shade of a building at a prearranged spot until a small caravan of Bedouins arrived on camels. Aldo roused Bruno, who was resting against the wall of the building with his eyes closed. Morell looked up at the group moving their way. He quickly hopped to his feet. "It's them. Let's move out."

They rose and walked out to greet the caravan of six

mounted Bedouins leading four additional camels. Boxer and his men were soon surrounded. Bruno called out in Arabic, *"Asalaam alaykem."*

"Alaykem asalaam," came the traditional reply. Peace be upon you, as Boxer understood it. He, Nicky and Aldo watched Bruno converse with the leader in Arabic, then returned in a few minutes to their midst.

"We follow them into the desert on the camels," he told them. "Ismal, the head man, brought along the proper clothing. Leave all your stuff in the Rover and put on these robes and headdresses."

The four men stripped in silence and replaced their clothing with traditional Bedouin robes and headgear. Then, with the help of Ismal's men, they ascended the huge beasts, slipping into the boxy, heavily padded saddles that the Bedouins had provided for them.

They made their way into the desert, and rode the camels for several hours before stopping to rest at a small oasis. There was a well and some palm trees, and several large tents set up in a semi-circle. Boxer felt the hot sand beneath his Arab sandals as he and Bruno followed Ismal into one of the tents. They removed their sandals at the threshold, and sat on their haunches on an ornate rug on the sand floor. Ismal introduced Boxer and Bruno to his superior, a gray bearded man with dark, leathery skin, named Khaled. After water was passed around, and the men snacked on dates and dried apricots, Bruno cleared his throat and came to the point. "Do you have the goods we asked for?" he asked the old man in Arabic.

"We have them." Khaled surprised them by answering in broken English. "Did you bring the gold?"

"Of course. After we see the merchandise, please."

Boxer appreciated Bruno Morell's courage. After all, these people could kill them and leave their bodies out in

115

the desert, and no one would be the wiser. The old man spoke to Ismal in Arabic, and the younger man left the tent. He returned with two of his men, and Nicky and Aldo, carrying two wooden chests. These were set down on the carpet before Bruno. Khaled nodded, and Bruno opened one of the crates.

"Very nice," replied Morell. The wooden chest contained four Uzis and an extra supply of ammo clips. The second box turned out to contain hand guns, knives, and U.S. Army issue hand grenades.

Bruno smiled and handed the old man a bag of gold coins which he removed from the folds of his robe.

Khaled smiled back, opened the cloth bag and fingered the coins, quickly calculating their value. "It is more than we agreed upon."

"Yes," Bruno replied. "I will need two of your men to act as guides."

"It shall be as you ask," the old man replied. "My nephew, Ismal, will go with you. And Ahmad," he pointed to a lanky young man, "will go also."

Boxer suggested they get a few hours rest. Their plans called for them to be at the slave auctions the next day.

Ismal took them to a small tent, where they slept for several hours. They awoke, and worked out a plan to capture Julio Sanchez, and at Boxer's insistence, free his illegal cache of slaves. The men left on camel shortly after dusk. To all but the closest scrutiny, they appeared to be six Bedouins. They travelled under the stars until they reached the ruins of a century-old stone building open on three sides, with only columns and archways left, where once they supported the roof. The six men took positions behind a dune on a rise overlooking the ancient slave market.

As dawn broke, a caravan of tarpaulin-covered trucks

wound their way to the site. Boxer watched through field glasses as several black-robed men freed eight or ten women per truck from their confines and led them into the closed-in section of the slave market. One of the robed women fainted at the sight of the hostile-looking building. She was rewarded by one of the men with kicks in her backside until she got up and followed the others inside. From what he could see, Boxer noticed that most of the women were either black or Asian. That meant that Julio Sanchez had not arrived yet.

Bruno touched Boxer's arm, and pointed to the half-dozen armed men fanning out in all directions around the slave quarters. One of them was heading in their direction. "Sentries," Bruno said softly.

Boxer nodded.

Ismal and Ahmad moved the camels further away from their position behind the dune. As the sentry got closer, they realized that he was coming directly at them. He, too, realized what a strategic position that they had taken. Bruno nodded to his men. Aldo and Nicky spread out, hiding behind neighboring dunes. Boxer and Morell crouched behind their original hiding place.

The black turbaned and robed sentry climbed around the back of the dune where the two men were hiding. The startled Bedouin came upon them suddenly and pointed his M-16 automatic rifle in their direction. Aldo Fagiole leapt from his hiding place and threw an eight-inch hunting knife into the sentry's back with such force that the man fell forward on his face, dropping his weapon into the sand.

Nicky Capoletti ran up and turned the body over with his foot. The sentry was still alive, barely hanging on, but with sense enough to point the barrel of his rifle at Nicky. Aldo reached over and tore the gun out of his hands, just as Nicky lashed out a kick to his jaw. Then Aldo removed his knife from the man's back and deftly slit the sentry's throat.

"Don't get blood all over that outfit," Bruno ordered. "We're gonna need it."

It took the two gunmen a while to catch on. Boxer had already summoned Ismal to their hiding place. Bruno told him to put on the dead man's clothes, and stand guard on the dune with the M-16. Boxer was pleased with the neat trick. Now no one from below would bother them.

As the sun continued its ascent, quite a few others arrived at the old slave market, some by camel, most by Jeeps and Land Rovers. Still no Julio Sanchez. Throughout the morning, Boxer and Bruno took turns watching the proceedings through a pair of high-powered field glasses. Women were being paraded out into the central clearing, made to turn around, show their teeth, and then the bidding would begin.

At one point, Boxer noticed Bruno staring intently at the goings-ons, a sardonic smile across his face. Boxer motioned, what's going on?

Bruno handed him the binoculars, and Boxer perched atop the dune alongside Morell. He stared at the objects of Bruno's fascination. One of the slave traders had a black woman by the hair at the back of her head. She was bare-breasted, wearing only a colorful sarong wrapped around her hips, and open to show a lot of thigh. The slaver began showing off her ample cone-shaped breasts to some of the buyers, eliciting taunts and jeers from them. Then he started tugging up the hem on the sarong, a little at a time, to more cat-calls. All were apparently amused, except for the hapless victim. Her face was a mask of terror.

Finally, the trader spun her around, grabbed a handful

of the skirt and lifted it clear up over the top of her high, firm behind. He traced up the back of her legs with a camel prod, slid it up over the swell of her backside slowly, very slowly, making sure all eyes were upon him and his subject. Then, with a swift movement of his wrist, he swatted her on the ass with the prod. She jumped about a foot. Boxer could hear the buyers laughter from there.

Suddenly, Bruno tugged him down. Boxer started to protest. Morell touched his fingers to Boxer's lips. He pointed to Ismal and then in the direction of the next nearest sentry. Boxer was so engrossed in the scene below at the slave auction that he'd failed to notice the other sentry coming over to converse with the one that Ismal had replaced.

"Don't kill this one," Boxer whispered in Bruno's ear. "Find out where Julio is."

Bruno nodded and motioned orders to his men. As the sentry approached, Ismal climbed down from his position and climbed down behind the dune. The two of them greeted each other and began to converse when Nicky threw a muscular arm around the sentry's neck and pulled him back off his feet. The others jumped out from hiding and bodily moved him farther out of earshot.

"Make him talk quickly," Bruno ordered Ismal. "Ask him where are the white slaves?"

Ismal removed a heavy, curved knife and moved to the man's side. He asked something in Arabic.

The sentry shrugged. How did he know?

That cost him an ear. Boxer turned away in disgust. Ismal asked him again.

Same reply, although the man was clearly in pain.

Ismal cut off the other ear. Blood ran down the man's face and neck. He was terrified, yet he would not speak.

Finally, Ismal called out something to Bruno Morell.

Bruno took Boxer by the arm and led him off behind a nearby dune. A few minutes later, Ismal returned, leading Ahmad, Nicky and Aldo. Ismal was wiping blood off his knife with the sentry's unravelled black turban. Bruno barked a command. Ismal's answer caused Bruno to grin, and turn to his men making a scissor movement with two of his fingers. They all chuckled.

Boxer was getting nauseated. "Well, what did he say?"

Bruno was still smiling. "Ismal says he just asked the bastard if he wanted to leave this world as a man or as a woman, and cut the crotch out of the guy's pants. The guy said that the white slaves aren't due till tomorrow. They're on a big white boat in the Red Sea."

Boxer shook his head in disgust. "The *Sea Breeze*. Julio Sanchez's yacht. We've got to get out there as soon as possible."

"Way ahead of you. Part of my escape plan was to have an inflatable with a powerful outboard waiting for us at the shore, for a fast getaway by sea if necessary. Well, we'll just use it to go after Julio. *Capice?*"

Boxer nodded his head. "Well, then, let's get the hell out of here. This place makes me sick."

The six of them travelled most of the day and into the night, in spite of the intense heat. They reached the shore of the Red Sea and found the place where Bruno had secured the inflatable. They bid farewell to Ismal and Ahmad, and then Bruno paid off the man guarding the boat. A small bribe bought them the whereabouts of the *Sea Breeze*.

They changed into the clothing that Bruno had stashed on the inflatable and took off at high speed down the Saudi coast. They headed south toward Yemen, where apparently the *Sea Breeze* was lying at anchor until the following morning. There was no time to lose.

At the southernmost extent of the Saudi coastline, the Arabian peninsula juts out into the Red Sea. The sea narrows at this point, and the shore becomes part of Yemen. This is where Boxer and his party first sighted the huge white hulk of Julio Sanchez's yacht. Bruno had his men cut the engine.

Nicky and Aldo each manned an oar on either side of the inflatable, silently rowing them closer to their target. Bruno handed Boxer an Uzi, and kept one for himself. Each man wore a 45 caliber pistol strapped to his side, and carried several grenades clipped to their belts.

Boxer noticed two guards standing watch on the yacht, one fore, the other at the stern. They seemed preoccupied with watching in the direction of the shore. Boxer had them approach from the sea.

Aldo had the best arm, so he got the call to hurl up a line with a rubber coated grappling hook over a side rail on the lowest level. The aft guard thought he heard a sound, gave a cursory glance over the side and, seeing nothing, he returned to his vigil toward the beach.

Nicky Capoletti scampered up the line, an Uzi strapped to his back. Aldo started up after him, but Bruno called him back. "You stay here with the boat. Me and Boxer got a score to settle with Julio."

Aldo shrugged and watched the others climb up the heavy rope onto the *Sea Breeze*. Then he used the dangling line to hold the inflatable close to the yacht.

The three others crouched low and made for the stairwell amidships. There, they had a chance encounter with a crewman who'd been drinking so heavily that he could hardly stand. Bruno took him out with a smash to the side of his jaw. The man fell backward, striking his head against a steel bulkhead. He dropped like a limp rag.

Nicky knelt beside the man and studied his face. The eyes had rolled back in his head. Nicky gave the thumbs down sign and they quietly climbed up the stairs to the main level. They split up onto each side of the deck, and made their way toward the stern. Bruno came from the seaward side and tossed a 45 caliber cartridge onto the deck behind the guard.

When the guard turned toward the sound, Nicky jumped him from behind and slit his throat. As the guard slumped silently, Bruno rushed in and took the rifle from him before it hit the deck. They tossed it overboard, and dragged the dead man behind a liferaft. Now they could safely look for Julio Sanchez.

From a previous attempt at capturing Julio they knew that his stateroom was on this level. That it was, in fact, a suite of three rooms, with a well stocked bar, and was usually heavily guarded. And all else being equal, the girls being held as slaves were probably one deck below, toward the stern. They decided that taking Sanchez had priority.

They removed their shoes and tiptoed forward, dropping to hands and knees when they spotted the first shotgun-wielding guard patrolling the deck in front of Julio's quarters. Bruno found a bucket and hurled it over the side within view of the guard's line of vision. As the guard hurried to the rail to see what had gone overboard, Nicky rushed him from behind, knife in hand. Before either Nicky or the guard could react, another armed man walked out of a doorway almost into Nicky's arms. The three startled men took a moment to focus on what was happening, and then the shooting started.

Nicky hit the deck. Boxer and Bruno opened up with the Uzis. The two guards fired their pump-action automatic shotguns. When it was over, both of Sanchez's guards were dead, one lying in a pool of his own blood on the deck, the other splashing into the sea below.

Boxer and Bruno ran to Nicky, who was lying there covered with blood. Bruno shook his man. "Nick, you okay? Speak to me, dammit."

Nick Capoletti rolled over on his side. "I'm hit, Bruno. My fuckin' leg hurts so bad."

Boxer noticed the leg was bent at an odd angle, probably fractured by a shotgun blast. The next thing he noticed was a group of men running in their direction, shouting and firing handguns. "In here," Boxer shouted. "Help me with Nicky."

Both men got down on all fours and dragged their fallen comrade inside the doorway. Boxer motioned for Bruno to cover the door. He was going after Julio Sanchez.

Boxer moved quietly through the second room of the suite, knowing that Julio would probably be armed and waiting for him inside the master stateroom. He could hear a woman weeping inside.

He cradled his Uzi, crouched, and kicked open the inner door. He ducked back just as two shots whizzed past his head from inside. Boxer jumped in belly first, firing a burst from his Uzi. A woman screamed.

Julio Sanchez sat on the bed in his shorts, pointing a lightweight Italian automatic pistol at Boxer. Boxer fired another burst, shattering the walnut paneling behind and just off to the side of Sanchez's head. "It's no contest, Julio. Give it up."

Sanchez stared at him a moment. He glanced at the buxom blond woman huddling naked on the bed next to him. He turned, and grabbed her hair, placed the barrel of his gun against her head. "I'll kill the girl."

Boxer snarled, "I'll shoot your legs off, Julio, and leave you here. How would you like to go through life like that?"

Julio looked hard at the petrified woman next to him, then, resignedly at Boxer. He took a deep breath, and as he let it out, it seemed as if his entire body shuddered. He just sat there on the edge of the bed, shoulders slumped down, the pistol dangling from his hands beneath his knees.

"Drop it, Julio."

The gun hit the floor at the same time as the burst of machine-gun fire coming from the outer room. Bruno was fighting off the rest of Sanchez's crew. Boxer had to come to his aid. He grabbed the top of the sheet partially covering the girl, and tore off a four inch wide strip. "Excuse me, Miss. I'd suggest you lie flat on the floor in the corner over there. You can cover yourself with this." He tossed the sheet after the terrified woman, who silently followed his orders.

"Turn around, Julio," Boxer commanded. "I'm going to want to question you in a little while. For now, this will have to keep you." With the torn strip of sheet, Boxer bound Julio's hands behind his back, winding a loop around his neck to keep him from trying to pull out of his bonds. Then he rushed to Bruno Morell's aid.

Bruno motioned to both sides of the doorway with his Uzi. Boxer nodded and unclasped two grenades. Morell smiled and did the same. They pulled the pins with their teeth, silently counted to five, laid flat on the floor and tossed the grenades in both directions, in rapid succession. They ducked back inside the room just as the grenades went off. Men screamed, windows shattered, and the stench of smoke and burned bodies permeated the area. Boxer and Morrell jumped out onto the deck and stood there back to back spraying anyone left standing with automatic fire.

Satisfied, Boxer returned to Sanchez's stateroom. "Cover me, Bruno. I've got some unfinished business with Julio."

Bruno Morell smiled, and stepping over Nicky lying there on the floor, returned to the doorway with his Uzi. Boxer went inside and turned to the naked woman cringing on the floor, shaking uncontrollably. "You can get up now, Miss. You're going to be okay. Please alert the other women to get ready to leave with us in a few minutes."

She nodded dumbly and stood up, the sheet falling to the floor. Big and blonde and buxom, Boxer thought. Just Julio's type, the little weasel. He reached down and picked up the sheet, handing it to the girl as she walked out of the room. Then he turned his full attention to Julio Sanchez. He walked over to Sanchez, grabbed a handful of shirt collar and twisted it until the man's face turned red. "Now, Julio, I want to know everything about Francine Wheeler's kidnapping. You'd better start talking."

CHAPTER ELEVEN

Igor Borodine and his exec, Viktor, rode in the spacious back seat of a brand new Zymcha en route to Admiral Gorshkov's quarters. It was a luxury that Borodine often bypassed, although it was a privilege much sought after by many of the senior officers. He realized, of course, that the boxy, unwieldy vehicle was merely a close replica of an extinct American Nash automobile of the early fifties, and therefore not worthy of the excitement it caused among his associates.

They were let off at the main entrance, and ushered to the office of the Admiral of the Fleet by two armed guards. They were even treated courteously by the admiral's jowly aide, the captain even hauling his great portly body out of his chair and saluting them. "Admiral Gorshkov is expecting you, Admiral Borodine. Please go right in."

Borodine and Viktor exchanged glances. There was never less than a half hour wait to see Gorshkov. Borodine wondered what the catch was; there had to be a reason for the cordial reception.

Old Admiral Gorshkov was standing behind his desk when the two of them entered. "Welcome, Comrade Borodine. And to you, too, Viktor Illyavich. Igor often speaks very highly of you." He indicated for them to sit down across from his desk.

They saluted smartly, and took the two wooden chairs

that had been proffered. Each of them carried with them thick leather briefcases filled with documents on the new *Sea Demon*. At last, Borodine felt, they had a good, workable prototype. "Viktor is as good a submarine captain as any in your fleet, yet he chooses to stay with me as my executive officer. And I am very glad to have him." Viktor was beaming from all the compliments being paid him.

"I hope," Borodine continued, "that when I am no longer able to command a submarine, that you will consider Viktor as my replacement."

Gorshkov ran his hand through his mane of white hair. "I see that you have brought along the documents that I requested. Let us go over them during lunch. I have ordered food set up for us in my private dining room. We can work and eat at the same time.

They followed Gorshkov into a medium sized room with rich mahogany paneling and wainscoting, and they took seats around a circular table set for three. There were embroidered linen napkins and tablecloth, and china that must have predated the Revolution. Two uniformed waiters stood at ready. Gorshkov nodded, and they went off to get the food. Then the admiral asked, "I presume you have overcome the flaw in the power plant?"

"I believe that we have, Comrade Admiral. First of all, I have ordered the thickness of all shielding material to be doubled. We have added an additional coolant pump operating on a separate, emergency power supply. And we have reinforced many of the moving parts. We have added a little weight, but we have a much safer nuclear power plant."

The two waiters returned, bearing silver dome-covered platters. "Ah, here comes lunch, comrades." He pointed to the table and addressed the waiters. "Just leave it here. We will help ourselves."

They placed the trays on the table, bowed perfunctorily and left. In a moment, one of them returned with a frosty bottle of 100 proof vodka and chilled tumblers. Gorshkov waited until the waiter made his exit, and filled three glasses with vodka. He handed one to each of his subordinates. "A toast," he said, uplifting his drink. "In honor of your new assignment as director of production for the new prototype. Igor, you and Comrade Viktor will leave for Polyarnyy to supervise the finish of the *Sea Demon*, and to take her out on her sea trials. Congratulations."

Borodine and Viktor looked at each other in surprise, smiled and downed their vodka swiftly. "Thank you, Comrade Admiral. It is an unexpected pleasure. I'll be glad to get back to sea after spending the last half year desk-bound."

Gorshkov refilled their glasses, and then removed the domes covering the food. "I'm just a peasant at heart, comrades. I hope you don't mind the peasant fare."

Borodine feasted his eyes on a tureen of cold borscht, accompanied by boiled potatoes and sour cream, black bread and butter. "I am just a peasant, myself, Comrade Admiral. There is nothing I like better."

Viktor nodded his agreement, and the three men dug into the food, consuming large quantities of the red beet soup and bread. When their hunger was sated, the old admiral buzzed for the waiters, and ordered tea.

The waiters returned with tea service consisting of glasses set into ornate silver casings, a silver tea pot, crystal dishes with sugar and cream, and a freshly made babka for dessert. Borodine watched in amusement as Gorshkov added cream to his tea, popped a sugar cube into his mouth and washed the steaming liquid over the cube, something he'd done himself as a small child. There's still some boy left in the old man, after all, he mused.

After washing down a second helping of the cake, Gorshkov patted his ample girth and said, "Now, comrades, I have something else that may please you. Comrade Colonel Portonyi, poor Kakusky's replacement in the Second Directorate, hand delivered it to me only this morning." He reached into his briefcase and came up with a thick document which he plopped in front of Borodine.

"Yes, too bad about Comrade Kakusky," Borodine agreed, knowing full well that they all equally despised the man. "Could it be true that a man of his stature met his demise at the hands of a jealous husband?"

"Jealous lover," corrected Gorshkov. "And one of his own people, at that. The fellow was lucky to have committed suicide before the KGB got hold of him. I hear they cut up his body and used it as herring bait."

Borodine smiled, and began leafing through the papers in front of him. At least he didn't appear to be a suspect. He slowed down on the second page. By page three, he came to a halt. "Comrade Admiral, these are plans for the new Yankee submarine class."

Gorshkov smiled. "We have the best intelligence agencies in the world. We have our own man in their shipyards getting this information for us at great personal risk. I hope you find it useful."

"Of course," Borodine turned another page. "The *Sea Demon*'s hull is already built, but the equipment, the electronics, the sonar alone is worth the risk. May I have these to study for a while?"

"That copy is yours to keep, comrade. Bring it with

you to Polyarnyy. You both leave on Monday. You have the remainder of the week to make your farewells."

Borodine's face suddenly fell. Gorshkov noticed and added, "I'm sorry, Igor, but our facilities at the submarine base have no accommodations for a wife and child."

When they got back into the Zymcha for the ride back, Borodine was a man possessed of deeply mixed emotions. He was saddened at the thought of leaving his wife, Tanya and newborn son for an extended period. But on the other hand, he was elated to be going back to sea duty. A double-edged sword, Borodine thought. He leaned back in the comfortable rear seat and closed his eyes. He still had to relay the news to Tanya.

Lori-Ann Collins was pleased with herself, as she primped in front of a boudoir mirror. Not only had she gotten Frumpkin the secret submarine documents he wanted, but with time to spare. For once, he couldn't complain about her, even complimenting her for a job well done.

She was sitting there in translucent pale pink baby-doll pajamas, nothing more than a pair of lacy bikini bottoms and a scant, frilly top with a deep, plunging neckline. The top barely reached below her waist, very provocative, she was sure. Henry would be putty in her hands. The thought tickled her as she skillfully applied makeup, which she finished off with a flourish of brush-on blush powder on her cheeks and the exposed tops of her full, pear-shaped breasts.

The door buzzer sounded three times, then twice again. Henry Tysin's signal to her. She tweaked her nipples to make them stand out and hurried to the door.

Tysin managed a smile as he stood there in a gray

tropical weight wool suit, with a burgundy colored silk tie pulled askew and his collar button open. He could already feel the stirring in his groin watching her framed in the open doorway wearing hardly anything at all. She was a knockout in that little pink thing, looking for all the world like the Museum of Natural History, or maybe like a slightly retouched photo. Anyway, just looking at her dressed like that had the desired effect on him. He just had to give her the bad news, let her cry it out on his shoulder, and take her to bed.

"Henry, darling, come in honey." She took him by the arm and led him into the apartment. "You look a little haggard, Henry. Is everything all right?"

"Sort of." He locked the door behind him. "I could sure use a drink."

"Oh, sure. You just make yourself comfy right here," she coaxed him into the sofa. "I'll just take your coat. Why don't you slip out of those shoes, and your tie. I've got some Glenfidich, darling. Your favorite."

Tysin followed the sway of her behind as she swished out of the living room. The filmy material clung tightly and followed the contours of her buttocks like a second skin. He held back on his information as long as possible, not wanting to break the spell. He didn't want to spoil his roll in the sack with her, and he needed all the help she could give him in that department. Why didn't he have a woman like her when he was a young man. She'd never let herself go the way his wife, Vivian had: all lard and heavy makeup covered up with expensive clothes. The fun had gone out of his marriage long ago. To Vivian, sex was a four-letter word. At least with Lori-Ann, he felt he could feel forever young.

Tysin stared at her unencumbered boobs beneath the flimsy fabric when she returned with two doubles of the

131

expensive scotch on ice. She sat down beside him on the couch and handed him his drink. She clinked her glass against his and said, "To us, Henry. You make me very happy, darling." She kissed him and they sipped their drinks.

He managed a weary smile. "You've made an old man very happy, Lori-Ann. I haven't felt this alive inside in thirty years." He downed his scotch in one long pull. "I'm sorry that I've got some unfortunate news for you. You got any more of this stuff?"

"Here, honey," she said, offering Tysin her glass. "I've hardly touched it."

"I'd better get a refill, Lor. I think you may need that when I tell you what I learned today."

"Oh, dear, Henry. Wait right here while I get you some more." She was gone and back in a flash with the bottle of Glenfidich, and poured him another double. She sat back next to him and rested her hand in his lap, massaging his crotch through the fabric of his pants. "Now, what could possibly be so terrible, darling, that a little love-making couldn't resolve?"

Tysin drank off half of his second scotch, leaned back enjoying her ministrations, and let out a great sigh. "I'm sorry to have to tell you this. It's about your husband."

"Richard? Is he all right? I hope he hasn't had an accident, or something terrible like that?"

"No, nothing like that. This trouble is something he brought upon himself. He's jeopardized his position with the State Department."

"Oh, no, the poor dear. He'll be so crushed. Is it something we can fix, Henry?"

"I'm afraid not this time, dear. He's . . . well, he's gone too far. Beyond the point of no return, actually, when State gets hold of the information I've got on him."

"What is it, Henry? What could he have done that's so horrible?"

"It's not so much what he's done, Lor . . . more what he is. You see . . . this is very difficult for me to tell you this. I don't want to hurt your feelings. But there is no other way. You see, Richard Baxter is — well, he's gay, Lori-Ann. I'm terribly sorry. Your husband is a homo-sexual."

Lori-Ann looked at Tysin as if he'd told her the moon was made of green cheese. "Richard? Don't be silly, Henry. I'd know it if he was. And I can assure you that he's a functioning male in every respect. Of course," she apologized, "he's nowhere near your equal in the sex department, Henry. You're a real bull where that's con-cerned." She ran her hand over his groin, and gave him her biggest smile. "But he still comes across once or twice a month, bless him."

Tysin shook his head, though still enjoying the good feeling in his groin where she was fondling him. "Don't you ever think it strange that a man would limit having sex with you to once or twice a month, especially being married to you? I sure wouldn't, I'll tell you." He patted her knee, then ran his hand up to the edge of her bikini bottom. "You'd have to fuck me into a coma before I'd let you alone."

"But Henry, where did you get such a nasty bit of gossip? I just don't believe it."

"I'm sorry, Lor." He reached into an inside pocket of his suit jacket which he'd draped neatly over the arm of the sofa, and produced a packet of photographs. "I think these will speak for themselves." He handed them over to her.

Lori-Ann recognized the pictures at once. They were

133

copies of the photos that Frumpkin had shocked her with that day in the park. Richard in bed with another man. No, two men, she realized. One at either end. He was taking them on in every way he could. Her mind drifted back a few years; she'd rather enjoyed that situation herself a few times. Now it seemed, Richard was becoming somewhat of a celebrity. She put on a stunned expression for Tysin's benefit. "Oh, Henry, this is just horrible. Take them away." She turned her head to the sexually explicit photos trying for just the right effect on Tysin.

"They say that a picture is worth a thousand words, darling. These tell it all. I'm afraid his bosses at State will be forced to dismiss him, in light of these damaging shots. There's nothing I can do about it."

"But there is, Henry. Burn them. Destroy those damning photos of Richard. Don't you realize that I'll be disgraced along with him? Do you think they'll allow me to continue working with you in the Company when word of this gets out? I'll be kicked out on my fanny. Oh, Henry, I'll just die of shame."

"There, there, Lor. Tysin patted the soft, white flesh of her upper thigh. "It doesn't matter whether you work for me or not. We can still go on seeing each other like this. I'll take care of you."

"Henry, don't you think I have any pride?" She removed her hand from his privates. "The Baxter family will be publicly disgraced. I'll be humiliated, shunned by the elite of D.C. society. I've wanted this kind of attention all my life, Henry. I've always wanted to be somebody, and finally I achieved that goal, as Mrs. Richard Baxter, married to the heir to the Baxter fortune. And now that Richard's parents are dead, all that is mine. Please, darling," she replaced her hand in his lap, tears

134

welling in her eyes. "Don't do this to me, now. I've got everything I've ever wanted. Please don't take it from me."

Tysin drained his drink and put the glass on the coffee table in front of the sofa. "I'm really sorry, Lori-Ann. But this involves government security. It's my job. I have to expose him for what he is. I'm sorry to have to hurt you in this. But there's nothing I can do about it."

Lori-Ann got up and stood in front of the TV. She undid the few buttons holding the front of her night-gown top together, letting her full breasts fall free. She looked at him dolefully, hands on her bikini bottoms, tugging them up between her legs until they forced her labia apart on either side of the filmy fabric. "Isn't there anything I can say or do to make you change your mind about this, Henry?"

He was tempted, sorely tempted, but resolved to do his official duty. "Sorry, hon. I have to do it."

"Well," she said, removing a video tape from its plastic container. "I can see that there's no sense in trying to entice you out of destroying me, is there, Henry?"

Tysin shrugged, a painful look on his face. He'd give almost anything not to risk destroying his relationship with Lori-Ann. But, after all, he was the director of the CIA. He had his duty to uphold.

"I think you should look at this, Henry," she said over her shoulder while she popped the tape into the VCR beneath the TV. It might just cause you to see things my way, after all." She turned on the television and the VCR by remote control and stood aside. In a moment there were the familiar color bars and tone. This was a professional job.

"C'mon, Lor. What's this all about?"

"People who live in glass houses, Henry, shouldn't be

so quick to throw stones at others. You shouldn't have forced me to do this."

Tysin watched in shock as he saw himself being drawn to the very sofa he was sitting on by a very naked Lori-Ann Collins. He was trying to walk with his pants dropped around his ankles, Lori-Ann tugging him across the screen by his penis. "Son-of-a-bitch," he shouted. "What the hell are you up to?"

"I'm an exhibitionist, Henry. I enjoy watching myself turning guys on. This was just going to be a little fun thing for my personal viewing pleasure," she lied. "To get me through those long periods between visits from you. But after what you've just done to me, I think a little trade-off is in order."

Tysin started to get up. "Damn you. Are you trying to blackmail me? If you are, it won't work. I'm no candy-ass like your husband. I'll just destroy that tape and the hell with you. I won't be bullied around by you or anyone else. Now give me that damn tape."

"Sit down, Henry. Do you think that this is the only copy that I have of this? I'm no fool, either, you know. I'm just trying to show you that Richard isn't the only guy to get caught with his pants down. Now the shoe's on the other foot."

Tysin was shouting at her. "You can't do this to me. I'm the director. I have the entire CIA behind me."

Lori-Ann pointed to his naked backside exposed to them on the TV screen. "I don't see any of your friends behind you now, Henry. I think you should think things over. Give Richard and me a break. He hasn't done anything so terrible, has he? True, he's been unfaithful to me. It's been a real blow to my ego to see him in action with another man, for God's sake. But he hasn't caused the government any trouble. He's just gay; he's not a

136

traitor," she lied again.

"I'll—I'll never forgive you for this," he sputtered. "Much as I hate to, I'm breaking off our relationship. And furthermore, you're fired. Don't bother cleaning out your desk. And," he added, pointing a finger at her, "you've got twenty-four hours to get the hell out of this apartment. Do you understand?"

She re-buttoned her top, and stood her ground, planting her feet slightly apart and staring him down. "Fuck you, Henry. I'll do nothing of the kind. I'm taking two weeks vacation, as of Monday. Just think about what you're doing, and reconsider. You wouldn't want your dear wife, Vivian to see you looking like this, would you?" She was pointing to the scene on the TV. Henry was on his knees, planting his face in her lap as she lay back on the sofa. I'm sure the *Post* and Channel Five News would be interested. Can you just see it on television? *CIA Director looking for lost contact lens.* Hah. You'd better re-think this one, Henry. And I'm keeping the apartment, but I'm changing the locks."

Tysin was trying to interrupt, but she wouldn't give him a chance.

"And you'd better be nice to me when I get back to work from my vacation. Now get out of here, Henry. And remember, I asked you nice. You did this to yourself."

Tysin grabbed his jacket and tie from the arm of the sofa and stormed toward the door. He called over his shoulder. "You'll regret this, Lori-Ann. You really will. This time you've gone too far."

"Oh, Henry," she called after him provocatively.

He turned back to face her.

She stood there, hip-sprung, facing him, the fingers of her hand toying with herself beneath the scant fabric of her panties. "You're the one who's going to regret this, darling. I was feeling real horny tonight."

CHAPTER TWELVE

"Henry Tysin." Julio Sanchez strained against Boxer's choke hold. "It was Tysin's idea," he blurted out.

Boxer let up just a little on Sanchez's shirt collar, and some of the deep red coloring left Julio's face. "Keep talking, Julio," Boxer said.

Sanchez coughed, fought to catch his breath. "It wasn't my idea," he wheezed. "Tysin offered me ten thousand to take her, to get rid of her."

"To sell her as a slave, Julio?"

"That, too, was Tysin's idea." He managed to say, "I swear it," before Boxer tightened his grasp around Julio's neck.

"Truth, Julio. If not, I'm going to turn you over to Mr. Morell. He's much better at these things than I am."

"No, don't."

Boxer eased off a bit.

"Tysin . . . I . . ." Sanchez stared into Boxer's hard gray eyes. "Okay, yes. It was my idea to sell her. I had to cover my costs. Tysin didn't pay me enough to cover my costs. I had to—"

Boxer squeezed Sanchez's throat and lifted him off his feet, fighting the urge to smash a fist into Julio's face. "And what about Admiral Stark? How much did you get paid for trying to kill him?"

"Don't, please," Sanchez gagged. As Boxer let up the

pressure a little, he continued. "He . . . he just got in the way. That was nothing personal."

Boxer backhanded him across the face, drawing blood from Julio's nose. Sanchez began to weep.

"Give me one good reason not to kill you, Julio."

"Please, Tysin wanted me to kill her. He wanted to hurt you. To get revenge."

Boxer tossed the slightly built man onto the bed. "Go on, Julio."

"It's true. Tysin wanted you dead. He tried to have you killed when he sank the *Barracuda*. But Bruno's men fucked it up."

"What? You'd sell out your own grandmother to save your worthless ass, Julio. You'd better not lie to me."

"It's true. I swear it. Believe me, I know how Señor Tysin operates. He would *kill* his own grandmother if she got in his way. And you got in his way too many times. He offered the job to me, but, of course, I turned him down."

"But why Bruno?" Boxer turned his head to see if Bruno Morell was within earshot. "Why would he be helping me now if he tried to kill me before? Besides, he had the drop on me, back in Rome, when your two goons got killed. He could have killed me then, no problem, and no one would have been the wiser."

Sanchez managed a weak smile. "Killing you was just a job with Bruno. If no one is paying him to do it, he has no reason to kill you. With me, its another thing. We're competitors. Killing me gives him a larger slice of the pie."

Boxer was having a hard time taking this all in. "You mean the CIA hires you both?"

"Si. CIA, KGB, what difference does it make. In

140

Libya, Bruno was working for the KGB. When he sank the *Barracuda*, he was hired by the CIA. Or, I should say, by Señor Tysin personally."

"Wait a minute, Julio. Bruno implicated you in that Libya fiasco."

Sanchez shrugged as best he could with his hands bound behind him. "Of course. What would you expect him to say to you, that he did it?"

Just then, Bruno Morell entered the stateroom. "What's that? Did I hear the weasel speak my name?"

Boxer just said, "I've been listening to some very disturbing information."

Two single pistol shots rang out in rapid succession, amidships. They were answered with a burst of machine-gun fire. A terrified woman screamed, and almost as if it were contagious, the screaming spread among the other women captives. "What the . . . ?" Boxer was out in the direction of the shooting in a flash.

Aldo Fagiole was firing from his position in the rubber inflatable, trying to keep under the protection of the inward sloping hull. Several crewmen were leaning over the side on the deck below, trying to get a better shot at him.

Boxer positioned himself so that he had a clear shot at the crewmen. "Okay, freeze right there. Drop those weapons," he shouted.

A tall man with a bushy mustache wheeled and fired at Boxer. The shot careened off the steel rail a foot away from him. Boxer answered with two quick shots at the crewman, hitting him twice, in the chest and shoulder. The man went down.

Two others leaned out to get a better shot at Boxer. At the same time, Aldo had pushed out from under the hull overhang and had both crewmembers in his sights. All four men fired simultaneously.

A shot narrowly missed Boxer again. One crewman's chest burst apart under a hail of fire from Aldo. And the other crewman got off several shots that struck the rubber raft. The starboard gunwale exploded, and the raft listed to the one side. Aldo found himself thrown into the water.

"I can't swim. Help me," he cried out to Boxer.

It was too late. Another shot found its mark, and Aldo Fagiole floated face down as his own blood soon colored the sea around him. Boxer shot the crewman, took a last glance at Aldo's body, to make sure that there was nothing left for him to do, and returned to Julio's stateroom,

That's when it hit Boxer. Bruno hadn't joined him in his battle with the remaining crew. That meant he was left alone and armed with Julio bound and defenseless. Shit. He raced back up to Julio's quarters.

He was met just outside the doorway to Sanchez's rooms by Bruno, who was carrying something that resembled a plum covered with blood, stuck on the tip of a six-inch stiletto. "There are many ways to make a man talk," Bruno boasted. "But this way never fails me. When I threatened to cut off his other testicle, he cried like a baby, and told me everything I wanted to know. He even tried to pin the blame for some of the things he did on me. That fuckin' weasel."

Boxer looked at Bruno Morell with his mouth agape, not believing Bruno's cruel, brutal treatment of Julio Sanchez. "That's inhumane, Bruno. And it's not the only thing that bothers me. Julio implicated you in the sinking of the *Barracuda* and that business in Libya. I still can't get out of my head the vision of my men impaled on stakes on the beach, and left to die slowly. And looking at you now, I keep drawing the same conclusion. That it was you, as we thought, and not Julio that was responsible. If that's true, Bruno, I'll kill you myself."

Bruno's arm dropped to the Uzi strapped across his chest, and he pointed it at Boxer. "You'd better think twice, my friend. Julio fed you a pack of lies."

"I wonder," Boxer said. "He made a lot of sense to me."

"He's lying."

"Prove it. Give me your gun, like you did in Rome. Then I'll believe you again."

Bruno hesitated. Then he tightened his grip on the Uzi and pointed it at Boxer's head.

A hail of fire rang out. The front of Bruno's head seemed to jump out at Boxer. A red stain covered the front of Bruno's shirt. A bullet tore through Bruno's throat, continued on and just missed Boxer.

Bruno Morell collapsed face down on the teak deck. Behind him, Julio Sanchez braced himself against the bulkhead, his automatic pistol smoking in his hand. He wore only a bloody pair of shorts, which told the tale of Bruno's barbaric torture. Julio lifted his head to stare into Boxer's eyes. "Why—" he managed. "Why did he—" and he collapsed in a heap.

"I just can't go on living like this, Richard." Bruce Symington leaned his naked body back against the headboard and drew deeply on the thin brown cigarette with the gold foil wrapper over the filtertip. He blew a

143

thin plume of smoke at the table lamp alongside the bed.

Richard Baxter lay facing him, propped up on his elbow, idly drawing his forefinger along the length of his friend's long, tan leg. "Don't be like that. This stupid submarine business will be over with soon, and we can go back to the way things used to be."

Bruce took another drag and looked away. "We can never go back, Richard. And sooner or later, someone's going to find out."

"About us? So what? Lori-Ann already knows. That's what got us into this in the first place. Besides, I hate asking you to do this as much as you do. Pass me a cigarette, will you?"

Bruce fumbled with the pack and shook loose a *Silhouette,* the latest trendy looking low tar cigarette to hit the market. Baxter took the cigarette and removed a match from the packet. The inscription on the matchbook read the Boston Park Plaza Towers. Eight hundred and fifty bucks a night for the suite, but it was worth it. The view of downtown Boston at night was magnificent. And they could easily afford it. Besides, Bruce charged it to the company, which in turn billed it to the Navy as part of their overrun. That's how the rich get richer, he thought, and lit up his cigarette.

"That snoopy bitch, Carson has been spooking me for the last week. I think she knows."

"Carson, the Navy lieutenant? She probably just has the hots for you, Bruce."

"That's not funny."

"But she can't have you, can she? You're mine," Baxter pushed on.

"Be serious, Richard. What if she finds out what I've

done? What if those plans are intercepted? They could trace them straight back to me. Do you know what my parents would do? Disown me, that's what. They'd probably lose the contract, maybe even be barred from ever doing any more business with the Navy. They could lose the shipyard." Bruce's voice rose an octave with each sentence.

"Calm down, Bruce, for God's sake. Let me make you a drink." He got up from the king-size bed and padded naked to the wet bar. "Johnny Walker Black or Wild Turkey?" he called back.

"The scotch, please." His eyes followed every movement of Baxter's body returning to the bed with the two drinks. He licked his lips.

Baxter handed him the drink and they clinked glasses. "Oh, Richard," he said. "I don't know what I'd do if we got caught. I think I'd die."

Admiral Chi-Chi Mason, Chief of Naval Operations, studied the set of eight by ten glossies arranged on his desktop. He let out a low whistle. "Good work, Captain. Very, very good. Just remember that this is for my eyes only. Understand?"

Captain Monroe Howard squared off his massive shoulders and stood at attention. "Absolutely, Admiral. No one else has seen these, yet. I developed them myself and brought them directly to you. As far as I'm concerned, I don't know anything about them."

"And the negatives?"

"Burned them myself, Admiral. You've got the only copies."

Mason scooped up the photos and slipped them back

into a manila envelope. Then he smiled at Howard. "How would duty in Honolulu sound to you, Captain?"

"Like paradise, sir. I put in a year at Pearl before signing on with Naval Intelligence. It's the closest to heaven I've ever been."

"Very well, then, you'll be assigned to Pearl. You'll ship out tomorrow, oh-eight-hundred. I'd suggest you get your things together tonight, son."

"Yes, sir."

"Oh, and another thing. I almost forgot."

"Sir?" Howard had expected some small reward for his part in trailing the guy from Langley to the sexy lady's apartment, but a tour in Pearl Harbor, wow. But now what? Captain Howard anticipated the other shoe falling on him.

"You'll present your orders directly to Admiral Dumont. Then you've earned a fourteen day leave. Enjoy Hawaii, son. And thanks for these."

As soon as Howard saluted and left the office, Admiral Mason shook the glossies from the envelope, and nervously arranged and re-arranged them again on his desk. Son of a bitch, but it looks like old Henry Tysin is digging a grave for himself. Fucking your own secretary is like pissing in the soup. It's something you just don't do. He tapped a finger on a picture of the director of the CIA. Son of a bitch, Henry, he said to himself.

He was momentarily startled when his intercom buzzed. "Admiral Jack Boxer here to see you, sir."

"Oh, yes. Tell him to have a seat. I'll be right with him."

"Yes, sir."

Mason tidied up the photos again and tucked them

146

back into the envelope. Then he locked them up in the top drawer of his desk. He selected a cigar from his humidor and carefully clipped off the tip. Lighting up, he switched on his intercom. "Send Boxer in, now."

When Boxer entered the CNO's inner sanctum, with Lt. Kit Carson in tow, he found Mason leaning back in his comfortable chair puffing smoke rings at the ceiling. Boxer and Carson stood at attention and saluted.

"Boxer, Lt. Carson. Pleasant surprise, Carson."

"Thank you, sir. We . . . uh, that is, we have a problem that . . ."

Mason raised an eyebrow. "Yes? Go on, Lieutenant."

"Well, sir, when we realized we might have a spy working with us on the *Manta* project, we sort of laid a trap for him. Or her."

Boxer interjected, "I had the specs for the *Shark* switched with the *Manta*'s and made them convenient to steal. That way, whoever wanted the plans would think he got them, and we could go on with our work on the *Manta*."

"What's that? You gave away our plans to the enemy?"

"No, Admiral," Boxer smiled. "They stole them. Only they stole the wrong specs. They already know everything they need to about the *Shark*. She's ancient history by now. And different areas got slightly different versions." Boxer started to chuckle. "All of them have fatal flaws in them. If the Ruskies ever do try to copy those plans, their subs will self-destruct."

Mason blurted out, "And why wasn't I let in on your little joke?"

Carson responded. "All respect, Admiral Mason. We weren't sure if someone from your staff would be in-

147

volved."

"And? Are you telling me that one of my own people stole the specs?"

"No, Admiral. The leak seems to have taken place at the shipyard in New London."

"Symington's? Their record is immaculate. We've done a lot of business with them in the past and never had any problems. You must be mistaken."

"Afraid not, sir," Boxer pushed onward. "It's pretty clear that someone checked out the blueprints and spec sheets for the version of the *Shark* with the faulty reactor at the shipyard. And it was someone with very high level clearance, who, if he didn't know we were on to something, would think he'd never be challenged."

Mason blew out a puff of smoke. "Someone in management, then."

"V.P. or higher, Admiral. Probably higher."

"I'd better get this to Henry Tysin right away."

Boxer's face turned hard. "Keep Tysin away from me, Admiral."

Mason furrowed his brow. "What the hell are you talking about, Boxer?"

"I have my reasons, Admiral. Someday, maybe I'll share them with you. At any rate, unless I've got the priorities mixed up, this is a job for the FBI. I'd suggest you notify them to check into this immediately."

"I suppose I'd better. Good work, both of you. Dismissed."

Boxer and Carson saluted and left Mason's office. When they were out of earshot of his staff, Boxer told Carson, "You know, that man has tried to have me court-martialled twice, kicked out of the Navy several times, and has done his best to get rid of me every chance he's had. This is the first time he's ever told me I did a good job. Kit, this calls for a celebration. How about I treat you to a fancy dinner tonight? It'll give me a chance to tell you about my sail down the Red Sea with a dozen harem girls."

Carson giggled, and said, "Yes, sir." She gave him a mock salute. "I never turn down orders from the boss."

CHAPTER THIRTEEN

Boxer walked the few short blocks from Francine'
townhouse to the tree-lined shopping district of smal
shops and boutiques on a quest that he knew woul
bring him immense pleasure. He was en route to one o
his favorite stores to buy a new supply of tobacco, hi
last chance before joining Kit Carson in New Londo
for the final preparations on the *Manta*. He rounded
corner, past the Paris Café, a quaint little coffee an
pastry shop, a book store, and then to the storefron
filled with racks and racks of pipes and humidors an
accessories. The gold leaf inscription on the plate glas
window read J. Schulte & Sons, Tobacconists, Est
1936. Boxer smiled and went inside.

The first thing that hit him was the wonderful fra
grances of the row upon row of pipe tobacco in clea
glass humidors. Most were imported, many custon
blends by the master, himself, Jules Schulte. Anothe
wall was laden with boxes of cigars of every kind, ligh
and dark, fat and thin, hand rolled, cedar wrapped
anything a cigar connoisseur could dream of.

Boxer was greeted by Herman Schulte, one of the "
Sons", behind the cigar counter. He seemed genuinel
pleased to see Boxer. "Ah, good afternoon, Admira
Boxer. It's been a while, no?"

"Hello, Herman. You're looking well. I've come for
couple of boxes of those fat cigars that Admiral Star
loves so much."

"Ah," Herman smiled. "He smokes too much,
think. But how can I blame him. He smokes Papa'

finest private label. As close to Havanas as you can legally get in this country. And I'm talking about the quality cigars before Castro came in and ruined the whole business." Herman took two wooden cigar boxes from under the counter and wrapped them in a heavy, masculine paper. "Give the admiral my regards, and that I said not to smoke so much."

Boxer smiled back. "This ought to keep him for awhile. I'll be gone for a month or two, and I want to make sure he's well supplied."

Herman's face got serious. "He is feeling okay, now? It's a shame what happened to him. You can't even be safe in your own neighborhood anymore."

Boxer nodded. "He's coming along pretty well, My son Chuck has been staying with him. They're good company for each other."

Herman handed the package to Boxer. "And what can I get you for yourself?"

"Well, I'm here for a supply of pipe tobacco. I was hoping Jules would be here, too."

Herman, who was in his mid-fifties, said, "Papa is getting a little old. He doesn't wait on customers much anymore. But he's in the back, and I'm sure he'll come out to see an old friend."

At that moment, a frail old man in his late seventies stepped into the shop, taking his place behind the counter display of pipes. "Ah, you see, I start to get a little bit old and already they talk about me."

Boxer beamed, "Jules, good to see you again." He took the old man's hand in both of his. "You're still the best, Jules. Whenever I'm in D.C. I come to see you."

"So what can I get for you? Some tobacco? I want you to try something." He turned around and gingerly lifted a glass tobacco jar from the shelf and placed it on the counter top between them. He took the humidor lid off and offered the jar up to Boxer's nose. "I think you'll like this one. My latest blend."

Boxer breathed deeply through his nose. "Smells wonderful, Jules."

"Try some."

Boxer took his worn Meerschaum from his jacket pocket and tucked a few pinches of the long cut tobacco into the bowl. Jules held a match to it until Boxer had a good ash going. Boxer took a long pull, savored it in his mouth and let the aromatic smoke waft upward past his nose. "Really great, this time, Jules. Wrap some of this up for me, please."

As the old man weighed out two one-pound bags of the tobacco he remarked, "Looks like you could stand a new pipe as well. I've got a beautiful straight-grained brier that I've been saving for just the right man."

Boxer laughed. By the time he was finished, he'd purchased a new pipe, four bags of tobacco for himself and the cigars for Admiral Stark. He paid for his purchases and bid the Schultes good-bye. He was feeling quite pleased with himself as he toted a shopping bag full of his new acquisitions past the bookstore. He didn't notice the angry woman who came storming out of the bookstore at that very moment until she collided with him.

Boxer's bag was knocked from his hands. The woman fell to the ground.

"Oh, excuse me, Miss. I didn't . . . Let me . . ."

"Why don't you watch where the f—"

"I'm terribly sorry. Say, aren't you Miss Collins from Tysin's office?"

Lori-Ann looked up at the bearded gentleman in

slacks and blazer standing over her. It took a few moments to register. "Why, Admiral Boxer. Oh, forgive me, shouting at you like an old fishwife. It was entirely my fault."

Boxer reached down to give her a hand up. "Not at all. I wasn't watching where I was going. Are you hurt?"

Lori-Ann brushed off the seat of her beige linen pants. "Just my pride, I'm afraid." She turned her head in the direction of the bookstore. "Some people just make me so mad."

Boxer picked his bag of purchases up off the sidewalk and straightened up. "Anything I can help with?"

Lori-Ann thought about that for a minute. She'd just love to pit Boxer against that bastard Frumpkin. Serve him right for blaming her because the submarine plans turned out to be worthless. Then she thought better of it. "Thank you, anyway. People can be so frustrating to deal with, sometimes."

"Well," Boxer said, "At least let me make amends for knocking you down. There's a nice little coffee shop on the corner."

Lori-Ann Collins gave him her best phony southern country-girl smile. "The Paris Café is very nice, thank you. But since it was my fault anyway, I'd just love it if you'd walk me home so I can make coffee for you. How 'bout that?" She slipped her arm through his.

Boxer looked around at the beautiful summer day, then at the beautiful woman at his side, thought about how pissed Tysin would be if he knew about it and answered with a big smile. "Sure, Lori-Ann. Why not?"

It was 0300 hours when the twin Sikorski helicopters

153

took off from Fort Richardson, Alaska, headed due east for twenty miles, skirted a mountain ridge and hovered above a snow covered plain. Each chopper carried six of the best fighting men the U.S. had to offer, three each of Rolly's Rangers and three of their counterparts from the elite Snow Troopers. A jumpmaster stood just inside the open doorway, fighting against the bite of the minus 30 degree blast of Arctic air. He had to shout at Rolly Jones to be heard only a few feet away. "Okay, Major, ready to jump. One of our guys will jump just ahead of each of yours. Just try to remember everything we've taught you and keep our cool."

Jones gave him the thumbs up sign, grinned, and shouted back," For sure we gonna keep your cool out there, Sarge. It's colder than a witch's tit outside."

Rolly took his place just behind the first Snow Trooper lined up to jump. Sgt. Rudy Bartell, the jumpmaster, placed a hand on Rolly's shoulder, checked that his release line was properly hooked to the overhead jump wire, and did a quick visual check to see that the major was dressed properly. Satisfied, he said, "You'll team up with Captain Dickerson's crew as soon as all the men have jumped. Good luck getting back to camp."

Rolly nodded his thanks. This was the big one, the final exam that he and his men had trained for the last month. In spite of the excellent survival gear and clothing, he wondered if he could ever get used to the incredible cold. Well, he would soon find out. It was twenty miles back to camp as the crow flies. More like forty miles to cover on the snow-covered ground, on skis and snowshoes, with each man carrying a seventy pound rucksack. He watched Sergeant Bartell pat the jump helmet of the lead-off man, and followed the Snow Trooper's flight for a full five seconds. Then he felt the tap on his own head.

He stood there in the hatchway, watched the parachute open below him and thought, well, it's now or never. Rolly jumped forward and downward, fighting the queasy feeling in his gut for his five second free flight. Then his chute lurched opened, and he enjoyed the floating feeling until he approached the ground. Landing was another thing.

He hit the snow-covered ground slightly off-balance and rolled forward head over heels, getting tangled up in his own chute. Pvt. Marty Coleman, the first trooper out of the chopper, ran to assist him. "You okay, Major?"

"Yeah, I'll be fine, dammit. Help me get this fucking thing off me, will you?"

Coleman helped him out of the harness and onto his feet. "The hardest part is the landing, sir."

"Yeah, but you made it seem so easy, I thought it would just come natural to me."

"You did just fine, sir. The rest of our team is on the ground. As soon as they drop our supplies we'll tie up with the captain."

Two more chutes containing all their gear were dropped from the helicopters. As the men rushed to gather their things, the choppers circled overhead one final time and took off to the west. Well, this is it, Rolly thought. The long walk home. He signalled to his men. "All right, guys, let's move out."

The men donned skis and trudged over to link up with Dickerson's team. Rolly and he shook hands. Jones was impressed by the man. Captain Richard Dickerson, thin and wiry, tough as nails, just under six

155

feet tall. He weighed maybe one-sixty, sixty-five, Rolly figured, but carried his seventy pound pack as if it were empty. He was the senior man among the Snow Troopers, and Rolly was glad to have his Rangers learn from him.

Dickerson produced a small map from his pocket and went over it with Rolly. "We're here right now," he said with a trace of a midwestern farm boy accent. "Figure we should make about twenty miles tonight, hole up for some rest, and touch home base within thirty-six hours. Think your men can take it?"

"We're here to find out, Captain."

"You can call me Dick, Major. The guys call me Double Dick, short for Dick Dickerson," he said with a smile. "Though not usually to my face."

"Might as well call me Rolly. My men usually do except when I'm chewing their asses out for something. Then it's back to Major Jones," he chuckled. "Why don't you lead on, Dick? We're here to learn all we can about cold weather survival. But I'll tell you the truth, I sure hope we never have the opportunity to try it for real."

"Just make sure your men keep bundled up. It's thirty below right now. Your skin will freeze if it's exposed for more than a minute. Make sure your men keep their faces covered with the balaclavas. And hope it warms up as the sun rises. If it gets much colder, your spit will freeze up when it hits the ground. And if it gets really cold, I'm talking about sixty, seventy below, forget it. Your spit will freeze up as soon as it leaves your mouth."

"Too cold for my liking."

"We'll buddy up. One of your men with one of mine. We'll show you how to check each other for frostbite, do finger and toe counts, and later, how to keep warm inside snow caves, and how to eat to survive up here."

Rolly turned to see his men already teaming up with the snow troopers, and he was pleased. They looked like ghosts in their white parkas and snow pants, especially with their breath freezing up as it filtered through their balaclavas.

"We're going to try to remain as invisible as possible on this maneuver. Just like the real thing. Cover our tracks, and all. Your men may as well learn what it's really like when we're in training."

"Okay by me, Dick. Looks like everyone's ready."

Dickerson signalled the men to move out, and the twelve of them set off on their journey back to Fort Richardson, laden with their heavy packs and M-16's.

"Double Dick," Rolly Jones said with a smile. "I always figured it'd be a cold day in hell before I'd wish I was back aboard a cramped submarine a half mile deep. And as I look around me now, I get the feeling that the cold day in hell is here."

"Why, Admiral Boxer, you are such a gentleman, holdin' the doors for me, and all. I wish more men would be like you."

Boxer shrugged and said nothing. He let Lori-Ann Collins pass in front of him and followed her up the stairs to the second floor apartment. At the landing, she handed him her keys and he let them in.

"Richard and I keep this small flat in town for those occasions when it's just too much bother to drive out to Silver Springs. I wanted to catch up on a little shopping today, and Richard is out of town with the limo. Some business up in Boston, I think he said."

Boxer took in the cozy apartment. "Very convenient. I live a short distance from here when I'm in D.C. Sure beats fighting the beltway."

"Please make yourself comfortable, Admiral. I'll fix us some coffee. I have some Bourbon Santos or a Mocha Java blend. Any preference?"

Boxer shook his head. "Whatever you like is fine with me, Miss Collins. And please call me Jack. Even my men don't call me Admiral Boxer."

"Okay, Jack," she smiled. "I think the Bourbon Santos will be nice. And please, all my friends call me Lori-Ann."

"Then Lori-Ann it is, if I may be counted among your friends."

She measured out some coffee beans into a coffee grinder. "You're climbing right up to the top of the list, Jack," she smiled again, and pressed the switch to start the pulverization of the beans. There was a raspy grating noise for about ten seconds. Boxer could smell the aroma of the coffee being unleashed as she removed the cover and emptied the grounds into the coffee-maker.

"Smells good."

"Nothing like fresh ground," she replied. "I always buy the beans whole and grind them at the last moment. Coffee will be ready in a few minutes. There's some good cognac in the dry bar in the parlor."

"Thanks. Can I get you one, too?"

"A true gentleman, I just knew it the first time I laid eyes on you, Jack. The first time I met you in Mr. Tysin's office I knew you'd be a man with a lot of class. There's snifters inside the cabinet."

Boxer busied himself with the drink preparation when a flash of light above the television and VCR caught his eyes. On closer inspection, he found it to be the lens of a camera of some kind, inconspicuously spying on the living room from behind the wall. Hmm, he thought. Might do well to check this out later.

"Coffee's ready, Jack. How're you coming along?" He stepped back into the kitchen with the two snifters of cognac in hand.

"Would you like sugar or cream?"

"Black will be fine," Boxer answered.

She wrinkled her nose. "I never could get used to black coffee. I don't know how you can stand it. Why don't you have a seat, Jack? I'll take that from you."

"Submariners live on the stuff. I guess it's an acquired taste. So how do you like working for Tysin?"

Lori-Ann swirled the cognac around in her snifter and brought it to her nose. Inhaling deeply, she paused to think about that with her eyes closed. When she opened them again, she said, "Henry is . . . Mr. Tysin is one of the most hard working, dedicated individuals I have ever known. It's an honor for me to work for him."

Boxer sipped his coffee. He watched her take down the cognac in one long swallow. "You know your boss has never liked me. He'd be very upset with you if he knew I was taking advantage of your hospitality. I'd better leave."

"Oh, poo. I'm not going to let Henry spoil our afternoon. I'm certainly not going to tell him about this."

"He just might be having you watched, Lori-Ann. As his secretary, he'd be concerned with whom you associated. Would you like more cognac?"

She slid her snifter across the table to him. "Yes, thank you. You're not afraid of Henry, are you? I didn't get that impression from your visits to his office."

159

Boxer retreated to the living room and returned with the bottle, a Couvoisier V.S.O.P. Nothing but the best, he thought. Back in the kitchen, he removed the cork and refilled her glass. He still hadn't touched his own.

"Why, Jack Boxer," she said. "Aren't you drinking with me?"

"I could do with some more of your wonderful coffee, Lori-Ann." She started to rise. "Don't get up. I'll manage."

"It's no problem, really." She rose unsteadily, bumping the table and spilling her coffee on her beige linen pants. "Oh dear. Now I've done it. Richard always says I'm such a klutz."

"Is there anything I can do? Perhaps I'd better go now."

Lori-Ann blushed, trying to blot the coffee from her pants with her napkin. "If you promise to remain a gentleman," she said, her eyes moving up to him, "I'd better get out of these and try to wash out the coffee before it sets. Else I'll have to throw them out."

Boxer didn't know what to say. Was it really an accident? Or was she trying to seduce him? Or both? He turned his back on her, and continued to sip his coffee.

"You're a dear, dear man. I'll just be a few minutes." She slipped off the pants and carried them to the sink. Above the running water he heard her say, "I sure hope they're not ruined."

He could make out her reflection in the glass door of a kitchen cupboard. Her silk blouse barely reached her hips, revealing, well . . . revealing just about everything. Her mini-bikini panties barely covered anything. And as the water ran, he could tell she was sneaking peeks back at him, to see if he were doing the same to her. As far as Boxer was concerned, he was going to just sit tight for the moment and take the first good opportunity to leave.

In a moment, she was parading past his line of vision with the wet pants in her hands. "Sorry," she giggled. "I have to hang these over the shower rod to dry."

When he heard the door to the bathroom open, Boxer decided that was his cue to leave. He placed his coffee cup on the kitchen table, got up from his chair and walked into the living room. As he heard her footfalls getting closer, he called out, "Thanks for your hospitality, Lori-Ann. I'll treat you to dinner next time I'm by to see the director." He headed toward the door.

At that moment, she walked into the room and almost into his arms. He noticed that she had unbuttoned two more buttons on her blouse, and she was clad in only the skimpy panties below the waist. Before he could object, she said, "Whew, I could sure use another cognac, now. Be a dear and pour me, would you?"

Boxer was not comfortable with sexually aggressive women, even when it was thinly veiled as in this case. Besides working for the director of the CIA, she was also a married woman. He decided to tell her his feelings. "Lori-Ann, you accused me of being a gentleman, before. Perhaps I am a bit old-fashioned, but I can't get comfortable with a half-naked married woman."

She took a deep swallow from her freshened drink, unbuttoned her blouse completely and let it fall open. With one hand, she unhooked her half-bra from the front and lifted the cups off of her marvelous breasts. "Is this better?" she challenged. "Besides, *Mister* Baxter is in Boston."

Boxer shook his head. "It's a matter of principle, not of distance."

Lori-Ann shrugged off her blouse and bra, and tossed them on the floor behind her. With a hand on Boxer's chest, she coaxed him toward the sofa. "Sit down, Jack. Please. And I'll tell you a little secret about *Mister* Baxter."

"I'd rather you didn't air your dirty laundry in my presence, Miss Collins." He had reverted back to formality.

"I just removed my dirty laundry, dear. What's the matter? Don't you find me attractive?"

Boxer noticed her maneuvering her body into position in front of the TV. "Miss Collins, I . . ."

"Lori-Ann, please," she retorted.

"Lori-Ann, I noticed the camera lens aiming at us from above the television. Are you trying to photograph us making love on the sofa?"

He caught her by surprise. She turned her head to verify that the camera lens was really visible. "Oh, silly me." She turned her back on him to cover up the camera, bending at the waist as she did to give him a birds-eye view of what was to come.

"I'm such an exhibitionist," she continued. "I just love to turn myself on by playing back videos of myself having sex. If it bothers you, we can use the bedroom." She glanced back at him over her shoulder to assess the influence she had on him. Good, she reflected. He seems like he's interested.

"Lori-Ann, I . . ."

"Oh, don't be such a party pooper, Jack. I'll go turn down the bed, and I promise that I'll show you a good time that you'll never forget. But first, close your eyes. I have something for you."

Boxer sighed, and closed his eyes. He heard her giggle and then press a trifle of silky material, sopping wet in the middle, into his hand. Then she said, "Don't go away, lover. I'll only be a minute."

True to her word, she returned to the living room a minute later, completely naked, fondling her love mound. She did a quick double-take around the room. "Jack? Where are you?" She padded into the kitchen. "Jack, are you hiding from me? Jack?"

Boxer paused in the stairway halfway down to the bottom landing. The cursing and screaming he heard coming from the apartment above was very un-ladylike. He thought he heard a lamp or a vase crash against a wall. Then the door opened.

"Jack, you son of a bitch, you come back here. Jack, please come back. Don't leave me like this."

Boxer continued down the stairs and out the exit door without turning back. Too bad, he said to himself, shaking his head as he walked down the street. What a waste of womanhood.

CHAPTER FOURTEEN

Natasha Sharnovsky was jolted out of her sleep by the harsh banging on her apartment door. She shook her husband awake. "Reuben. Wake up. Quickly. Something's wrong."

Reuben Sharnovsky rubbed the sleep from his eyes in time to hear the second barrage of hammering on his door. "What could it be? We have done nothing . . . Natasha, darling . . . Have you done something to cause trouble? You promised me you'd stop helping the Refuseniks, dear. Are they coming to take you?"

Natasha shrugged her shoulders. She pulled the covers up to her neck as the banging on the door became louder and more persistent. "I have done nothing, Reuben. I promise . . . I . . ."

"Open up," came the shouts from the hallway. "Open the door, Comrade Sharnovsky. Do not force us to break it down."

For a moment, the Sharnovskys contemplated trying to escape down the back fire escape. A glance out the back window was enough to rid their minds of that thought. There were two husky men blocking that avenue of escape below.

"Open up. This is the last time I will ask you."

The couple hugged each other in fear. Then Reuben summoned up all his bravery and proceeded to the door before his wife. "Just a minute. I'm coming." He was dressed only in blue striped broadcloth pajamas. Natasha quickly grabbed up a robe to pull on over her nightgown, and slipped into a pair of slippers. She had heard that when the KGB comes to arrest you, they don't even allow you to get dressed. And Siberia is a very cold place . . . if they don't kill you at once.

Reuben Sharnovsky opened the door and immediately realized his worst nightmares were about to come true. The bald, stout man dressed in a black suit at two o'clock in the morning was undoubtedly KGB. "Please, Comrade. We haven't done anything."

The stout man ignored him and announced in a gravelly voice, "I am Ivan Pisanya of the Second Directorate. I have business here with Natasha Sharnovsky."

"She hasn't done anything." Reuben pleaded. "It was all my fault. She had nothing to do with the Refuseniks, I swear. It was my doing."

Pisanya glared at the little Jewish man made even smaller by his cowered posture. "Quiet, fool. Do you wish to confess imaginary crimes against the state to the entire neighborhood?"

"But . . . but . . ."

"Butt out, before I give you cause to be fearful of me. I said I have business here with your wife."

"Please, Comrade. Come in. Forgive my manners. Have a seat. Would you like some vodka, perhaps?" he asked, pulling a kitchen chair over for Pisanya to sit on.

The KGB man ignored him. He stared directly at his wife. "You are Natasha Sharnovsky?"

"I am. Please forgive my husband. He's just trying to protect me. What am I being charged with?"

"So far," Pisanya said, moving into the tiny apartment, "only stupidity. I have important news for you. You must sit down and listen to me. And stop acting like you are being arrested."

Natasha sat at a kitchen table. Her husband moved around to stand behind her. She noticed the doorway being filled with the bulk of two more men in dark suits. There was no doubt in her mind who they were. But what did they want with her?

As if reading her mind, Pisanya, who now towered over the seated woman and her diminutive husband stated, "You have been chosen by your superiors to take part in a scientific project for the Motherland. Your work as a nuclear physicist has been given the highest rating. You have been hand picked for this undertaking. Do you accept?"

"Do I have a choice?"

"Yes," Pisanya smirked. "There is always a choice, though not always a pleasant one."

"May I ask what this project is about?"

Pisanya solemnly shook his head. "It is top secret. You will know what you have to do when you get there. You will be able to tell no one. I'm sorry to say, not even your husband."

Reuben sputtered. "But . . . but . . . but . . ."

Ivan Pisanya's menacing glare cut him off. "If you do an exemplary job for the Motherland, you will be rewarded, Comrade Natasha. We might even consider ignoring your previous dealings on behalf of the traitorous Refuseniks." He made certain that the implications of what he just said sank in with both of them. "Well?"

"I accept."

Reuben glanced at his wife, his eyes pleading with her to decline. She did not meet his eyes, and he knew there was nothing more that could be done. He knew that she had no way out of this predicament, that he might never see her again, and, alas, that he would probably be placed under detention as insurance against her performing as directed, and to ensure his silence about the matter. And he felt certain that she knew it also. The great arms of the bear had them in their grasp. There was nothing that could be done to stop them.

"Good," Pisanya announced. "Quickly take a few personal things with you. You don't need much. Everything will be provided for you."

Natasha got up resignedly, and went to gather her things. Pisanya clapped Reuben on the shoulder, nearly knocking the smaller man off his feet. "Congratulations, Comrade. Your wife is going to be a hero of the state. This calls for a celebration. I'll have some of that vodka you offered before."

Boxer handed over the package to Admiral Stark, who began to neatly unwrap it. "Oh ho, what a pleasant surprise, Jack. Schulte Specials, my favorite cigar." He smiled at Boxer. "Thanks very much, Jack. You sure know how to make an old sea-dog happy."

Boxer made a mock-serious face. "Remember, now, your limit is three a day. Doctor's orders."

Stark removed one of the beauties from the wooden cigar box, snipped off the tip and lit up. He offered the box to Boxer, who declined. "A man my age, and in my position doesn't take orders." He blew a plume of smoke toward the ceiling. He thought a moment about Francine Wheeler, how she used to good-naturedly chide him about his excesses, while at the same time nursing him through his ailments and treating him like an honored guest in her home. "I really miss her," he said, as if Boxer had been privy to his thoughts.

"Huh? Oh, Francine. I'm afraid she may be lost to

us. My last visit didn't go very well. Those bastards made her fearful of all men, even the male doctors at the sanatarium. My only regret is that I didn't kill her abductors more slowly."

"You let Julio Sanchez get away?"

"I traded him his life in return for an even bigger fish."

"Meaning Tysin?" Stark asked.

"Meaning Henry Tysin," Boxer replied. "It seems like he personally ordered the sinking of the *Barracuda* in the hopes of killing me and making it look like an accident."

"A lot of good men lost in that. To say nothing about a billion dollar sub."

Boxer removed his newly purchased pipe from its wrappings and filled it with Mr. Schulte's newest blend. He soon had an ash glowing and the fragrant aroma of the smoke filled the living room of Francine's townhouse. "Cowly," he said. "The best. Left his newly married wife a young widow. Anyway, Julio claimed that he had turned down Tysin's offer to do the *Barracuda* job, but that Bruno Morell took it on for a price."

"Wouldn't surprise me at all." He took another pull from his cigar and let the smoke drift out. "Hey, you look like you could use a drink. Double Stoli on the rocks sound okay?"

Boxer smiled. "Sounds good to me." Over the sounds of Stark fixing the drinks, he said, "Trouble is, how do I get anyone in a position to help believe me? Take the word of a scumbag like Julio Sanchez over a pillar of national security like Henry Tysin."

"Seems to me, Jack," Stark said, carrying in two rocks glasses, and handed over the vodka to Boxer. "That we've got to convince the president, himself, that Tysin's dirty. Get him to launch an FBI investigation of

168

Henry."

Boxer sipped his vodka. "Sure, just call up Spooner and tell him Henry Tysin paid to have me killed, and is responsible for the kidnapping and rape of my fiancée, and for almost killing you . . . and destroying the *Barracuda* and the score of the men who went down with her. I wish I had that much clout with the president. Even my Medal of Honor wouldn't be enough of a wedge to gain his ear."

"Maybe not, Jack." Admiral Stark stirred his Chivas on the rocks with his forefinger, and downed a half inch of the scotch. "But Billy White and Jay Corless Archer sure have the inside track. Why don't we get in touch with them."

"Good idea. I think I'll call up Jay at his ranch in Texas. We're overdue for a visit, anyway." He walked into the kitchen and dialed the Archer Ranch. After several moments, he was connected to Jay, himself.

"Jack Boxer," Archer responded in his big, booming voice. "How the hell are ya? How they hangin' boy?"

Boxer chuckled. "Pretty well, Jay. You and the wife?"

"The missus and me been doin' just fine, Jack. And ol' Billy's got hisself engaged again. Pretty young thing."

"Blonde, and about twenty-three years old, I'll bet."

"Right on the money. You sure know how ol' Billy is all right. Heh, heh, heh. Well, what can I do for you, Jack? I'm sure you didn't call up just to reminisce about Billy's sexual preferences."

Boxer didn't waste any words. "I need a private audience with the president, Jay. Can you arrange it?"

"Whoa. That's a tall order. Might I just find out what it's all about? I'll have to give Dick Spooner something to sink his teeth into so's he can make up his mind about a meeting."

"Sorry, Jay. Not over the phone. Just take it on faith that it's important enough to go through all the trouble. We may have a national security problem."

"Why, hell, Jack. That's what we got an FBI and a CIA for, ain't it?"

"They won't do, Jay." Boxer took a drink of his vodka. "Well, Jay, are you with me or not?"

"Let me see. Tell you what, Jack. Spooner's planning to spend tomorrow here at the ranch. We're havin' a barbeque in his honor. Suckling pig and all that. You still got that boy of yours with you?"

"Yes, Chuck has graduated from high school, and is staying here with Admiral Stark and me in D.C. when he's not visiting his aunt in the old neighborhood on Staten Island."

"Well, why don't the three of you come on down to the ranch and join in the festivities. I'm sure once you're here I can arrange a sit-down with the president."

Boxer finished his drink, and clinked the cubes around in his glass. "Thanks, Jay. That's very kind of you. I'm sure I can arrange it on my end. It will be my last chance for R & R before I head back up to New London for sea trials the end of next week."

"Great. Just make sure to give a holler when you get down to DFW airport, and some of the boys will pick you up."

"In the big Caddy convertible with the giant steer horns on the hood?" Boxer chuckled to himself. "I can hardly wait, Jay."

Lt. Kathleen Carson was seated behind an immense oak desk in the Department of Defense office at the Symington Electric Boat Works compound. The contractor spared no expense to make the government officials feel comfortable, a subtle gesture on their part to influence Carson's quality assurance people in their favor. The walls of the office were elegantly panelled, with expensive water-color and oil paintings of ships at sea, including several prototypes built at Symington.

Carson was poring over a stack of documents, running her stockinged feet through the plush carpeting beneath her. She was chewing on a yellow pencil, her brow furrowed, re-reading the same page for the third time that day. Something was bothering her, something not quite right . . . something . . . and then it hit her. She jammed her forefinger on the intercom buzzer on her desk. "Haroldson, Painter . . . My office, please. Now."

Two civilian employees of the Dept. of Defense Procurement Office were in her office within 30 seconds, huffing from the exertion. Carson was a nice enough boss to work for, but they'd long since learned not to cross her. Several of their colleagues had been transferred to less pleasant working places because they were reluctant to take orders from a female boss. Haroldson, the more corpulent of the two men, was breathing heavily. He slicked the few remaining wisps of hair in place across his shiny dome. "What's up, Lieutenant?"

"Look this over carefully, men. I'm not pleased with these Q.C. reports on the propeller shaft housing. We've got sea trials in a week and I don't think those seals will hold up, considering this data."

The two men sat across the desk from Carson and read the material she had circled. "The breakdown rate on those bushings is much too frequent. Imagine yourself aboard a submarine several thousand feet below the surface, and you spring a leak in the propeller housing. Talk about being up a creek without a paddle."

"Holy shit . . . Oops, sorry, Lieutenant. This doesn't look good. Can we postpone the launch date?"

"Not a chance. Admiral Mason made it very clear that he's coming up here next Friday with the skipper and crew for a shakedown run. Mrs. Spooner, the president's wife is going to christen the *Manta*. There's no turning back now, men. We'd better get Chet Symington up here for a meeting, right away. We've got no time to lose."

"Old man Symington, himself?" Painter was plainly impressed.

"It's his plant. He's responsible. There are serious financial penalties involved if the *Manta* isn't finished by due date, so he'd better get his ass up here and personally make sure we're in good shape by next Friday."

Haroldson straightened his tie. "I'll call him right now. I'll be back in a couple of minutes."

Painter sat there uncomfortably, pretending to re-read the data while he waited for his immediate supervisor to return from his phone call. After what seemed like forever, but in reality was only a matter of minutes, Haroldson returned to Carson's office. He was visibly upset.

"What's wrong, Haroldson?" Carson asked him. "I'm not about to take any excuses from Symington or anyone else at this late date."

"They're having a serious problem downstairs, Lieutenant Carson. There's some FBI people here talking to Mr. Symington. I think you'd better go down and join them."

"You sure?"

"Yes, ma'am. Mr. Symington suggested it, himself."

Carson wasted no time getting to the chairman of the board's office. Chester Symington was seated behind his desk, his complexion ashen. Two well-groomed men in gray flannel suits and with neatly trimmed hair stood on either side of the desk facing him.

Policemen, Carson thought. Somehow, they all look alike, though these two render a neater appearance than most that she'd known. She entered the room, and extended her hand. "I'm Lt. Kathleen Carson, in charge of procurement here. How do you do?"

The senior man, in his forties, Carson figured, with just a trace of gray running through the temples of his thick black hair, gripped her hand firmly. "Special Agent Frank Ward," he said, presenting his credentials from a leather wallet he'd produced with his other hand. "FBI." He motioned to his partner with a head movement. "My associate, Thomas Collins. We've found some disturbing problems here at the plant."

"I'm aware of a breach in security, Mr. Ward. Admiral Boxer and I suspected a problem and baited a trap. I presume we were successful in flushing out the culprits."

"At this point, we have only one suspect, although we're not absolutely certain he acted alone."

Carson glanced from Ward's face to Symington's, and back. Apparently the problem was very close to the old man. Too close, she guessed.

"Bruce Symington," Ward continued, "was seen making copies of some documents he had no business with. He didn't realize that we have hidden time-lapse cameras through the government offices."

"Must have been the data we used as bait. Admiral Boxer and I substituted the specs from a much older submarine for the *Manta*'s and left them where they could be stolen by someone who tried hard enough. And we didn't ask Symington's for any money to set up the surveillance system, so they wouldn't necessarily realize that we were taping everything."

Ward nodded, and turned to Chester Symington. "Sir, I'm afraid I've got to arrest your son, Bruce. It would be better if he'd come along with us voluntarily."

"I suppose so," the old man said, his usual sonorous voice now weak and shaky. "I believe he checked out of the plant shortly after you two arrived this morning. Unusual for him. Perhaps he wasn't feeling well and went home. I still can't get over this." Symington was fighting back the tears welling up in his eyes.

"We gave him everything, his mother and I. Lord knows I tried to make a man out of him. Sent him to the best private military schools. I wanted to help him overcome his . . ." The words choked coming out. He said to them apologetically. "He was gay, you know. I think that was his undoing. The types of people he associated with."

Carson went over to the sunken figure of a once great man and tried to comfort him. Special agent Ward said, "Perhaps it would be best if you came with us, sir."

"I'd better come along, too, if you don't mind," Carson said. As Symington rose from his chair, Carson helped him on with his suit jacket. The FBI man nodded his assent and led the entourage toward the waiting pale gray government car parked in a no-parking zone in front of the plant headquarters building.

Agent Collins drove, with his partner, Ward, sitting next to him in the front seat. Lieutenant Carson rode with Symington in the back. No one spoke during the half-hour ride to the Symington estate. They drove up a long drive and pulled behind a Mercedes convertible under a porte-cochere at the entrance. The vanity license plate on the rear of the sportscar simply read BRUCE.

A butler met them at the door. "Yessir," he told his boss. "Mr. Symington came home about two hours ago. Been upstairs quiet since then."

Ward looked at his partner, then at Symington and Carson. "We'll go on upstairs, sir, with your permission. It would be best if you and Lieutenant Carson wait down here."

Chester Symington nodded his consent. The two FBI men climbed up the long curving staircase and walked to a room at the end of the hallway. There was no response. They knocked again, then entered the room.

Carson was waiting with the old man in the foyer when the FBI men returned downstairs several minutes later. Special agent Ward's face was very grim. He approached them and placed a gentle hand on Chester Symington's shoulder. His words nearly choked coming out. "You'd better sit down, sir. I have some very bad news to tell you."

CHAPTER FIFTEEN

The big open Caddy barreled along County Line
Road with Boxer and Admiral Stark sharing the spacious back seat. Boxer's adopted son, Chuck, rode
shotgun for the driver, a lanky cowboy dubbed Pecos
Slim, while George Strait belted out *"All my exes live
in Texas"* on the car radio. Slim turned off the freeway
onto a dirt road at a small wooden roadsign bearing
the stylized JCA brand of Jay Corless Archer's ranch.
He pushed the big car to almost seventy, leaving a
dustcloud in their wake for the remaining mile to the
ranch.

Boxer was glad when the ride was over. He wondered if Pecos Slim rode horses the way he drove cars.
He got out and brushed the red dust from his clothing. Chuck jumped out and helped the driver with the
bags. Stark got out of the car slowly, muttering under
his breath.

"Whyn't y'all go on around back while me an'
Chuck take care a your bags. Jay's fixin' up some grub
back at the barbeque pit."

Boxer led Admiral Stark around the back of the
ranch house. The older man begged off from any further walking when he spotted a swing chair on the
expansive back porch. "You go on without me, Jack. I

need to rest these old bones after that ride from the airport. I thought we'd never get here alive."

Boxer proceeded down a sloping lawn to where several people were milling around under an enormous live oak tree. He spotted Jay Archer among them, and ambled over.

"Why, Jack Boxer," Jay roared when Boxer came into view. "Ah see that Slim got y'all here safely." He wiped his hand off on a towel and extended it toward Boxer.

"Just barely, Jay. You're looking good."

Jay Archer was dressed in light gray western tailored slacks tucked into handmade lizard-skin boots, a white cowboy shirt with yellow embroidery, and a string tie held in place by a silver and turquoise slide. His shock of white hair was mostly tucked into a nine and a half gallon hat with a fancy feather in the sweatband. "Feel good today, boy. Welcome to the Archer ranch. I was just showin' these dudes how to make the best ribs you ever tasted. It's all in the slow cookin' and my special recipe sauce."

Several cooks dressed in starched whites looked on, embarrassed. Jay continued, "We got a suckling pig been roasting underground since sunup." He pointed to a rock-covered trough a short distance from where they were standing. "She'll be finger lickin' good by dinner. Melt right in your mouth." He licked barbeque sauce from his fingers. "How's the Admiral . . . and the boy?"

"They're back at the ranch house. Stark's resting up on your back porch, and Chuck's helping Pecos Slim with the luggage. He's quite the cowboy, isn't he?"

"Slim? One of the best hands I ever had workin' for

177

me, since the day I sprung him out of jail. He's been forever grateful."

"Jail?"

"Shhh. Not so loud," Jay admonished. "Some folks around here still don't know about it, and with the president's security men makin' themselves right at home here today, Slim might feel a bit uneasy. No sense rilin' him up. He's really a good ol' boy, that Slim."

"What was he in for? Nothing serious, I hope."

Jay said, "Some big, dumb Oklahoma roughneck made the mistake of pickin' a fight with him one night at a bar in town. Guy played defensive tackle for Oklahoma State for a year or two, and was pissed because nobody was payin' him much attention. So he slaps our boy on the back and says, 'Bein' as a Virginia Slim is a name for a faggot cigarette, then what's a Pecos Slim?'"

Boxer shook his head.

"Well, Slim showed him what's a Pecos Slim. Just the meanest, toughest son-of-a-bitch in these parts, that's all. Busted that Okie up so bad they had to take him to the hospital. Sheriff picked him up, Judge gave him thirty days or three hundred dollars. Slim was flat broke, so he got the thirty days."

"And you paid his fine?"

"Yeah. Billy found out about it through a friend and we paid off the fine, plus a little campaign contribution for the judge, and the sheriff. Say," Jay said, looking up at the sky beyond the house. "You hear that?"

Boxer listened intently. "Sounds like a helicopter."

"Good, the president's arriving early. Give you a

178

chance to get your meeting out of the way before the festivities."

Two helicopters swooped over the ranch house, and hovered over a clearing on the back lawn not far from the live oak. As the first bird settled down, four Secret Servicemen jumped out and ran toward the second chopper. Two more security men toting attaché cases climbed out of the president's helicopter, followed by Spooner, himself, and a man Boxer knew to be his personal physician. The entourage headed toward Jay and Boxer under the huge tree.

Jay gave the racks of ribs he'd been tending a final turn, and handed the utensils to one of the cooks. He waved to hail President Spooner, and said, "Howdy, Mr. President."

"Jay. Nice of you to have this fund-raiser for me. You know I appreciate it."

Jay Archer was all smiles. He loved playing the part of power-broker. "It's mah pleasure, Dick. We got some of Dallas and Fort Worth's finest out here to pay their respects, and a hundred dollars a plate to meet you today." He nodded to Boxer. "Ah'm sure you remember Admiral Boxer, here."

Spooner held out his hand. "Of course. How you doing, Jack. Keeping your Medal of Honor polished, I hope?"

"Thanks to you, Mr. President," he said, shaking the extended hand.

"Jack's got something to say to you, Dick. Top secret stuff. Wouldn't even give me an inkling of what it's all about. I hope you don't mind a quick pow-wow with him before the festivities?"

President Spooner looked serious for a long moment,

causing Boxer to wish he hadn't been so impertinent. "I suppose I can squeeze a few minutes in with Boxer between you and Billy and the potato salad."

Jay nodded. "Billy's up at the house entertaining some debutante, right now, Dick. If you like, you and Jack can have your little meeting now while I rustle up the guests for drinks and hors d'oeuvres."

Spooner removed his dark blue suit jacket and slung it over his shoulder. He loosened his tie and top shirt button, turned to Boxer, and said, "Let's take a walk down by the creek, Jack. My legs could use a good stretch after that long chopper ride."

Boxer nodded and fell in alongside the president. Spooner was a tall, handsome man, a few inches taller than Boxer, with a thick shock of wavy brown hair, an aristocrat who liked to mix it with the good ol' boys like Jay Archer and Billy White. Boxer thought him a shoo-in to win re-election in November, and told him so.

"Ever think of entering politics, Jack? You've got the makings of a fine U.S. senator. National hero, honest as can be, now that's a real rarity up at the Hill these days. You've got the right stuff, Jack."

"I'm afraid politics isn't for me, Mr. President. I like to do my small part for the country at the command of a submarine. I'd be like a fish out of water as a politician."

"You ought to think on it awhile, Jack. You know, with my influence, and the financial backing of Jay and Billy, you'd stand a real chance. Hell, Ike made it all the way to the White House based on his military record."

Boxer was a little embarassed. "Thanks for your

180

kind words, Mr. President. I think I'd find it hard to take some of the people I'd have to deal with along the way. Which brings me to why I wanted to speak to you, sir."

"Well, son, might as well spit it out. I can see you're about to bust. But consider what I said about running for office. I think you'd do just fine."

"Sir, over the last year and a half or so, there's been a campaign mounted to destroy me."

Spooner grunted, "Happens to people in power all the time, Jack. Hell, if you can't take the heat, get out of the fire before you get burned."

"I'm not worried about myself, Mr. President. A lot of innocent people have been destroyed along the way."

"Meaning?"

"I'm very sure that the same person responsible for kidnapping my fiancée and almost killing Admiral Stark was the man who ordered the sinking of my sub, the *Barracuda*, in order to have me killed."

Spooner thought back a moment and came up with, "If I recall correctly, FBI Director Kirby told me a man named Moran was responsible for the *Barracuda*."

"Morell," Boxer corrected. "Bruno Morell. He was hired to kill me by a very high government official."

Spooner stared hard into Boxer's eyes. "Well? At least I hope it's one of my political opponents."

"One of your appointments, Mr. President." Boxer let out a deep sigh. "Henry Tysin."

"What? Henry's the head of the CIA. Why would he commit treason by destroying a U.S. Navy ship just to get at a small-fry like yourself? No offense, Boxer, but your story just doesn't wash."

Boxer shrugged. "He's been out to get me from the

181

moment he took over from Kinkaid. He started out by trying to ride roughshod over our super-sub program, and put me on notice I was on his enemies list."

President Spooner smiled. "If memory serves me, Jack, you've had the reputation of being sort of a pain in the ass, even going back to Kinkaid's days."

"Yes, sir. I have a pretty good sense of right and wrong. Kinkaid and I fought over that many times. But we respected each other. And, in the end, Kinkaid left his entire estate to me. In his heart, he always knew I had the best interests of this country in mind." They paused by the bank of the creek. Spooner tossed in a twig and watched it being carried downstream, back in the direction they'd come from. Boxer followed the twig, also. His eye caught the images of two of the president's bodyguards a short distance away, and he instinctively lowered his voice. "With Tysin, I never had one bit of respect. He never did anything to earn it."

"Henry came to me well recommended. He was widely respected in the intelligence community." He paused, and looked deeply into Boxer's eyes. "Are you certain about your allegations?"

Boxer kept the eye contact. "Yes, Mr. President. The man whom Tysin hired to abduct my fiancée, Julio Sanchez, is near death by torture for having told me."

"I'll want to question this Bruno Morell myself."

"Bruno Morell died for his troubles, sir. Sanchez killed him."

Spooner's tone became angry. "So all I've got is hearsay to go on? I'm not pleased by that, Boxer."

"He is not all he seems to be, sir. I think you should discreetly investigate him. If you turn over the right rocks, you'll uncover the slimy insect that lurks

182

beneath the surface."

"Humph. Well, you've sure dealt me a kicker, Jack. I just hope you know what you're talking about." He tossed another stick into the creek and watched it float along in the current. After awhile, he said, "Let's go back and join the others. I can smell those ribs cooking from here."

CHAPTER SIXTEEN

The big Texas Air 747 touched down on schedule at Dulles International Airport at 8:30 PM, as night descended upon the nation's capital. Boxer and Admiral Stark retrieved their luggage and headed for the long line of green and white cabs just outside the arrivals gate. "Sure was nice of Jay Archer to let Chuck spend the summer there on the ranch."

"Yes, it was," Boxer replied. "It'll keep him occupied for the next month and a half before he enters Annapolis."

They reached the lead taxi. Boxer opened the rear door for Admiral Stark, walked around the back and got in behind the driver, and gave his address. The driver, a skinny young man wearing a rock group t-shirt and a Baltimore Orioles baseball cap put down the comic book he was reading and pulled out onto the access road. A short while later, he was maneuvering the cab in and out of downtown traffic. It was a beautiful, clear summer night, and the city was still wide awake.

A few blocks from Francine Wheeler's brownstone traffic ground to a halt amid the wailing of police and ambulance sirens. The street seemed familiar to Boxer, and he peered out of the window to verify it. Sure enough, this was the very block where he'd visited Lori-Ann Collins, Tysin's secretary. Several blue and white D.C. police cars were double parked in front of her apartment building, with their overhead lights ablaze. "Find someplace to park," Boxer commanded the taxi driver. "I want to check this out."

"I ain't got all night to spend with one fare, mister. You get out here, you pay the meter, and I'm gone."

Boxer strained to see what was on the front seat of the cab. "What's that you're reading?" he asked the driver.

"This?" the young man asked, lifting up the comic book. "Oh. This is *The Adventures of Submariner.* It's about this guy who can live underwater and saves the world from the bad guys, usually the Russians or the Commie Chinese." He looked admiringly at his treasure. "Nothing you'd probably know anything about."

Boxer looked at Stark and the both of them broke out in a laugh. Boxer produced a hundred dollar bill and waved it in the driver's face. "Want to make a hundred dollars while you sit and read your book?"

The driver's eyes lit up and he stared greedily at the bill. "You bet." Then he was pensive for a moment. "Do I have to give up my comic book when I'm done?"

"You keep it," Boxer assured him. He tore the bill in half, tucked one part in his pocket and handed the other to the driver. "Find a place nearby to park and wait for me. And take good care of your other passenger."

"Yes, sir. The C-note bought you the rest of the night."

Boxer stuck his head into the rear of the cab. "Admiral, I know someone who lived in that building. I'm going to make sure everything's all right."

"You go ahead, Jack. I'm going to catch a nap. That long flight wore me out."

Boxer crossed the street, walked to where a crowd was gathered, and shouldered his way to the front. He watched two paramedics wheel a gurney to the opened rear doors of an ambulance. Strapped to the stretcher was a corpse encased in a black rubberized body bag. He strained to take a closer look.

"Hey, Buster, get the hell back out of the way." A uniformed policeman was pointing his nightstick at Boxer. "You need a special invitation or something?"

A rotund plainclothes officer, with tie askew and shirtsleeves rolled up, ambled over to see who was aggravating the policeman. He overheard Boxer explain, "I know someone who lives in that building. I just want to make sure everything's okay, there."

"Boxer? That you?" The plainclothesman shielded his eyes from the glare of the emergency lights to get a better look. "Hold on, Donovan. I know this guy," he told the cop, and walked closer to where Boxer was standing.

"Detective Murphy?" Boxer asked, recognizing the portly policeman who investigated the kidnapping of Francine Wheeler.

"Detective Sergeant Francis X. Murphy, at your service. What can I do for you, Boxer?"

"I know a woman who lives here. Lori-Ann Collins is her name. When I came upon this commotion, I stopped to make sure she was okay."

"Collins? Nice looking babe with long, black hair down to here. I'm afraid you're looking at her." He jerked his thumb in the direction of the body bag.

Boxer shook his head, his lips pressed tightly together.

Murphy took a little notebook from his back pocket and scribbled something on it. "What's your relationship with the deceased?"

"She worked at the CIA office in Langley. I had some dealings with them in the past, I'm sorry I can't reveal any more about that, and I recently bumped into her on the street, nearby. Literally. She . . ."

"That's him. That's the man, officer," a woman shouted. "I'd recognize him anywhere."

Boxer looked up to see a middle-aged woman pointing an accusing finger at him. He started to protest.

"He's the one I told you about . . . That's the man."

"Okay, lady, thanks. Everything's under control," Murphy told her. He took Boxer by the elbow and walked him out of earshot of the crowd. "We were interviewing the neighbors. That old busybody lives down the hall from the deceased. Smelled something foul coming from the apartment and called nine-one-one. The boys recognized the stench as coming from a stiff, and called for a meat wagon.

"Anyways," Murphy continued, "the old lady was telling me about a well-dressed guy with a beard who she seen coming out of the apartment a few days ago. The deceased was shouting obscenities at the guy, but he just kept walking down the stairs and out the door."

"That was me. The day I bumped into her, we were shopping on the same block, she invited me to her apartment for coffee."

Murphy noted this in his little book. "You sure it wasn't for coffee, *and?*"

"No, but if it was, you'd be the first one I'd tell, Sergeant," Boxer chuckled. "Seriously, the lady made a pass, but I told her I wasn't interested in having sex with a married woman. She decided to make a try for it anyway, and I walked out." He motioned with his head in the direction of the old woman from the building. "Miss Collins didn't appreciate that, and I guess the neighbor was snooping and caught her shouting after me as I left. That's a guess. I didn't look back."

187

Murphy wet the tip of his pencil with his tongue and made a note in his pad. "So I'm supposed to believe that the deceased offered it to you, and you very nobly turned it down?"

Boxer frowned his displeasure. "Believe what you want, Sergeant. I told the truth."

"The truth," Murphy said. "That's my job. To get at the truth." He had his pencil poised to write in the little notebook. "I suppose you got an alibi for the last couple of days?"

"As a matter of fact, I have. I just came from the airport. I've been in Texas over the weekend. I should have my copies of the plane tickets somewhere." Boxer came up with the tickets in a jacket pocket, smoothed them out, and handed them to Detective Murphy. "Here you are."

Murphy looked them over, and made some notations in his book. "These look okay. Course you could a flew home, killed the deceased, and flew back to Texas, then back home again on these tickets."

"Admiral Stark was with me all weekend. He's back in that green and white cab, taking a nap."

"Admiral Stark. The old guy that got pistol whipped when your ladyfriend got snatched?"

"The very same, Sergeant. I can account for my time for the entire stay in Texas."

"Name names. The old man don't count. He's too close to you for me to consider him as an unbiased witness."

"I'd rather not do that. The people I was with would not like the publicity they'd get."

Murphy shook his head. "Then consider yourself a suspect, Boxer. Stick close to home, in case I need to question you again."

Boxer looked at the stout detective incredulously. "You can't be serious? I'm an admiral in the U.S. Navy. I go where they send me."

"You leave without my okay, and I'll put out a warrant for your arrest. As far as I'm concerned, you're a suspect in a homicide investigation."

Boxer shook his head. "I'd think you'd be better off looking for a real killer, Detective Murphy. Meanwhile, if you need me, you know where to find me." Boxer turned on his heel and walked back to the taxi. He shook the cabdriver, who was dozing with the comic book cradled against his chest, awake. "Let's go," Boxer said, and got in the back seat.

At Francine's townhouse, he paid the driver the fare on the meter, plus the other half of the hundred dollar bill. To the young man's surprised face, Boxer said, "Consider the hundred a tip."

As the cab pulled away into traffic, Boxer said to Stark, "Before we turn in for the night, I'd better make a phone call to Jay Archer in Texas."

Detective Sgt. Francis X. Murphy walked into the darkened viewing room, quietly closed the door behind him, and stood with his back against the rear wall. On the giant television screen at the front of the room, Lori-Ann Collins was leading CIA Director Henry Tysin by his genitals to her sofa, as he half walked, half hopped with his legs hobbled by his trousers dropped around his ankles. The three other detectives were laughing and making lewd remarks.

"Hey, Ozzie, run that back again, will ya? Geez, did you see her pull the old guy around by his dick? Can you believe that?"

"You just wish it was you, Busko. If she could find yours."

"Awright, knock off the crap," Murphy commanded. The others immediately shut up, surprised by their sergeant's sudden appearance. "Quit jerkin' around," Murphy continued. "I don't need to remind you that this is a serious murder investigation."

"Sorry, Sarge," Ozzie Newberg said. "We was only kidding around."

"Yeah, Sergeant. We didn't mean nothin' by it. It's just that, shit, Sarge, did you see this thing yet? I mean, it's better than the stuff you see at the movies," Stanley Busko said.

Murphy switched on the lights, and the men squinted to regain their day vision. "What Busko really means, Sergeant," Sal Ianello, the third detective in the room added, "is, would you mind very much if we ran off a duplicate of this before we return it to Property?"

"Not funny, Ianello," Murphy growled. He scowled at all three of his men to show them he was serious, and to knock off their levity. "Seems like the deceased recorded all the men who came to visit her in the apartment. Or someone else recorded it for her. From the looks of those videos, she may have had blackmail on her mind. Anyways, the lady in question had the foresight to make copies for herself. The forensic boys found them in the false bottom of her dresser drawer when they tossed the joint. Otherwise, you guys would be out on the streets with no leads, playin' with yourselves." Murphy stared down each of his men. "Instead a sittin' in here watching dirty movies, playin' with yourselves."

They chuckled at their boss's returned good humor. "By the way, Sarge, we ran into a dead end on who was

190

paying the rent on the apartment."

"Yeah, Ozzie and me traced it back to some blind corporation that don't really exist, except to pay the lady's rent on the first of each month. Really spooky."

"Hmmph. Sal, rewind that tape, will ya? Now, let's see. What we got so far." He took his little notebook from a back pocket. "We got the deceased, Lori-Ann Collins, age twenty-eight, five-six, one-oh-seven pounds, otherwise in excellent health . . ."

"I'll say."

"Butt out while I'm talking, okay, Ozzie?"

The room fell silent, again.

"Awright. Now it starts to get sticky. The deceased worked for the CIA. Worked for the head man, himself. Future looked . . ."

"Excuse me, Sergeant," Sal Ianello said. "Funny you should say that. Me and the guys were joking how the john she was tugging around by his joint looks like CIA Director Tysin. It's hard to say without his clothes on."

The others chuckled.

Murphy said, "Run that part of the tape again, Sal. And no wisecracks from you guys."

"Sure, Sarge. My pleasure."

Ianello fast-forwarded to the desired portion of the video tape. The detectives settled back in their seats. "Here you are, Sarge. The Detective Bureau's entry in the Academy Awards."

Amid the laughter, Murphy said, "Awright, pause it right there. Can you get a copy of that? Good. You'd better crop it to just the face. If it really is the director, we wouldn't want his dick on the front page of the *Post*. And we also want face shots of all the other guys in these tapes. All of them are to be considered suspects. One of them is our killer."

191

Stan Busko said, "That guy Boxer never took his clothes off, just like he told you. All it shows is him drinking coffee, and talkin' to the broad . . . I mean the deceased."

"That still doesn't rule him out," Murphy emphasized.

"And the tall blond guy turns out to be her husband, Richard Baxter."

"Works for the State Department," Ozzie Newberg added.

"Wait a minute," Sal interjected. "Ain't he the same guy in the movie with that all male orgy?"

"Yeah, the queer party. Son of a bitch, that's the same guy."

Murphy scratched his head. "Looks like the deceased had quite a porno collection. And it looks like too many coincidences, to suit me. Has forensics got back to us with the fingerprints, yet?"

"Nah," Busko said. "I know they dusted everything in the place. They're probably still with the FBI."

Murphy placed his hands on his corpulent belly, and smiled. "Gentlemen, I think we may get to the bottom of this very soon. We got at least three suspects, maybe more when the prints get back. If we can turn up the blunt object she got bludgeoned to death with, and match up the prints against any of these guys . . ."

Just then, the door opened, and the smiling face of a uniformed policeman peered inside. "Uh, excuse me, Sergeant."

"What are you smiling about, Donovan? The missus been good to you last night?"

"There's a call for you, Sergeant, about that Boxer guy."

"Well?"

"Uh, Sarge, did you move your bowels yet today?"

The detectives giggled. Murphy said, "What the fuck you talking about Donavan?"

"Well, Sarge," Donovan was grinning from ear to ear. "You're gonna shit when you hear who's on the phone for you."

CHAPTER SEVENTEEN

Boxer rode in the back seat with Monty, while Pierce rode up front with the driver of the gray government sedan. They pulled up at the main entrance to the Symington Electric Boat Works where Monty rolled down his rear window and handed the guard his credentials.

"Go right through to the headquarters building, Mr. Montgomery. We've been expecting you." The security guard told their driver, "Pull up to that tall building with the blue trim, and park in one of the VIP visitors spots. The section is labeled RESERVED."

Monty gave his thanks and they made for the headquarters building. They checked in with Lt. Kit Carson, and were immediately led to Chester Symington's office. The old man looked awful as he stood to greet the government contingent. Boxer shook hands with Symington, and offered his condolences.

The old man shook his head and said, "Thank you for your kind words, Admiral. It's always a terrible loss to have to bury your children. On the other hand, I'm terribly shocked and embarrassed by what he did. I knew the boy was . . . was running with the wrong crowd, but I'd never have suspected him of being a traitor."

Boxer said, "It seems there was some blackmail involved, sir. The Russians had a mole working in the CIA, as a personal secretary to the director. The FBI found evidence that she married a high ranking staffer at the Department of State, and then set out to blackmail her husband, Richard Baxter."

Old man Symington nodded his head. "Sure. It begins to make sense, now. Baxter and my son were fellow Yale graduates. My son took an MBA and came to work here for me. Richard went on into government. They'd remained friends through the years."

"That's the link, Mr. Symington," Boxer told him. "The mole put pressure on her husband, who then turned to your son, Bruce. It was a vicious scheme that almost worked." Monty and Pierce nodded in agreement.

"We were forewarned, and set a trap for whomever turned out to be the spy. I'm sorry, but your son just fell into it."

Symington sat down behind his desk, his head hanging, his eyes close to tears.

"Don't blame yourself, Mr. Symington," Monty said. "The Department of the Navy doesn't hold what happened against your company. And we're really sorry about your personal tragedy, sir."

The old man raised his head, then noticed the time on the wall clock. "Eleven-thirty already, and we launch at noon. Your men are already checked in aboard the *Manta,* Admiral Boxer. And Mrs. Spooner is standing by with the champagne bottle." He shrugged. "Too bad we can't have the traditional ceremony, with all the bunting and hooplah."

The three government men smiled. This was to be a top-secret launching, with the ceremony to take place in a heavily fortified bunker, into a deeply dredged channel which led out to sea. The launch time was carefully arranged to take advantage of the orbit schedule of the Russian spy-in-the-sky satellite over North America. "Well, we should be getting on with it, sir, if you don't mind."

The four men led the way to the bunker complex, followed by several high-ranking Symington executives, and Lieutenant Carson and most of her staff. Boxer was pleased to see his entire crew in dress whites standing in formation on a removable deck specially constructed for the occasion. Mrs. Spooner was standing nearby, escorted by the Secretary of Defense, Sidney Weintraub. Boxer took his place at a small reviewing stand, with Monty and Pierce on one side of him, and Mr. Symington, Mrs. Spooner and Wientraub on the other.

Boxer hadn't gotten an official send-off like this in years, so important was the *Manta* project to the government that it provided this little breach of secrecy for the sake of ceremony. Weintraub said a few words about the stout-hearted men whose gallantry would preserve peace in the world, and then Mr. Symington presented the president's wife with the champagne bottle tethered to the bow of the *Manta* by a long ribbon. "Mrs. Spooner, would you please do the honors?"

She gripped the bottle by the neck, took a long windup, and swung it in an arc toward the new submarine. A cheer went up among the crew as the bottle shattered, sending shards of glass and foamy champagne into the water below. Monty took the stand, opened a manila envelope and produced a two page document. He officially congratulated Boxer as skipper of the *Manta,* named Captain Mark Clemens as his executive officer, and to everyone's surprise, announced that Lt. Kathleen Carson would be joining the crew as technical advisor during the sea trials.

Boxer was both pleased that Carson was so well thought of by the Navy brass, and somewhat ill-at-ease because there were no special accommodations for a woman aboard the *Manta.* Boxer snapped a formal salute to his men, to the dignitaries, and to Kit Carson, who returned the salute with a big smile. "My gear's already on board," she said. "I wanted to surprise you."

"Well, you succeeded at that," he said with a grin. "We'd better get aboard."

Boxer was handed a second envelope, his orders, along with the special codes they'd be using during the test run. He shook hands with everybody who came to see them off, and escorted Carson on board the new sub. As they went below, the temporary planking was removed, and the *Manta* slid down a launch ramp into an estuary to the Atlantic Ocean.

Boxer went immediately to the conn. He was very impressed with how well his ideas had been implemented by Carson and her staff. "Well done, Kit. I'm very pleased."

"Thanks, Skipper. Everything should feel familiar to you and the crew. I adopted whatever I could from the *Barracuda* and some of the previous prototypes, and adapted it to the *Manta*'s configuration. The major differences are the smaller turning radius due to our shorter length, and the superior electronics. And, of course, the turtle shell. Did you see the way that champagne bottle shattered? I wonder if anyone else noticed."

Boxer smiled. "I didn't think the First Lady was that strong."

Carson walked around the command center, turning on all the various consoles that comprised the COMM-COMP, the master computer that allowed the *Manta* to be run so shorthanded. Banks of LED lights flashed from red to amber to green. Boxer keyed the MC mike. "Chief White, please stand by the diving planes."

"Aye, aye, Skipper. Standing by."

Boxer took them down to periscope depth, watching their progress on the UWIS, the UnderWater Image Screen that showed a three dimensional image of their surroundings, and also on the sonar screen set at a much larger perimeter. Mark Clemens, the EXO, and Carson looked on.

Boxer called, "Five degrees on the diving planes, Whitey."

"Aye, aye, Skipper," he responded from his nearby diving station. "Five degrees on the planes."

"Helmsman, right rudder ten degrees."

Mahoney answered, "Aye, aye, Skipper," glad to be back at his familiar position.

Boxer followed the dive on the CIC screen. At periscope level, he watched the image of the submarine level off, corresponding to the bubble on the depth gauge mounted on a nearby bulkhead coming to the null position. The ship was following the course of the channel. The UWIS showed them to be approaching its convergence with the ocean. "Good work, men. That was really smooth."

"Aye, aye, sir," Whitey said, still used to answering his captain somewhat more formally than the hands that had been with Boxer longer.

"Thanks, Skipper," Mahoney answered. "This baby can turn on a dime. My compliments on the hull design."

Boxer smiled at Kit. "All compliments go to Lieutenant Carson. She's done an outstanding job. I'll take the blame for any faults that may show up. That would be due to shortsightedness on my part. The lieutenant's given me everything I've asked for, and more."

Kit Carson beamed. She'd been handed a grand compliment in front of most of the crew. Most senior officers she'd known kept all the glory for themselves, and passed on the blame to others. Not the Skipper. Not Boxer.

"We're out of the channel, Skipper," Clemens announced, pointing to the display on the NAVSCREEN. He'd also been following their course on a backup chart, manually, and the two positions coincided.

"We've been making five knots," Boxer said. "Let's

pick it up a bit. Looks like the channel was dredged along the contours of a natural trough along the sea floor."

"Roger that," Clemens replied, checking the UWIS.

Boxer switched on the MC microphone. "EO, make good ten knots."

"Aye, aye, Skipper. Coming to ten knots."

As the *Manta* gained speed, Boxer noted that the noise level wasn't appreciably greater than it had been at five knots. A very good sign. He said to his exec, "We're approaching deep water, Clem. Stand by to lower the sail."

"Aye, aye, Skip." Clemens stood by a red wheel overhead in the command center, called the attack center when engaging the enemy. "Ready when you are, skipper."

"Lower sail."

Clemens spun the wheel, and with a hydraulic whoosh, the sail lowered into place around them. The *Manta* immediately picked up speed due to the reduced drag of the streamlined hull without the sail acting as a brake. "Sail lowered."

"Conn, EO. Making twelve knots," the engineering officer reported. "It's really quiet back here. The reactor's humming like a baby."

"Roger that, EO." They were now traveling sixty feet under the surface at twelve knots. There was no sensation of depth except visually on the CIC and the UWIS. The ocean outside the hull made no noise as they slipped out to sea. "Maintain course and speed," Boxer ordered.

When they passed by Block Island, Boxer pointed it out on the screen to Carson, who'd never been aboard a sub at sea before, though she'd been involved with every aspect of the *Manta,* and had personally inspected every inch of her, inside and out.

"Let's see what this baby can do on her own," Boxer said. "Going to AUTONAV," he announced over the MC. "Lieutenant Carson, would you like to do the honors?"

"Would I? Thank you, Skipper. Actually, there's nothing to it."

"Take her down to one hundred feet."

"Aye, aye, sir. Going to one hundred feet." Carson switched a large-handled lever from Manual to Auto, punched in the desired depth on a keypad on the AUTONAV console, and followed it up with the turn of an illuminated dial. Automatically, the rudder centered amidships to reduce drag, a measure of compressed air was blown, and the ballast tanks filled with a corresponding volume of seawater, and the diving planes adjusted for the dive.

"Rudder amidships," Mahoney reported.

"Diving planes at zero five degrees, sir," Chief White announced.

Boxer could feel the ship tilt forward slightly, and verified their status on the depth gauge and the inclinometer.

"Diving planes null, Skipper. Approaching one zero zero feet."

"Good work, Carson," Boxer said, placing a hand on her shoulder.

"Smooth as a baby's ass, you don't mind my saying so, Skipper," Whitey said. That brought a round of smiles and laughter from those present in the command center.

"Passing by Martha's Vineyard, Skipper." The island showed up on the UWIS to their port side.

"Increase speed to twenty knots, Carson. Take a heading of zero eight three degrees and maintain course and speed till we pass by Nantucket Island."

"Aye, aye, Skipper. Coming to course zero eight three," she tapped in the three digits and set the dial on the navigation console. Then she entered the required information in the computer that governed the power plant. "Coming to speed of twenty knots, Skipper."

In a few minutes, "Making twenty knots, Skipper. Steady as she goes," EO reported.

"Most of the systems can be handled from right here with the COMMCOMP, Skipper."

"Well, I'm impressed, Lieutenant," Clemens stated.

"If you're impressed with this, Mr. Clemens, wait till you take a shower," Carson said with a smile. "A Hollywood shower for all with the same amount of water as you'd use on any of the earlier subs."

"A real Hollywood shower? With running hot water the entire three minutes? Now, that's something to look forward to," Clemens agreed. "On the other subs, you wet down, soap the walls of the shower stall, and spin around to get clean."

That brought a round of laughs and knowing smiles from the crew.

Fifteen minutes later, "Passing by Nantucket Island, Skipper."

"Roger, that, Clem." Boxer checked the digital LED readout on the date and time display. "Time to unseal our orders."

He went to his quarters, just behind and to starboard of the command center, and opened the small safe under his bunk. Boxer removed the manila envelope and returned to the COMMCOMP. He took a pocket knife from his pocket, slit the envelope and removed the top sheet of paper. It took him a minute to look it over. Then he said, "We're to make our way through the Northwest Passageway among the northern Canadian islands, and rendezvous with Rolly's Rangers in Alaska."

"Whew, some shakedown cruise," Clemens remarked.

"If you want to put a submarine through a torture test, you take her up to the Arctic. And I think the *Manta*'s up to it," Boxer said. "Thanks to Lieutenant Carson."

"I think the men are, too, Skipper."

"We'll soon find out, Clem. We'll soon find out."

Before long the CIC and the depth finder showed deeper water, and Boxer once again gave the orders to dive. "I want to stay with the AUTONAV," Boxer told Carson and Clemens. He switched on the intercom. "Now hear this, this is the captain speaking. All hands prepare to dive. Repeat, prepare to dive."

Carson and Clemens waited for further orders. Boxer said, "Okay, Carson, you're on a roll. Take us down to four zero zero feet, speed four zero knots. Clem, you'll have your turn many times over before this passage is over."

"Aye, aye, Skipper," they both responded. Kit Carson performed the necessary steps on the AUTONAV computer and the *Manta* nosed downward.

In thirty seconds, Whitey announced, "Passing through two zero zero feet. Passing through two five zero feet . . . three zero zero feet . . ."

"Making good four zero knots," EO reported.

"Leveling off at four zero zero feet. Diving planes are at null."

The entire maneuver took less than two minutes. To those standing, it felt like downhill skiing.

"Secure from angles and dangles, Skipper." Carson had used the slang for a quick dive to evade an enemy.

"Excellent, Kit. Set a course of zero seven five degrees and maintain it until we reach fifty-one degrees thirty minutes longitude."

"Aye, aye, Skipper."

"We'll maintain that course till we're past the tip of Newfoundland Island, then head north-northwest and make our way around the hump, through the Hudson Strait, up along Baffin Island and head west. There's some deep water along the way to practice our diving drills."

The next twenty-four hours went uneventfully. Then, at 1900 hours, between Nova Scotia and Newfoundland Island, Howard "Hi Fi" Freedman signalled the command center from the tiny sonar room. "Conn, sonar. I just picked up three distinct pings, Skipper. Someone out there's got a fix on us. Can we slow down enough for me to give a listen?"

"Roger that, Hi Fi." He switched on the intercom. "All hands, going to manual systems. Repeat, going to manual."

Clemens was on watch with Boxer, and immediately lifted the AUTONAV lever to manual.

Boxer continued, "EO, reduce speed to zero four knots. Helmsman, full right rudder. Come to course one six zero degrees."

The engineering officer immediately reduced the demand on the reactor, thus cutting the speed. "Aye, aye, Skipper."

Mahoney swung the wheel hard to the right, keeping an eye on the Rudder Position Indicator and the Navigational Bearing Display in front of him at the same time. "Right full rudder . . . Aye, aye, sir. Coming to one six zero degrees."

The *Manta* came about and slowed to a crawl, maintaining just enough power to make steerageway. Freedman reported again. "Conn, sonar. I think I've got him, Skipper. A Ruski *Alfa,* from the sound signature."

"Good work, Hi Fi. Can you get me a bearing?"

"Sure thing, Skipper." Hi Fi did a quick calculation and entered it into his computer. "Target bearing zero eight five degrees . . . Range twenty thousand yards . . . Depth three zero zero feet . . . Speed . . . three zero knots, Skipper. Our sprint and drift caught her off guard."

"I wonder when she picked us up?" Boxer asked.

"Second target bearing zero eight four degrees, Skipper. Range twenty thousand yards . . . Speed zero three knots on the surface. We've got us a big one, Skipper. By the sound of her, I'd guess a trawler."

Boxer rubbed his beard. "Assuming Hi Fi's right, and it is a fishing trawler, than that *Alfa* could be along to protect it."

Clemens looked puzzled. "Protect it from what, Skipper? Why do you need an *Alfa* to protect a harmless fishing boat?"

Boxer had taken out his pipe and was lighting up. He blew a wisp of smoke out and said, "With the Ruskies, there's no such thing as a harmless anything. Virtually all of their fishing trawlers double as spy ships. They have some of the most sophisticated listening equipment in existence. My guess is he's much too close to the Canadian coast, and fishing in forbidden waters, besides monitoring any naval traffic in the area. That *Alfa* is riding shotgun for it."

Clemens asked, "How do you want to handle it? Do we notify the Canadian authorities about the illegal fishing?"

"Can't do anything about it. We can't risk having that *Alfa* find out that we're anything but a *Los Angeles* sub. They already know the *Manta* exists. If they get an inkling that we're it, they'll have every ship they've got in the North Atlantic looking to sink us. Too bad, but we'll just have to lose them. We can't take the risk." He spoke into the intercom, "Going to manual systems. All hands man battle stations. Repeat, battle stations."

The men scurried to their assigned battle stations in less than a minute. Boxer gave the orders for evasive action. "EO, give me four zero knots."

"Aye, aye, Skipper. Four zero knots."

"Whitey, take us down to one thousand feet."

"One zero zero zero feet, aye, Skipper. Diving planes at one zero degrees."

Boxer said, "Helmsman, left rudder ten degrees. Make course zero nine five degrees."

Clemens and Carson plotted their course as they plunged deeper and faster on an easterly course, hoping to outrun the Soviet *Alfa*. "The Ruskie sub will have to leave the trawler to chase us, and it's my guess that it won't," Boxer advised them.

"Conn, sonar. Enemy sub changing course. Target bearing zero two seven degrees . . . Range sixteen thousand yards . . . Depth five zero zero feet . . . Speed three eight knots, Skipper. That *Alfa* is chasing us."

Boxer spoke into the MC. "EO, go to four five knots. Let's lose them."

"Aye, aye, Skipper. Going to four five knots."

"Target bearing zero three five degrees, Skipper. Range fourteen thousand yards . . . Depth seven zero zero feet . . . Speed four zero knots and closing."

Boxer turned to his EXO. "Clemens, prepare a firing solution for tubes one and two."

Clemens raced to the Fire Control Console of the COMMCOMP and entered the reported coordinates and speed of the enemy sub. "Aye, aye, Skipper."

"Kit, I'd like to test the drone. Set it on a simulated course of one seven five degrees and a depth of twelve hundred feet. As soon as the *Alfa* latches onto its track, we'll head north, again."

"Yes, sir," she said, and relayed her directions to the aft torpedo room.

"Conn, sonar. Twin targets bearing zero four zero degrees . . . Range nine thousand yards . . . Depth nine five zero feet . . . Speed seven zero knots and closing fast, Skipper. Killer darts."

Boxer was quick to react. "Mahoney, left full rudder. Come to course zero eight zero degrees. Whitey, dive. Bring us down to twelve hundred yards."

"Aye, aye," they chorused, and the *Manta* plunged and veered left, rolling onto the port side as she maneuvered out of harm's way.

"Target's closing on us, Skipper. Range four thousand yards and following on our heading."

Boxer followed the trajectory of the projectiles on the UWIS, and realized that a collision was inevitable. "All hands, brace for explosion."

The killer darts were upon them in a moment. The *Manta* took the twin blasts simultaneously on the port beam. The explosions shook the ship.

"DCO, report damages," Boxer ordered.

The Damage Control Officer flipped the switches on his DC screens. Section by section, each major area of the sub came into view, along with a description of any damages. "Damages negative, Skipper. It seems the killer darts exploded harmlessly off the *Manta*'s hull."

"Anybody injured?"

"Negative, again, Skipper."

Boxer and Carson looked at each other and smiled. The polymer turtle shell protecting the hull held up against the killer darts. They had taken away one of the Soviet's key anti-submarine weapons. "Prepare to release the drone, Kit. Send it down to the bottom and have it explode on contact."

"Aye, aye, Skipper. Drone fired."

"Helmsman, come around one eight zero degrees."

Mahoney spun the wheel hard right. When the sub had completed three-quarters of its turn, he back-spun the wheel to slow its rotation. "One eighty turn completed, Skipper. She turns on a dime."

"Good job, Mahoney. EO, cut speed to zero five knots, and drift."

"Aye, aye, Skipper."

Boxer's face became grim. "'Clem, prepare to fire one and two. If that *Alfa* comes for us instead of the drone, we'll have to take her out. I'd like to avoid an international incident if possible, but that *Alfa* has fired on us for the last time."

"Yes, sir," Clem replied. He was itching for some action.

Several tense minutes went by while they followed the *Alfa*'s progress on the UWIS. After floundering for a moment, it went after the drone, following it to the bottom, two thousand feet below the surface. Then, Whoomp! A violent explosion sent fragments of the drone hurtling in all directions. The force of the blast flipped the Soviet *Alfa* on its side and bounced it off the ocean floor. It was fortunate to escape the beating intact, and slowly made its way back to its mother ship.

Boxer guided the *Manta* on a wide tack around the enemy ships, drifting deep at five knots until they were well clear. Finally, Boxer ordered a course that would take them up through the fabled Northwest Passage to Alaska. He spoke to his crew on the intercom. "We were tried . . . and we were proven ready, men. Good work. I'm very proud of you." He placed a hand on Carson's shoulder and smiled at her. "That goes especially for you, Kit. You built a damn good ship."

CHAPTER EIGHTEEN

The gray military transport jet sat alone on a secluded tarmac on the far reaches of the Soviet Air Force base, surrounded by a contingency of KGB vehicles and personnel. Deputy Director Ivan Pisanya was personally herding his cadre of physicists into the plane like a mother hen clucking after her scared chicks. That's just what they act like, Pisanya thought. I have given them the chance of a lifetime to become heroes of the state, and they act as if I were sending them to a forced labor camp.

Maybe that's what they think their fate is to become. After all, they were being sent to Northern Siberia, but not to toil with their hands and their backs. Merely to test a new nuclear device away from the prying eyes of the foolish Americans. It's one thing to agree to a bi-lateral nuclear disarmament as a propaganda measure, but to actually cease testing? Ridiculous. After all, it was his job to see that the testing continued to take place, and that the Yankee imperialists were none the wiser for it. Besides, they have their damn star wars satellites.

Natasha Sharnovsky huddled in her seat between the hulking figures of the two KGB men who flanked her. She noticed that her three other esteemed colleagues received similar treatment. She was sure that her work with the Refusenik movement earned her a life sentence in a Siberian labor camp, despite assurances to the contrary from Comrade Pisanya. Who could believe a word that he says? If only her poor husband, Reuben, could somehow sneak the word out about her sudden departure to one of the human rights groups, then, maybe . . . But why think of something as hopeless as that.

Maybe we are really going on a secret mission for the Motherland. Something that required the special talents of herself and Pilchik and the Schmendrikovas. Talents such as nuclear fission specialists, biologists, and in Misha Schmendrikova's case, the foremost nuclear power plant designer to emerge since the Chernobyl disaster back in the eighties.

A dozen more burly KGB guards climbed aboard the plane, filling most of the seats. And, finally, Pisanya, himself, followed two men carrying a heavy wooden crate with fragile markings stenciled on all sides. The boarding hatch was dogged shut behind them, and the twin engines revved up while Pisanya directed the two men to secure the heavy container. As soon as this was accomplished, Pisanya shouted an order to the pilot, and the plane began to taxi slowly down the runway.

Pisanya walked back to Natasha Scharnovsky's row of seats, and motioned for her guard in the aisle seat to get up and let him sit next to the woman. He buckled in, and placed a hand over Natasha's white-knuckled grip on the armrest. "Relax, my dear. You'll see, you have nothing to fear. I will personally take you under my wing, and see that no harm comes to you."

The plane picked up speed and in a moment, the ground gave way beneath them. Natasha peered through a porthole sized window as they gained altitude, and gripped the armrests even tighter. "I'm terrified of flying," she confided to him.

Pisanya smiled and began to stroke and soothe her hand and arm. "There is nothing to worry about. The pilot is one of the finest aviators in the entire Air Force," he told her. "A full colonel. And the co-pilot and navigator are also extremely competent. I would have it no other way, considering the precious cargo that we carry."

"Your important box?" she motioned with her head.

"Ah, the detonator? Yes, that. And four very capable, and I might add, expendable, scientists. You and your colleagues will have the opportunity to share in the making of a great moment in history. Or, if you fail . . ." Pisanya shrugged his shoulders. "You will be that much closer to your God, which you hold in higher regard than the state." He continued to stroke her hand.

"Where . . . where are you taking us?" she managed.

"You are questioning *me* as to where we are going? Ha. My little chicken has summoned up some courage, I see. Well," he said, taking her hand in his, and holding it against his side, "we are flying first to Leningrad, to refuel. Then, on to Franz Josef Land, for more fuel and supplies, and to pick up a few more passengers. And finally, we fly over the pole to the New Siberian Islands. And, if you do your work well, back home again." He was actually smirking.

Natasha sat back in her seat, closed her eyes and prayed, trying to block out the ministrations of the evil man beside her, hoping either to die, or, dear God, if it's not too much to ask, for someone to learn of our plight and rescue me.

The *Manta* continued to ply her way through the straits separating Canada's northern island groups above the Arctic circle. Every forty-eight hours, at precisely midnight, Boxer brought the sub close enough to the surface for the sensitive ELF antenna to pick up messages beamed off a satellite through the Extra Low Frequency range.

Sitting in the tiny sonar room, Hi Fi Freedman recorded the excruciatingly slow message, dubbed it onto another tape at high speed, and signalled Boxer on the MC. "Conn, sonar. ELF message received, Skipper."

Boxer turned the conn over to Clemens, who had just come on duty. He headed to his cabin through the galley, checking with the night cook to see what there might be to eat. His nose told him, at the same time that the cook did, that tonight's mid-rats were pizza. He opted instead for a piece of apple pie, and a steaming cup of black coffee, and brought them into his quarters.

Hi Fi had placed the speeded-up version of the message on Boxer's navigation table, along with a headset and recorder. Boxer closed his door, took a bite of the pie and a long sip of coffee, then set up the tape and ran it through the decoder. It has been learned, the message stated, that the Soviets are planning to set off a nuclear device in one of the islands off the Arctic coast of Siberia, in violation of the Reykjavik Accords of 1990. The *Manta* is to pick up its assault force at Point Barrow and proceed to 145°15′ W long, 76°12′ N lat, and destroy the Soviet operation. There is to be no, repeat, no prisoners taken, nor any survivors left behind. The destruction must be made to appear to be a nuclear accident. It was signed by the CNO.

"Son of a bitch," Boxer cursed. The whole deal reeked with Tysin's scent. Well, he'd learn more about it when he rendezvoused with his men in Alaska.

At the Naval Arctic Research Laboratory at Point Barrow, Boxer was re-united with Major Rolly Jones and his Rangers, and introduced to Dick Dickerson's Snow Troopers. Combined, they made up an assault force of one hundred men. Together, they had to penetrate Soviet waters and destroy a military installation and who knows how many Ruskies, and make it look like an accident. He wondered how Tysin dreamed up his schemes, and shook his head. He had his orders, and he would do his best to carry them out. And when he returned, he would deal with the director of the CIA personally. There was severe payment to be extracted for all the damage that Tysin had inflicted on him and his friends.

Boxer and most of his men were enjoying their first real meal in a week, compliments of the captain in charge of the Naval Station, when they received the Mayday relayed from Ice Station Omega, situated near the North Pole. Captain Eric Dawson called Boxer aside and briefed him on the emergency message. "It seems as if a Soviet airplane has gone down on the ice cap very near the pole, around eighty-eight degrees North latitude. Our weather people are going to see what they can do to help."

Boxer nodded. "Maybe our flyboys can get out there to help."

"If the weather holds up, I suppose so. Maybe Dick's Troopers can 'chute down to the ice cap and perform the rescue."

"Sorry," Boxer told him. "They're assigned to the *Manta* on another project."

"But this may be a matter of life or death."

Boxer shrugged. "I agree with you, Captain. But without orders to the contrary, those men are moving out with me at oh-eight hundred tomorrow."

Ivan Pisanya cursed the incompetents at the airplane assembly plant who built the faulty engine, while he struggled to unlatch his seat belt, thankful that he'd kept it buckled during the final hop over the Pole. Surely, it had saved his life. The woman in the next seat was still in shock, whimpering and moaning over and over, "Oh, God . . . Oh God . . ."

He patted her hand reassuringly. "It is all right, Natasha. We are still alive, as are most of the others. I'm afraid I can't say as much for the pilot and the flight crew."

Pisanya ached all over from the impact of the crash. He stretched his arms and legs. Everything seemed to be working okay. He quickly went over a mental checklist. The detonator, first. He crawled up the incline of the floor toward the tail section, where the crated device was secured. It looked unscathed. He unlashed it and pushed it down toward the gaping hole in the fuselage where the starboard wing had been torn away. He looked around for assistance. Isn't anyone else in here capable of any action? He pushed with all his strength until the heavy crate was wedged between two rows of seats.

Now, the cockpit. The pilot lay face down, his body crushed against the icy ground from the force of the crash. The co-pilot and navigator were broken men, their limbs askew, heads cocked at odd angles. Well, too bad about them. There were more important things to do than to mourn for them. Ah, the radio.

He fiddled with the dials, and after an initial sputtering and squawking, he was able to get it to work. So far, so good. With some luck, they'd be able to reach the outpost on Zemlya Frantsa Josifa, and wait it out right here in the wreckage. There was enough cold weather gear to go around, and enough food to last for a week. Good. Now to get those stupid oafs up and around. And hope that nothing else goes wrong.

213

When he returned to his seat, Natasha Sharnovsky was still in shock. He administered several sharp slaps to her face. That seemed to bring her back.

She started to cry. "Oh, Comrade, what shall become of us? We will surely perish in this God-forsaken place. I don't want to die here."

"Don't talk of dying. We have food and water and shelter. And, hopefully, some vodka."

"But," she whimpered, "nobody knows we're here."

Pisanya put an arm around her and hugged her to him, deliberately pressing her breasts against his chest. He smiled at her discomfort. "I told you I would take care of you. We have a radio that works. It is just a matter of time until we find the correct frequency, and help is on its way to us."

Several of his men began to arouse, and he put them to work helping the injured, doling out the extra parkas and sleeping gear to ward off the terrible cold, and to prepare a meal. In a little while, one of his subordinates reported back to him, "Comrade Pisanya, I count seven dead, not counting the flight crew."

"Throw them off the plane."

"What?"

"You heard me, Comrade. I gave you an order. Throw their carcasses off the plane before they begin to decay and stink. Do I have to do all your thinking for you?"

"Yes, Comrade, at once."

"You . . . and you, there. Help him move the dead out of the plane. It's too late for them, anyway. Now move. Quickly."

Soon, the survivors were huddled in the center of the fuselage, bundled up in warm clothing, and helping themselves from tins of marinated herring, cold cabbage soup and black bread. Pisanya took a long swig from a bottle of vodka, and passed it to the KGB man next to him. After all they'd been through, they had reason to celebrate. They'd been able to transmit their situation to their forces on Franz Josef Land, and given their coordinates from the plane's navigation system. With a little luck, they'd be safely out of there within twenty-four hours. Now, finally, all is well. There was nothing else to go wrong. Pisanya took the bottle back and helped himself to another pull on the vodka.

The reverie aboard the wreckage of the plane was punctuated by a cry from outside the hull. "Ahoy, inside. Anybody there? I say, is everything okay in there?"

The Russians looked at each other in bewilderment. It sounded like English-speaking voices outside calling them. Or is it their imaginations playing tricks on them because of the severe cold.

"Ahoy, in there. Is anybody still alive?" There was a banging on the metal fuselage.

Pisanya composed himself quickly. "Listen," he said to his charges. "We are Russian civilians who were en route to Vladivostok by way of the Pole. We all have papers to prove it." He turned to Natasha. "And you, my dear, shall be my beloved wife. So act accordingly. Remember, you still have family and friends at home, so you'd better not give away our real status. Understand?"

Natasha meekly nodded her head.

"Schmendrikova, do you understand what I have just said? We are all civilians who have survived the plane crash. Your wife is dead, true, but things can be made much worse for you and your kind if you do not cooperate."

Misha Schmendrikova looked up from the chunk of

215

pumpernickel he'd been munching on and nodded. "Yes," he said. There was much bitterness in his voice. "I understand."

Pisanya made his way to the hole in the plane's hull and called out a greeting in Russian.

"Charlie, did you hear that? Someone's alive in there. The markings on the plane are in Russian. Anyway, that's what the guy's voice sounds like."

Though Ivan Pisanya spoke fluent English, albeit with a heavy accent, he chose to speak a few words in pidgin English to dupe his rescuers. "Here. Up in here," he shouted.

The first of five red-clad American rescuers from Ice Station Omega filed aboard the wreck. He sized up the situation, and called for food and medical supplies. He approached the stout, balding man who seemed to be the spokesman for the group and extended his hand. "Hi, I'm Charlie Andrews. From the American weather station about twenty miles from here."

Pisanya shook hands, smiled broadly and nodded his head. "American?" He turned to his men and pointed at Charlie Andrews and the others who were soon lugging supplies into the cabin of the plane. "Americans." And then he went on in their native tongue, careful not to betray their true identities in case any of the Americans understood their language. Pisanya turned his attention back to Andrews, pounded his chest with a fist and proclaimed, "Reuben Sharnovsky." He put a beefy arm around the only woman present and crudely pulled her to his side, grabbing a handful of her breast as if by accident. "My wife, Natasha."

Still smiling and nodding his head, he ordered her to follow suit. She did. "Natasha Sharnovsky," she told them.

Charlie Andrews noted the seemingly fearful expression on the woman's face when the heavy guy pulled her to him. Was there something fishy going on here, he wondered?

The Americans passed out chocolate bars, and prepared a large meal of noodles in broth and pemmican, a calorie-laden mixture of dried meat and fat. All of the Russians took the chocolate; some partook of the other food, while others twitched their noses at the strange mixture and declined. Lloyd Wright, the Omega Station's medic, set about treating the various cuts and bruises suffered during the crash, and set a few broken bones with the help of his colleagues. One KGB officer was visibly relieved when his broken leg was set with an inflatable cast, and smiled his gratitude while being injected with Demerol to stop the pain.

Charlie Andrews told Pisanya, "We have snowmobiles and sleds outside. We will take you to our weather station and notify your people. They can fly in and pick you up there."

"You take us to military station? You are to arrest us? We have done nothing."

Andrews laughed. "Hell, no. We're not going to arrest you. We're going to help you get someplace nice and warm and dry. We'll feed you and provide shelter until we can get you turned over to your people. Understand? We're your friends," Charlie told them.

"Friends. Ah, friends," Pisanya acknowledged, all smiles. He turned to the other Russians and spoke rapidly in his native tongue. "Friends," he said several times, pointing in the direction of the Americans.

After eating and attending the wounded, the five Americans helped the dozen Russians onto sleds hitched to snowmobiles, and headed northwest to Omega Station. There was a heated discussion between Pisanya and Andrews about bringing along a strange wooden crate, but Pisanya insisted that it was a much needed heating unit for his family in Vladivostok. Reluctantly, Andrews agreed. They reached the weather station five hours later. Late evening, except that you couldn't tell by looking. The sun never sets on the pole at this time during the summer.

Omega Station consisted of a series of double-walled inflatable Quonset huts, an eighty foot tall antenna alongside an insulated concrete-block building which was the radio shack, and several outbuildings. The radio tower had four receiving dishes attached, as well as radar scanners and reflectors. Closer to the base, a hand-made sign read, WELCOME TO THE NORTH POLE, and in smaller letters, UNITED STATES WEATHER STATION OMEGA.

The bright orange of the huts, and the red foul weather parkas on the Americans were the only flashes of color on the otherwise white surroundings all the way to the horizon on a 360° azimuth.

Another meal was prepared, and the guests were provided sleeping quarters in the huts. The radioman, a bearded hulk named Bernie Baer went out into the cold to call in the successful rescue. Bernie, who dressed in overalls and a heavy red-plaid flannel shirt looked like one of his namesakes, a grizzly with an almost human face added.

When it came time to bed down for the night, Pisanya insisted on zipping two sleeping bags together for himself and his "wife," Natasha. Again, Charlie Andrews thought it a bit strange, but the woman seemed to be going along with him against her will. She did not seem at all happy with the sleeping arrangements, but said nothing. Well, marital disputes were not Charlie's concern, and so they all went to sleep.

Andrews was awakened roughly at 0700 by one of the Russians sitting on his arms and chest, and with a 9 mm automatic pistol an inch from his right eye. A furtive glance sideways told him the fate of his associates was the same. The Russians had pulled a fast one on them.

Pisanya stretched out, scratched his groin, and strode over to where the leader of the American team was entombed in his sleeping bag. Pisanya pointed a finger at Andrews's head. "You and your men are our prisoners. Do as we say, and you will not be hurt. And when our comrades come to rescue us from this place, you will be given an opportunity to become our guests, in our country."

"What the hell . . . ?" Charlie Andrews was stopped short by the pistol barrel pressed against his lips.

"We simply did not want to be turned over to our people by your military. It might prove a problem if they discover who we are. And I'm sure my close associates will be very interested in the observations of you and your men at the station here. I think they'll learn a lot more than just the weather from you." Pisanya was smiling down on him.

One of the KGB men said something to Pisanya in Russian. Ivan nodded. "Yes, we must radio our position and the situation to our outpost. Wait . . . where is the big one that resembles a grizzly bear? I don't see him here."

Pisanya took in the entire hut. There were four Americans now tightly bound in their sleeping bags. A fifth bag was empty and rolled up against a wall. "Where is he?"

growled Pisanya. He looked down directly at Andrews.

Charlie stared up the barrel of the gun pointed at him, but kept silent.

Pisanya nodded at his man sitting on Andrews.

The barrel of the gun cracked sharply across Charlie's face, closing an eye, and drawing blood from a gash on his brow. "I said, 'Where is he'?"

Charlie Andrews said nothing.

A Russian said something, and Pisanya nodded. "Of course. He's the radioman. Marko," he called to one of his men standing nearby. "You and Anatoly go to the radio shack and take care of the bearded one. A shame. He looks like he could be a Russian."

The two KGB men bundled up and walked to the radio shack. When they walked in, Bernie Baer was pouring himself a steaming cup of coffee. He was surprised to see the Russians in the radio room without an escort, but figured maybe Charlie sent them with a note to try and reach their people, let them know all was well.

Bernie held up the coffee pot and cup, an offering to the guests. He was answered by two automatic pistols drawn and pointed at him, not five feet away. Well, he figured, desperate times call for desperate actions. He splashed the cupfuls of hot coffee into the face of the nearest Russian, and threw the pot at the other. He dove for cover behind some equipment.

Marko screamed and held his hands to his face. The hot coffee scalded his face, and he was temporarily blinded. Anatoly overcame the surprise and pain of being hit in the head by a hot coffee pot, and fired off several shots in Bernie's direction. Then there was silence.

Something clinked on the floor to Anatoly's right, and he wheeled and fired at it.

220

A massive forearm wrapped across Anatoly's neck, lifted him a foot off the ground, and was choking the life out of him. His gun dropped impotently to the floor. His hands went up to pry away the arm that was killing him, his eyes bulged, his face turned a deep purple and his tongue hung out of his mouth. He pleaded wordlessly with his partner to save him.

Marko stood ten feet away, one hand covering a badly burned eye, the other hand pointing a pistol at the two of them. The massive American had poor Anatoly dangling like a puppet, all the while inching closer and closer to Marko.

Two shots rang out. Anatoly's body twitched and went limp. A surprised Bernie Baer dropped the Russian and placed a hand over a burning sensation in his chest. The hand came away bloody. "Why you crazy bastard. Kill your own man to get me? Why you—"

The next two shots stopped the charging bear of a man three feet from Marko. The KGB man emptied his gun in panic. The hulk toppled him over and covered him, the final gesture of a dying man fighting for his life.

Marko lay there under the weight of Bernie's body, the bulk crushing him. The Russian pushed the body off and stood on shaky legs. He was filthy, and covered with the American's blood. The bear was dead. Now, he had to tell this story to his superior. He knew Pisanya would not be pleased by their blundering. He sighed heavily and made his way back to the main hut.

CHAPTER NINETEEN

Borodine passed the conn to his exec, Viktor, and climbed the stainless steel ladder leading to the outside bridge. Though it was summer, he was conscious of the blast of cold air coming from the north. Must be a storm brewing over the Pole, he figured, turning up his jacket collar. He scanned the horizon with a pair of powerful glasses. To the north and east, nothing but deep blue seas, clear skies with an occasional puff of cumulus cloud, and bright sunshine in spite of the chill. To the south and west stood the approach to the fjord which led to the shipyards and naval base at Polyarnyy. The craggy cliffs acted as buffers against the blustery wind as he guided the *Sea Demon* home.

The intercom crackled, and then the voice of the radio officer came on. "Comrade, greetings to you from Admiral Medvezhka. Over."

"Thank you, Comrade. Patch him through to the bridge. I'll take the message up here."

Another crackle and Medvezhka's voice was heard. "Welcome home, Igor. How went the trials?"

Why is he calling me on the sub when we are only five miles from the base, Borodine wondered. "Excellent, Comrade Admiral. The *Sea Demon* has done everything I have asked of her. She is a good ship."

"And the crew?"

"They have performed admirably, sir."

"Good. Good. Igor, please come to my quarters as soon as the *Sea Demon* is dockside. There is an assignment for you, and I want to brief you personally."

The hairs on the back of Borodine's neck prickled. Was it the Arctic breeze? He said, "Yes, Comrade Admiral. I will see you as soon as we dock." But Medvezhka had already switched off. What could it be that the Admiral of the North Fleet deems so important, he wondered. Well, we will find out soon enough, won't we. And, whatever it is, I'll be ready for it.

Borodine guided the *Sea Demon* into the holding area on her own power, ever so slowly, with just enough speed to maintain steerageway. He disdained having the giant sub towed into its berth by tugboat. It was the mark of a captain's seamanship to handle a tricky task such as this. He eased the *Sea Demon* gently alongside the long wharf. Immediately, two of his crewmen tossed lines ashore. These lines in turn were attached to heavy hawsers which were attached to immense iron stanchions.

Satisfied his ship was secure, Borodine turned the preparations over to Viktor and headed directly to the Admiral of the North Fleet's quarters. He was admitted forthwith. He saluted his superior, and Medvezhka motioned him to a seat. "Igor, I have an assignment for you of the utmost urgency. I must order you to depart immediately to the North Pole. A planeload of nuclear scientists accompanied by a KGB detail have crashlanded near an American weather station. We must get them out before the Yankee imperialists get to them."

Borodine shrugged. "Why not simply fly them out?"

"That is now impossible. There is a severe storm over

223

the polar region. The only way to get them out is by submarine."

"But, Comrade Admiral, my men have just returned from an intense two week training period. They need to be rested."

"Comrade, they are Soviet sailors, and they will do as they are told. As will you. Our people were on a highly sensitive mission, the nature of which we can't have fall into the hands of the enemy. And there is some equipment with them, very secretive, that would give the Americans a great propaganda victory over us, should they recover it. It is imperative that you and your crew leave immediately. The *Sea Demon* is being resupplied now. You leave at eighteen-hundred hours."

"Eighteen-hundred hours, today?" Borodine couldn't believe what he'd heard.

"That's correct, Comrade. Your orders are to safely return our people and their special equipment. And you will also bring back any American survivors from the weather station."

Borodine shook his head. "But that is in violation of international law. It could start a war. Surely, you don't . . ."

Medvezhka slammed his fist on his desk and shouted, "Surely you will follow your orders, Comrade Admiral, or you will just as surely be brought to trial and found guilty of treason against the Motherland. Is that quite clear?"

"I understand what you have said." Borodine tried to reason with Medvezhka. "But please try to understand the implications of . . ."

"Igor," the older man said. "Those Americans may already know too much about our aborted mission.

And they are the only direct proof of what went on up there. With them in our possession, the imperialists can only conjecture. So you see, Comrade, it is imperative that you proceed at once and remove all traces of our people being there."

Borodine knew that any further argument would be fruitless. With a sigh he said, "We will need a landing force."

"Done," smiled Medvezhka. "There are a hundred men of the elite Arctic Wolves standing by to go aboard the *Sea Demon*. And you will have an escort of two hunter-killer subs to assist you. The *Yalta* and the *Sevastopol*."

"Very well, Comrade. I'd better go help with the reloading. Is there anything else?"

"Yes, one other thing, Igor. If the Americans resist leaving with you, kill them. That's all. Dismissed."

Borodine saluted, did a sharp about-face and walked out of his superior's office. This time, he knew, the bristling on the back of his neck was not caused by a frigid blast from the Arctic.

0700 hours. Boxer was supervising the final preparations before embarking for the New Siberian Islands from the sail's bridge. Dick Dickerson's Snow Troopers and Rolly's Rangers were already aboard with their equipment, and several of the *Manta*'s crewmen were preparing to cast off. The conning tower's intercom crackled and Hi Fi Freedman's voice came through. "Conn, sonar. I have a message for you from Captain Eric Dawson, Skipper."

"Patch him through, Hi Fi."

"Aye, aye, Skipper."

"Admiral Boxer, Dawson here. There's been a change in your orders. It seems that the plane that went down over the Pole was carrying the very same hot shot Ruskies that you were going after. And they've taken over Omega Station, sir. The radioman up there died trying to get out the message to us. The CNO's been advised of the situation, and the severe weather over the Pole, and issued the new orders. I'll send over a courier at once."

"Roger that, Captain. And thanks."

"Aye, aye, sir."

Upon receipt of his orders, Boxer went below, ordered the sail retracted, and the *Manta* slipped below the Beaufort Sea. He gave orders to Lieutenant Carson, and she dialed in a depth of two hundred feet. The ballast tanks flooded, the diving planes adjusted accordingly and they slowly angled downward at the bows until they reached the desired depth. The sub leveled off smoothly.

Boxer keyed his MC mike. "Helmsman, come to course one five five true."

"Aye, aye, Skipper. Course one five five," Mahoney replied.

"EO, go to flank speed."

"Flank speed, aye, aye, Skipper. Going to five zero knots."

"Roger that," Boxer answered. He called Mark Clemens and Kit Carson to the plotting screen, and pointed out their projected route. "Basically," he said, "we'll be following the same route as the *Nautilus* did on the very first underwater passage to the Pole in 1958. But we'll have to make much better time. Omega

226

Station's been taken over by a group of Russians. And you can bet that they've sent for help getting out."

"We'll have to get there first," Clemens added.

Boxer nodded his head. "And possibly have a fight on our hands if we don't."

"But they can't just hold our people like that. That goes against international law," Carson said.

Boxer smiled wryly. "That's being naive, Kit. The Ruskies are notorious for doing that."

"What do you figure our ETA, Skipper?"

"Well, Clem. We've got a thousand miles ahead of us. If we can maintain flank speed all the way we should be in the vicinity of Omega Station by oh-three hundred tomorrow morning. Then we'll blast our way to the surface and rescue our people. That is, if the Ruskies haven't snatched them first."

Boxer set the course of the *Manta* on AUTONAV, and they raced flat out toward the North Pole at nearly 50 knots, continually diving deeper under the polar ice cap. After twenty hours, as they approached 88° N. lat., they first picked up the sound patterns of other submarines. "Conn, sonar," Hi Fi reported. "We've got company, Skipper."

Boxer walked back to the sonar room and stuck his head inside. "What's up, Hi Fi?"

"Multiple targets, Skipper. From the noise profile, I read two Soviet *Alfa*s and something bigger. Sorta like a boomer, only different."

"Good work, Hi Fi. What's your best guess?"

Freedman tossed an extra headset to Boxer and they listened together. "Hear that, Skipper? That's twin screws. The Ruskies use them extensively."

Boxer nodded. He already knew that, but he let the

young sonarman continue.

"The sounds are very similar to our *Barracuda,* Skipper. Even closer to the *Shark.* We learned about that prototype in our history of submarine warfare class."

Another wise-guy heard from, Boxer mused. Was he really getting that old that several of his young officers studied his original supersub, the *Shark,* in a history class? "Well, if it's a supersub you hear, Hi Fi, and it's got twin screws, then it has to belong to the Ruskies." Boxer smiled at the thought. "Maybe even my old friend, Comrade Admiral Igor Borodine."

"Borodine? He still around? Learned about him in history class, too," Hi Fi said, very seriously.

Boxer rolled his eyes heavenward. Ah, youth, he sighed. A shame it's wasted on young people. "If it is Borodine, let's hope he hasn't found us yet."

Boxer returned to the command center and issued several orders. "EO, slow to zero five knots."

"Aye, aye, Skipper. Slowing to zero five knots."

"Roger that. Carson, switch over to MANSYS."

"Going to manual. Aye, aye, Skipper."

"Mahoney, come to course two four zero degrees."

"Coming to two four zero, Skipper."

Boxer said to his EXO, "Clem, you've got the conn for now." Then he went to the sonar room. "Hi Fi, let me know the moment you pick up any communication between those subs and Omega Station. I want an exact fix on it."

"Aye, aye, Skipper."

Boxer went into the midships area occupied by the assault troops. "Rolly, Dickerson, bring your squad leaders and meet me in the ward room, now."

"Yes, sir," they chorused, and gathered up their team

228

leaders. Rolly Jones showed up with Mean Gene, Snappy and Long John Silverman. Double Dick came with three of his men, and they each took seats on either side of a rectangular table mounted to the deck. Boxer stood at the head of the table, drawing a diagram on a green chalkboard behind him. He turned to his men.

"It seems that the Ruskies have beaten us to the punch. We've got to assume that they have control of Omega Station, and that our people there are prisoners. According to Captain Dawson, this is the layout of the weather station."

The board had a sketch of two rows of three attached inflatable Quonset huts, running parallel. A concrete block radio shack was set two hundred feet to the west, adjacent to the antenna tower. There were several outbuildings dotting the camp. And beyond the tower, there was a cleared off stretch of ice used as an airfield.

"We picked up the Ruskie subs around here. This is about thirty degrees east longitude, but the lines get very close up this far north. My guess is, the station is between us and them. As soon as I get confirmation of that, we move out."

Dickerson cleared his throat.

"What is it, Dick?" Boxer asked.

"I'd like to make a suggestion, Skipper."

Boxer nodded his assent.

"If those positions turn out to be correct, I would hit them with a two pronged assault. My Snow Troopers could circle around behind the Ruskies and draw them off, away from the *Manta*. Then Rolly's Rangers could charge them in a frontal assault, rescue our men, and fight their way back to the sub."

Rolly nodded his agreement. "Good idea, only one thing still bothers me."

"What's that?" Boxer asked.

"What happens to Double Dick and his guys? They'd have to fight their way back through the entire enemy line. They'd be too far away for us to help them."

Boxer looked at Dickerson. "Dick?"

"We'll take our chances, Skipper. This is the kind of job we do best. Besides, it will give you time to get the Russian scientists, too, if you want. Maybe if we give them the opportunity, they'll defect."

"Good thought, Dick. And we could give you covering fire from the *Manta*'s heavy machine guns. And we could launch the chopper to give you some air cover."

"He'd be a sitting duck up here, Skipper," Dickerson warned.

Boxer shrugged. "We'll take our chances on that. Now, are we agreed on the plan?"

"Fine, Kit. The ice looks to be no more than a foot or so thick. No problem for the *Manta*." He keyed the MC. "Mahoney, left rudder ten degrees. Come to two one zero."

"Aye, aye, Skipper."

"EO, keep her at zero four knots."

"Zero four knots. Aye, aye, Skipper. Steady as she goes."

Boxer called to Chief White, seated at the Dive Center. "Whitey, bring her up very slowly. I want to just break the surface, then periscope up."

The COB repeated back the orders and then gently coaxed the diving control lever back. The *Manta* shivered and rose up several feet. A scraping, crunching sound was heard throughout the ship, and they broke surface.

"Good job, Whitey. Periscope up."

Clemens activated the periscope mechanism, and Boxer took his place at the eyepiece. "Bitch of a storm brewing outside," Boxer commented. "Visibility's almost nil."

"The better for us," Dickerson remarked. He turned to his white parka clad troopers and said. "Let's move out, men."

A good deal of the Snow Troopers ability to elude the enemy lay in its maintaining absolute radio silence. As long as they didn't transmit, they wouldn't be detected. Therefore, at the end of one hour, precisely, Rolly Jones led his Rangers out onto the ice without any assurance that Double Dick's men were in position to draw off the enemy. They would simply do their assigned job, and hope that Dickerson's men did theirs. Boxer watched the last of them disappear from view into the snowstorm, and climbed below to the inside bridge.

Double Dick gave the thumbs up, quickly followed by his squad leaders doing the same. Rolly sat there silently for a moment, looked into the eyes of each of his NCOs and finally said, "Okay by me. Let's do it."

Hi Fi knocked on the bulkhead separating the ward room from the mess hall. "Excuse me, Skipper, but there's been quite a bit of radio activity among the three subs, and between the boomer and the station. That puts Omega station between us and the Ruskies."

"Just as we suspected. Okay, men. We'll find a Pollyanna or some thin ice to surface. Dick, how much time do you need to get into position?"

"An hour too much?"

"Okay, an hour it is. Synchronize your watches, men. And get your battle gear."

Boxer returned to the COMMCOMP and activated the hydraulics systems that raised the sail. Boxer knew that the Arctic ice cap was a constantly shifting mass, breaking apart, drifting in more or less preset patterns, and grinding together, leaving open leads of water and raised pressure ridges that mottled the surface. Hopefully, these raised projections would offer some protection to the Snow Troopers.

He called Carson over to the UWIS screen. "Kit, find us a lead to surface in. We're letting off Dickerson and his men."

"Aye, aye, Skipper." She studied the screen for several minutes. "Skipper, this looks promising."

Boxer joined her in front of the console which displayed the area directly overhead. She pointed to a lightly shaded area on the screen. "This looks like a recently frozen over lead." She tapped the suspected area on the console.

Mark Clemens came over with two cups of steaming black coffee, and handed one to Boxer. "Thanks, Clem." He took a sip of the piping hot brew. "All we can do now is wait for a signal. And hope."

Clemens nodded and they both sipped their coffee. Carson joined them and said, "The chopper is ready in the launch well. It gets propelled skyward just like a missile. In fact, we copied the same technology. At fifty feet, the rotors spring open, already rotating."

Boxer smiled. "You've done a good job, Kit."

Suddenly, the intercom squawked, and Hi Fi's excited voice came on. "Conn, sonar. Two targets approaching,

Skipper. Bearing zero three five degrees and zero four zero degrees . . . Range ten thousand yards . . . Speed four zero knots and closing."

Boxer switched on the klaxon siren and began giving a series of commands. "Dive . . . dive," he began.

CHAPTER TWENTY

Captain Dick Dickerson knew that the storm was his ally, not his enemy. His well trained troops were fanned out behind the enemy encampment, just outside the perimeter of Omega Station. His watch read zero minus two minutes, and the Russians hadn't spotted them yet. Good thing, he thought, for he'd recognized the uniforms of the infamous Arctic Wolves, their Soviet counterparts.

Dickerson had a mortar unit flanked wide to the right, to draw off the bulk of the Russian assault force. Then two of his squads would move in behind them, cut off the Arctic Wolves from the mother ship, whose black fifty foot sail towered above the ice, betraying its position to the Snow Troopers. His remaining men would swing around to within the station's perimeter and keep the Ruskies clear so Rolly could do his job.

It was T-minus ten seconds . . . nine . . . eight . . . the seconds ticked off slowly . . . a knot tightened in Dickerson's gut, a good sign; his system was pumping adrenaline . . . he was ready. Whump . . . whump . . . whump. The mortar-fired rockets walked a path through the Arctic Wolf bivouac, exploding, throwing chunks of ice and bodies through the air. Three more rockets disturbed their brief respite, sending shards of ice and shrapnel into unsuspecting Russian troopers, elite no longer, now very dead.

"There. Over there." A Russian commander barked at

his men. He pointed out the trajectory of the rockets, yet another round incoming while he shouted to his men, "Move. Move. Over there. Get them."

Ivan Pisanya watched his rescuers take off away from the station, and ran shouting after them. He caught up with Captain Alexandrovich, their leader. "I am Deputy Director Ivan Pisanya, of the Second Directorate. I demand that your men return to the station to protect us."

Alexandrovich pushed him off. "Keep back, you fool. You will get us all killed."

"I gave you an order, Captain."

Alexandrovich wheeled around to find Pisanya aiming a handgun at him. He called over his shoulder to some of his men nearby. "Gregor, Josef, if this fool shoots me, kill him." The captain turned his back and ran after his troops, leaving Pisanya standing there with a pistol in his hand, staring down the barrels of two AK-47 assault rifles. He growled at the fleeing figure and pocketed his gun. Dejectedly he went back to the camp, swearing revenge on the impertinent leader of the Arctic Wolves.

At the sound of the first concussions of the mortar rockets, Rolly directed his squad leaders. "John, radio shack. Carlos, your men cover him. Mean Gene, you and Snappy take the Quonset huts. Do it." They slipped away from the *Manta,* and silently made their way to Omega Station, encountering no resistance. The defenders were busy fighting off the Snow Troopers off to the east.

Long John Silverman's team took the radio shack. They surprised the lone occupant, Marko, who was too slow getting his gun out. He died with a bullet in his forehead, a shocked look on his face and his hand in his pocket, still wrapped around the butt of a 9 mm automatic.

Silverman tagged two of his fighters. "Baker, Szabo, man the radios. The rest of you, come with me." With that, they left the only formidable shelter in the station to join up with Carlos Rivera and his team. The other buildings were made up of double-walled nylon fabric, inflated over support frames. They were meant to ward off the cold, not enemy fire.

Snappy motioned Mean Gene around the far side of the twin rows of huts. His own men split up at the front entrances, poised to strike. Five men burst through the entrance to the east wing, and dropped to the floor. There was no resistance. The hut seemed empty. Mean Gene's men charged through the rear and encountered the same.

Snappy gave a signal to his squad, and kicked open the door. "Now," he shouted, and led the charge into the hut.

The KGB men were hiding behind the Americans still tied up in their sleeping bags. Pisanya shielded himself behind Misha and Natasha, the two surviving scientists.

Snappy hesitated for a moment, in fear of hitting a non-combatant. It cost him dearly. The KGB men opened fire immediately. Snappy went down. He managed to get off a shot. A KGB man yelped in pain. Another KGB volley cut down the next two Rangers, and cut off Snappy's life.

Some of the Arctic Wolves were alerted to the action at the Ice Station by the gunfire, and returned to investigate. Rolly Jones fired an M-16 burst, downing the first man. "John, Carlos," he yelled. "Set up a perimeter here and hold them off."

The two squads set up between the huts and the regrouping Arctic Wolves. The fighting soon became intense. Rolly crouched and ran to Mean Gene, at the west wing of huts. "What's going on here?"

Gene shook his head. "Stalemate. The fuckers have hostages in there, so we can't get off any clean shots. They got Snappy and two of his guys."

Rolly tossed an idea around in his head for a moment. "Torch 'em."

"What the . . ."

"You heard me, torch the huts. With that flimsy nylon

236

fabric, and the air wrap between the layers, those huts will go up like a tinder box."

"But what about our people inside?" Gene asked.

Rolly replied, "They're in little danger. The flames will be well over their heads. But if we do this quickly, we'll have the element of surprise, and those KGB bastards will have nowhere to hide."

"Right." Mean Gene passed the word along and within minutes, a dozen men stood along both sides of the west wing of nylon huts waiting to light their makeshift torches.

"Now," Rolly shouted. Torches were lit, touched against the orange fabric, and with a tremendous roar, the huts seemed to disintegrate in a sea of flames.

Mean Gene yelled, "Drop."

Pisanya immediately sensed what was happening, and fell to the floor. Natasha and Misha watched him, and followed suit, dropping alongside him.

The KGB men stood up, fanned out into a semi-circle and began to fire. It was of no avail. Rolly's men let loose with the M-16's, firing staccato bursts into the Russians. In less than ten seconds, it was over. Eight KGB men lay dead. The Americans from Omega Station lay safe in their sleeping bag cocoons.

Ivan Pisanya slowly rose with one hand raised over his head. With the other, he dragged up Natasha beside him. The other bewildered scientist got up also. Pisanya smiled broadly and nodded his head while saying, "Reuben Sharnovsky." He tapped his chest with his fist. "My wife, Natasha." He held her tightly to him by her coat sleeve. In Russian, he said to her, *sotto voce,* "Smile and nod, you twit or I will kill you right now." Pisanya continued, pointing to Misha, "Misha Schmendrikova, good man, scientist, yes? We thank you for save us from KGB."

One of the Rangers, Pete Smirnov, recognized the few fragments of Pisanya's speech from childhood memories

237

of Russian spoken at home, and nudged Rolly, whispering his premonitions in Jones's ear. Rolly noticed the fear in the woman's eyes, and said to her directly, "We will protect you. Is he telling the truth?"

Pisanya glared at her, an unspoken warning of what might happen to her husband and others she left behind if she betrayed him.

"Yes, yes," she blurted out.

Misha stared at her in disbelief. Now is your chance, Natasha, his eyes seemed to say.

Natasha broke down in tears. "No. No," she cried, breaking away from Pisanya. She dropped to her knees, blubbering, "He is one of them. The worst."

Immediately, a dozen M-16s pointed at the KGB man. "Freeze, motherfucker," Gene shouted.

Pisanya stood there with his hand in his pocket, gripping the butt of a 9 mm automatic pistol.

Natasha continued, "He is Ivan Pisanya, Deputy Director of the KGB Second Directorate," she continued in her halting English. "He threatened to kill us."

"I know," Rolly said, casting a glance at the grinning Pete Smirnov. "You have nothing more to fear from this man." He turned to Mean Gene. "Okay, take him."

In moments, Pisanya was bound with his arms behind him, gagged and blindfolded. The Americans from Omega Station were released. Rolly took one last look around and said to his Rangers, "Good work, men. Now, let's get out of here and make our way back to the *Manta.*"

"Piece of cake, Rolly," Mean Gene said. "Nothing to it."

Silverman came running to the burned out huts, and reported to his CO. "Rolly, we've got us a problem here."

Rolly Jones looked at his squad leader, as if to say well, what is it?

"There's no sub, sir. The *Manta*'s disappeared."

"Dive . . . dive . . . All systems on MANSYS," Boxer ordered. "Whitey, bring her down to one zero zero feet."

"One zero zero feet, Aye, aye, sir," the chief of the boat repeated, and pulled back sharply on the diving lever. Simultaneously, Lieutenant Carson flooded the forward ballast tanks.

Boxer and his exec, Clemens watched on the UWIS screen as they slipped below the ice cap. The polar ice took on the shape of many upside-down valleys among the many inverted ice ridges caused by the constantly shifting, grinding movements of the ice floes. A nuclear submarine could hide out interminably within them.

"Targets bearing zero four zero and zero four five degrees, respectively, Skipper. Range six thousand yards . . . Depth zero five zero feet . . . Speed four five knots and closing fast."

Boxer keyed the MC. "Helmsman, hard right rudder. Come to course zero nine five degrees."

Mahoney replied, "Zero nine five, aye, aye, Skipper."

"EO, give me all you've got. Now."

"Aye, aye, Skipper."

Hi Fi interjected, "Four new targets, Skipper, bearing four zero zero degrees . . . Range five thousand yards . . . Depth one zero zero feet . . . Speed seven zero knots and fast approaching."

"Roger that, Mahoney. At seventy knots, that can only be those damned killer darts. Whitey, dive to two zero zero feet."

"Aye, aye, sir. Coming to two zero zero feet."

"Skipper, all four targets are following our wake. Range now three thousand yards."

"Damn," Boxer cursed. "All hands brace for a hit."

The first killer darted narrowly missed the *Manta*. The second struck the base of the sail, and exploded. The

Manta rolled on its starboard side.

"Hold on," Boxer shouted. Those that did not were thrown to the deck or crashed into the bulkheads or the equipment.

The third killer dart found its mark on the portside hull, just amidships, and the last Soviet projectile struck directly below, on the newly exposed underbelly of the sub. The *Manta* shuddered violently, and spiralled downward.

Boxer had strapped himself into his seat at the first warning of attack. He shook his head clear, aware that the firing could resume momentarily. He checked around the attack center. Clemens was strapped into his seat, but slumped over the UWIS console. Carson lay prone on the deck. Whitey was secured into his swivel chair in the Dive Control Center, and seemed to be okay. Boxer switched on the intercom. "DCO report on damages and casualties."

"Conn, DCO," the Damage Control Officer replied. "The sail is jammed, Skipper. Part of the sealing flange is caved in and pressing into the tower. Also, there's some leakage showing on the DC computer."

"Go on."

DCO continued, "The other two hits didn't do any damage to the hull, Skipper. The turtle shell held up."

"Good. Thank God for that."

"There are at least ten men injured, Skipper. At least a few of them serious."

"I've got two hurt in here, DCO. Carson's unconscious and it looks as if Mr. Clemens is just coming to."

"Roger that, Skipper. I'll have Doc get to them as soon as I can. Over."

"Tend to the worse wounded first, DCO. The dead will take care of themselves."

"Aye, aye, Skipper."

Boxer knew that he could live with the sail jammed in the raised position. At worst, it would cut five knots off their flank speed, and cause some loss of maneuverability. He was very concerned about Carson. He unbuckled his safety harness, and dropped to where she lay prone on the deck. "Kit? Kit, are you okay?"

No response. Boxer touched his fingers to her neck and felt for a carotid pulse. He checked the seconds display of his chronograph. The pulse was slow and weak, but at least it was present. He placed his face next to her lips and was pleased to feel her breath against his skin. She seemed to be all right for the moment.

He got up and checked on his EXO. Clemens was trying to sit up, his hand pressed against the flow of blood from a scalp wound. "You okay, Clem?"

Clemens smiled weakly. "Roger that, Skipper. I guess I banged my head on the UWIS console."

Boxer placed a grateful hand on Clemens's shoulder. Clem looked up, cocked his head and listened intently. "Skipper, you hear that? You're being paged on the MC."

"Now that you mention it, Clem. My ears have been ringing since the first hit."

Over and over in a frantic monotone, came Hi Fi's voice. "Conn, sonar. Do you read me? Come in, Skipper, please."

Boxer grabbed the mike. "Sonar, conn. I read you, Hi Fi."

"Whew. I was afraid you were . . ."

"What's up, Hi Fi?" Boxer interrupted.

"The original two targets have turned away from us, Skipper. They must presume we're goners."

"Well, their presumption is a bit premature, don't you think?"

"Aye, aye, Skipper." There was new life in Freedman's voice.

"Then I think we'll have to teach them a lesson in manners. See if you can raise them on the UWIS."

"Sorry, Skipper, I tried to tell you, the UWIS is out.

241

Did something hit against it?"

Boxer looked at his exec, pressing a handkerchief against his bloody scalp. "You might say that, Hi Fi. It might have been worse if Mr. Clemens hadn't used his head."

Hi Fi couldn't understand the laughter in the attack center at a time like this. "It's very difficult to find them on sonar, Skipper. The image of the subs and the under-surface of the ice cap are too similar. Wait. I could try to track them with the HSID."

"The what?" Clemens asked.

"The Heat-Sensitive Imaging Device," Hi Fi told him. "One of Lieutenant Carson's babies. I'll try to raise those two hunter subs with their heat signatures. They'll stand out like sore thumbs against the ice pack."

"Do it, Hi Fi. We've got to take them out if we're to get out of the Arctic alive."

"Aye, aye, Skipper."

"Excuse me, Skipper." It was Chief 'Doc' Calahan, the ship's quartermaster, and acting medical officer. "You've got casualties in here?"

Boxer pointed to Carson, still lying on the deck. "Lieutenant Carson's taken a spill."

The medic knelt besides Kit and ran one hand over her cervical spine, while checking for a pulse with the other.

"Pulse was fifty and weak," Boxer helped out. "And she's still breathing."

Calahan looked up at him. "That's about what I get. Her neck doesn't appear to be broken. I'm going to try to turn her over." He called to an assistant who had just arrived in the attack center. "Give me a hand with her, will ya?"

Together, they very carefully turned Carson face up. There was a large bump on the center of her forehead. Suddenly, her eyes twitched, then opened. "What . . . wha . . . ?"

"Take it easy, now," Doc Calahan said softly, pressing her down with a gentle hand. "I think you've suffered a concussion. You need to rest."

Calahan looked up at Boxer. "The sick bay is full, Skipper."

"Put her in my cabin, Doc. And take good care of her." As Carson looked at him, he smiled back. "She's one of the best men I've got."

"Skipper, targets bearing one six zero degrees . . . Range eight thousand yards . . . Speed ten knots. They seem to be drifting to the surface."

"Probably think they sank us, the bastards. Let's teach them some manners."

"Yes, sir."

"Whitey, I want to take us up using only our own buoyancy."

"Aye, aye, sir."

"EO," Boxer spoke into the MC. "Keep her under zero four knots."

"Aye, aye, Skipper. I'll give you just enough to steer by."

"Roger that, EO." He turned to his exec, who was having his scalp wound bandaged by the medic. "Okay, Clem. Let's teach them a lesson."

Clemens smiled broadly. Boxer keyed his MC mike and said, "Mahoney, right rudder ten degrees. Come to course zero four five."

"Aye, aye, Skipper. Coming to zero four five."

"FTO," Boxer ordered, "Arm tubes one, two, three, and four with heat seekers."

The Forward Torpedo Officer repeated back the orders while operating the electronic torpedo loading mechanism. One by one the fish slipped into their tubes, ready to be launched by the turn of a dial and press of a red switch.

Boxer said to his EXO, "Clem, figure out a firing solution for those two *Alfa*s as soon as Hi Fi reads you the

243

coordinates."

"Aye, aye, Skipper."

"Targets bearing zero three zero degrees, Skipper. Range eight thousand yards . . . Speed zero five knots. They're hovering just below the ice cap, Skipper. I don't think they've heard us yet. I haven't heard their active sonar yet."

"Roger that, Hi Fi." He placed a hand on Clemens's shoulder. "Slave the fish in on those coordinates, Clem, and fire when ready."

"With pleasure, Skipper." Clemens punched in the coordinates, spun a dial until a red LED display lit up over his console. He turned a lever, and they listened. They could barely detect a pop as the torpedo hatches opened, and a hiss of the compressed gas that expelled the torpedoes from the tubes. They watched the heat image of the fish converge with the two larger images on the Fire Control screen. Suddenly, twin explosions. The force of the sound waves sent the *Manta* careening downward.

"Bulls-eye, Skipper. We did it. We got the two *Alfa*s." Boxer yelled, "Whitey!"

The COB replied, "Under control, Skipper."

Boxer watched on the DDRO screen as the *Manta* leveled off at two hundred feet. The depth gauge on the bulkhead overhead verified that. "Good work, Whitey." And to Clemens, "We'd better go back and pick up the assault force before they get into trouble."

CHAPTER TWENTY-ONE

Soviet Captain Alexandrovich came to the same realization as Major Rolly Jones, at almost the same moment: The American submarine had disappeared. A quick glance behind him assured the Russian leader that the huge black conning tower of the *Sea Demon* was still where they left it. They had only to retreat to their sub to be rescued. But Alexandrovich would not leave without the scientists, and any remaining KGB men.

He ordered a dozen men to dig in and hold off the Snow Troopers for as long as they could. With the remainder, he would re-take the weather station in a surprise turnabout attack. The Americans would expect him to retreat. Instead, he would storm their position.

With the dozen men defending his back, Alexandrovich rallied the others. It was his sixty against, what, maybe two dozen Americans. Divide and conquer, Caesar, the master tactician had taught. So be it. "Charge," he shouted, and led the attack against the entrenched squads of Silverman and Rivera.

The fighting became furious. It was M-16s against AK-47s. Grenades exploded. Shrapnel, ice spicules, flesh and bone spewed everywhere. Rolly, Mean Gene's squad, and the remnants of Snappy's command took a firing position behind the concrete block radio shack, surrounding the Omega crew, the Russian scientists and Pisanya. The Snow Troopers were cut off from Rolly's

Rangers, caught between the rear guard of the Arctic Wolves, and the Soviet submarine.

Borodine watched the battle from behind the safety of the bulwarks of the *Sea Demon*'s conning tower. He ordered a deck detail to fire at the backs of the Snow Troopers. Men were cut down where they fought. Red blood stained white uniforms and snow. The Americans were in dire trouble.

Mean Gene spotted it first. He tugged on the major's sleeve. "Rolly, it's the *Manta*. Boxer's come back for us."

There was a good two hundred yards of clear ice, the size of two football fields, between the *Manta* and Rolly's crew. Rolly quickly assessed the situation and said, "I'll keep these three men with me to cover you. Get the Russians and the Omega people back to the sub."

Gene said. "I'd rather stay here with you. You need me more than they do."

"You're the best man for the job. Now do it."

"It looks like you need me more than they do right now."

Rolly blew his cool. "Getting them back safely is the mission, *Sergeant*. Now get the fuck back to the sub with these people. Now."

"Yes, *sir*," Mean Gene spat, and joined the others already heading toward the submarine.

"And send us some air support, if you can," Rolly called after him.

Mean Gene armed the Omega crew and had them lead the dash back to the *Manta*. He and his Rangers formed a protective phalanx behind them. He held up his right hand.

Rolly looked at each of his remaining defenders and said. "Open fire. Fire at will."

With the burst of covering fire behind them, Gene

swung down his arm and shouted, "Now. Go for the sub."

Boxer was first up the sail to the outside bridge. He could see that his men were taking a beating. He switched on the intercom mike. "Lieutenant Cooper. Report immediately to Chopper One."

"Aye, aye, Skipper. I been waitin' for some action." Vance Cooper, a lanky Kansas farm boy turned Marine aviator, donned his flight helmet and dashed forward to the helicopter launch tube. He fastened himself onto his seat, dogged shut the hatch and signalled his readiness. "Chopper One ready for launch, Skipper," he radioed to the bridge.

Boxer said to the DO, "Bring us up a bit, Whitey. I want the hatches above water."

"Aye, aye, Skipper," came the COB's reply and the *Manta* climbed a foot higher, buckling the sea ice as she rose.

"Launch Chopper One," Boxer ordered.

The Forward Torpedo Officer was in charge of the helicopter launch. He spun a wheel overhead, popped a lever and the 'copter was catapulted skyward. "Chopper One launched, Skipper," the FTO reported.

"Roger that," Boxer replied.

At fifty feet, the overhead rotors sprang open and the tail assembly dropped into place. After two uneasy spins, Chopper One was airborne under its own power. Vance Cooper set out to even the odds. He swooped low over the Soviet's rear guard, and strafed them with his twin machine guns.

A cheer went up among the entrapped Snow Troopers, and they stormed the vestiges of Soviet resistance. Now, on to the main body of Arctic Wolves, who were in the process of wiping out Rolly's Rangers.

247

Boxer watched the orderly retreat toward the sub and signalled orders below. "Open forward hatch. Deck detail out on the double. Get those people inside."

A deck crew quickly opened the forward hatch and positioned a steel mesh bridge between the *Manta* and the ice shelf.

Boxer called down to his men on the deck, "Man the heavy machine guns. I want you to cover those people coming in."

Four men did his bidding, two at each station.

Silverman's and Rivera's squads watched the Snow Troopers come to their rescue with a rear assault. They regrouped their forces and led a frontal charge against the Russians. The tide of battle was turning for the Americans. The Soviet Arctic Wolves were again caught in a pincer, cut down from the front and behind.

Charles Andrews was the first man to reach the *Manta,* and helped the Russian scientists and his men aboard. The deck detail guided them down the steel ladder belowdecks. Mean Gene dragged Pisanya with him by the scruff of his coat collar. He shoved the deputy director in the direction of the sub and sent him sprawling with a kick to the backside. "Drag that lump of shit on board the sub before I drown him," Gene barked. When all his men were aboard the *Manta,* Gene threw a salute up at Boxer and sped off in a running crouch toward the radio shack.

Rolly couldn't believe it when the wiry squad leader showed up at his side. "What the fuck you doin' here? I gave you an order."

Gene flashed a grin. "Everybody else's aboard the sub. Besides, you know you can't make it without me."

Rolly grimaced and sputtered for a moment. Then he, too, flashed a smile and gave Mean Gene a big high five.

"Okay, let's go. The boys need a hand."

Dick Dickerson's Snow Troopers were being sprayed by fire from the *Sea Demon*. Borodine had ordered rocket fire when the Americans had retreated out of machine-gun range.

Vance Cooper watched from the vantage point of Chopper One, and radioed back to the bridge. "Attack that sub," Boxer ordered. "Vance, see if you can knock out that gunnery battery."

"Aye, aye, Skipper." He swooped in low and fired two air to surface missiles at the *Sea Demon*. One knocked out the machine gun. The second found its mark on the sail, sending burning metal and debris everywhere. "Get him," Borodine shouted, and clambered below.

A Soviet rocket struck Chopper One in the fuselage, right behind the cockpit, ripping a gaping hole in its side. Flames surged inside the cockpit. Cooper radioed, "I'm hit, Skipper."

"Eject," Boxer cried. "Bail out. Bail out."

The forward momentum of the chopper kept it on a collision course with the enemy sub. A sardonic smile creased Cooper's lips. He lined up his failing machine with the Soviet rocket battery. The gunners tried to jump away, but were too late. "No way, Skipper," Cooper said, and smashed the 'copter into the *Sea Demon*. The gunners and the gunnery disappeared in a ball of flame.

"Dive . . . dive," barked Borodine. "We must stop the American submarine before it gets away. We must somehow salvage this mission, Viktor."

The exec sounded the klaxon siren. The *Sea Demon* slipped below the ice and nosed downward, as compressed air was blown from the ballast tanks and replaced with sea water. He watched the sonar blip of the *Manta* on his sonar screen and cursed, "You will pay for this."

Clemens signaled the bridge. "Skipper, the Ruskie sub has dived."

"Shit," Boxer said, and dropped through the hatch below his feet. The chief of the watch followed him below, and dogged the hatch shut. "Dive . . . dive," Boxer shouted.

Whitey pushed the diving lever all the way forward. Clemens cleared the ballast tanks and the *Manta* dropped like a stone.

"Whitey, one five degrees on the planes," Boxer ordered.

"One five degrees, aye, aye, Skipper."

The *Manta* nosed downward at a forty degree angle. The men in the attack center braced themselves.

"What about the men we left behind on the ice, Skipper?"

Boxer's face turned grim. "They'll have to fend for themselves, Clem. If we survive, we'll go back for them. Right now, we've got an enemy sub right on our tails trying to bugger us. And they will if they get any closer."

"Sorry. I guess I knew the answer to that before I asked it."

Boxer picked up the MC mike. "EO, give me everything you've got."

"Aye, aye, Skipper. Full speed ahead."

The *Manta* dove ever downward, its speed approached fifty knots, and still could not shake the *Sea Demon*. "EO, can't we go any faster?"

"We're at full ahead right now, Skipper. If I push any more, the reactor might blow."

"If you don't, we're goners anyway."

"Aye, aye, Skipper. I'll see what I can do."

"Conn, sonar. She's still right on our tail."

"Roger that, Hi Fi." He looked at Clemens. The EXO just shrugged.

Boxer keyed the aft torpedo room. "ATO, launch the drone. Do it now."

"Aye, aye, Skipper."

"Mahoney, as soon as the drone is launched, hard right rudder. Go to zero nine zero."

"Yes, sir. Ready when you are."

"Drone ready to launch," ATO reported.

"Launch. Launch," Boxer commanded.

They heard a faint thump of a hatch opening and a hiss of compressed air as the drone escaped. "Now, Mahoney. Hard right."

The drone continued on the original course of the *Manta*. The sub veered a sharp ninety degrees.

Boxer breathed a sigh of relief. "That ought to do it."

"Target bearing zero nine zero degrees, Skipper. Range four thousand yards . . . Depth three five zero feet . . . Speed zero four zero knots. We're gaining on her, Skipper, but the Ruskies didn't go after the drone. They're still on our tail."

Boxer rubbed his salt and pepper beard. "Not many Ruskie captains are that good, Clem. I wonder if it's Igor Borodine trailing us?"

Three miles back, aboard the *Sea Demon*, Borodine clapped his exec on the shoulder. "Good work, Viktor. We didn't lose them." He switched on his intercom. "EO, give me full speed ahead," he ordered, knowing that they were already at flank speed.

"Yes, Comrade Admiral. At once," came the reply from the engine room.

Borodine managed a thin smile, and rubbed his beard. "Very clever, that American captain. You know, it wouldn't surprise me to find out that our old friend

251

Comrade Admiral Boxer is at the conn."

Three nautical miles ahead, Boxer said, "Let's try to lose them, Clem. Head toward the surface. We can try to hide out between the ice ridges."

"Roger that, Skipper." Clemens turned the dial that blew water from the ballast tanks. The *Manta* began to rise.

"Whitey, one zero on the diving planes."

"Yes, sir. One zero on the planes."

The *Manta* nosed upward.

"Comrade Admiral Borodine," the SO called. "The American submarine is surfacing."

"We've got her now," Borodine exclaimed. He switched on his intercom. "FTO arm forward tubes."

"Yes, Comrade." In a minute, "Forward torpedo tubes loaded and armed, Comrade Admiral."

"Viktor, work out the firing solution."

The exec did a quick calculation and punched the data into his fire control console. "Ready, Igor."

"FCO, fire one and two."

"One and two torpedoes launched, Comrade."

Borodine and Viktor watched the two blips streak toward the larger image on the dull green screen. "We've got her, Viktor."

Aboard the *Manta,* Clemens watched in horror as the two fish streaked toward them on the sonar screen. "Geez, Skipper, they've got us."

"Mahoney, hard right . . . hard right." Sweat dripped from Boxer's forehead. He wiped his brow with a sleeve, and turned to Whitney. "Pull it back, Whitey." Boxer mimicked the surfacing gesture as his DO tried to respond with the diving lever.

The first torpedo narrowly missed the *Manta,* gliding through the sea a mere thirty feet below the keel, at the exact location that the *Manta* just vacated. The second fish caught the propeller shaft at the point where it entered the stern.

The *Manta* was hurled ass over end, spiralling downward out of control. Boxer struggled to hold on to a console. He read the terror in his exec's eyes.

Clemens pointed to the screen. "The Ruskies are closing in for the kill, Skipper."

Sure enough, the *Sea Demon* was moving in on them even as Whitey struggled to bring the craft level. "What do we have loaded?"

"One and four, Skipper. But they're armed with nuclear warheads. We could all be blown to hell."

"FTO, you still there?"

"Aye, aye, Skipper."

"Roger that. Stand by." To Clemens he said, "Arm one and four."

The exec froze for a moment, caught Boxer's determined gaze, and turned a dial until the red LED display came on. "One and four armed."

Hi Fi's desperate plea was heard on the intercom. "Target closing fast, Skipper. Wait. They've just fired two more fish."

Boxer calmly switched on his mike, and brought it to his mouth. He placed his other hand on Clemens's shoulder. To Clem, it almost seemed as if the skipper was smiling.

"FTO, fire at will," Boxer ordered.

"One and four away, Skipper."

It was not known whether the *Manta*'s fish found their mark on the enemy torpedoes, or vice versa. The ensuing explosion was picked up by sensitive listening devices on Greenland, Ellesmere Island, the Norwegian Svalbard Island, and in several of the Soviet Union's Arctic Island groups. All those aboard the two submarines who were not knocked unconscious by the blast sat or lay there too dazed to think, too stunned to question their fates. The *Manta* and the *Sea Demon* settled uncertainly toward the ocean floor.